The Wonder Chamber

Also by the Author

Fiction

Lizzie Manning mysteries:

The Wandering Heart

Paradise Walk

Nonfiction

Devil on the Deep Blue Sea: The Notorious Career of Captain Samuel Hill of Boston

Souvenirs of the Fur Trade:
Northwest Coast Indian Art and Artifacts Collected by American Mariners

"Boston Men" on the Northwest Coast:
The American Maritime Fur Trade, 1788-1844

A Most Remarkable Enterprise:
Lectures on the Northwest Coast Trade and Northwest Coast Indian Life by Captain William Sturgis

The Wonder Chamber

Mary Malloy

A LIZZIE MANNING MYSTERY

Leapfrog Press
Fredonia, New York

Published in 2014 in the United States by

Leapfrog Press LLC
PO Box 505
Fredonia, NY 14063
www.leapfrogpress.com

Distributed in the United States by
Consortium Book Sales and Distribution
St. Paul, Minnesota 55114
www.cbsd.com

First Edition

ISBN 978-1-935248-42-2

Library of Congress Cataloging-in-Publication Data

Available from the Library of Congress

Printed in the United States of America

This book is dedicated to the memories of three people I loved who died while I was writing it.

My aunt, Gladys Paxton
My uncle, William Newman
My cousin, Dale Gonsalves

Enthusiastic readers and lovers of history all, they are much missed.

Prologue

The corpse had been packed in salt for forty days, following the ancient prescription, and dehydration was complete. One of the men cried when he first saw her face. The gums were drawn back from her teeth, the jaw wide open, and the eyelids bulging, where his assistant had removed her eyes and stuffed the empty sockets with linen soaked in resin. He had not been able to look when that part of the process was done, or when the bits of what had been her brain were pulled with a long hook through one of her nostrils.

It had been his job to remove her organs, however, and that he had done with loving care, pulling her stomach, liver, lungs and intestines carefully through the incision he made in her side, washing them all carefully and packing them in salt. Her heart had been left in her chest, as it was the seat not only of love and other emotions, but also of intelligence—all thoughts both good and awful.

His assistant had been angry through the whole process, both when they made the original preparations for mummification and now, as they washed the salt off the body.

"She was evil," he said. "She doesn't deserve this attention."

There was no use arguing, she had done things with terrible consequences. But that did not mean that they could simply dispose of her like a common person. She had to be carefully prepared to lie in the sarcophagus that was waiting to receive her. And so they rubbed the body with scented oils and began the long process of wrapping her tightly in strips of linen.

Chapter 1

The headline on the society page of the *New York Times* spoke volumes: "Boston Heiress to Marry Italian Prince." Whatever else one wanted to know could be seen in the grainy black-and-white picture of the unhappy couple. She was a frightened teenager with a rich father; he was a middle-aged man with an impressive title and a grim expression. The story was by now thoroughly familiar to Lizzie and she quickly scanned the description of Paddy Kelliher's rise from poor Irish immigrant to American textile tycoon. He had used his new money to buy himself respectability, first by founding St. Patrick's College in Charlestown, Massachusetts, and then by marrying his daughter to a European nobleman. Every article about him in his lifetime, including this one—which really ought to have been about his only daughter—told the story of his rise to riches.

Lizzie Manning looked up from her computer and through the library window to the campus green, where the grass that gave it its name now lay under a thick layer of snow. There was a larger-than-life statue of Kelliher there, which students dressed for every season and special occasion. Today it wore a bright red puffy jacket, a woolen hat with earflaps and a pompom, and a yards-long muffler in the school colors of green and white.

"Poor Maggie Kelliher," Lizzie said, turning to her friend Jackie Harrigan, who sat at her desk at one end of the reading room.

"You mean the Principessa Della Gonzaga?" Jackie asked, impressively giving the title a rhythmic Italian cadence. "She might have been the unfortunate victim of a couple of grasping men, but she left you a fortunate legacy. I can't believe the college is paying for you to have a vacation in Italy."

"Please," Lizzie answered sternly, "it is *not* a vacation. How many times do I have to tell you that my trip to Bologna—with its fabulous food and great collections—will be hard, hard work."

Jackie laughed. "Oh yes! I'm glad you reminded me how hard you will be working so that I can think of you with real sympathy while I shovel snow and layer on the sweaters."

"It's not all that warm in northern Italy, you know. I'll be wearing a sweater," Lizzie responded, and then corrected herself. "Well *maybe* I will wear a sweater. But of course I won't be shoveling snow. They have servants for that kind of thing at the Palazzo." She mimicked her friend's Italian accent as she said the last word.

Jackie had spent a semester in Rome during college and now gave a rapid soliloquy in Italian, from which Lizzie captured only two words, and they were not ones introduced on the Rosetta Stone computer program she was using each day to prepare her for the project.

"Luckily for you my friend," she said, turning back to her work, "Italian sounds quite lovely even when you are saying ugly things."

"There was nothing ugly about it," Jackie said. "Only my best wishes for your work, and curiosity why they didn't give this project to me, who actually speaks the language."

Lizzie kept her back to her friend and smiled, watching through the window as a snowball flew across the green and smacked Paddy Kelliher's statue in the side of the head.

"I don't need to speak the language," she said. "As I will have my own personal full-time translator always at the ready. And besides, one has to know about ancient collections for this particular project."

There was a grumbling sound from Jackie's end of the room that was neither Italian nor English and Lizzie smiled again.

The two friends took up the conversation again at lunch, where they were joined by their colleague, Kate Wentworth, and their friend Rose Geminiani, who owned the restaurant where they ate every Thursday. Jackie immediately repeated her complaint that she spoke Italian and ought to make the trip.

"If that's the criteria," Rose interrupted, "then I should be the one to go. I speak better Italian than you, and my father is from Bologna, so I even have the right accent—you speak Roman." She nudged Jackie's arm with her elbow as she spoke, and put a plate in front of her.

"I'd love to bring you all," Lizzie said, "but the college will only be paying for me."

"How long will you be gone?" Kate asked.

Lizzie explained that she would be in Italy for about three weeks, selecting objects from the Gonzaga collection to bring back to Boston for an exhibition at St. Patrick's College the following September, as part of the college's centennial celebration.

"Explain to me again, this relationship between the Gonzagas and St. Pat's," Rose said, sitting down for the first time since her friends had arrived.

"Don't you know the famous story of our founder, Paddy-boy Kelliher, marrying his daughter off to the Italian prince?" Jackie answered.

"Famous to whom?" Rose asked, pouring wine into each of their glasses.

"Well, it's famous at St. Pat's, of course," Kate offered, "and Lizzie wrote a book about it."

Rose turned to Lizzie. "You wrote a book about a local girl marrying an Italian prince and you never gave me a copy?"

Lizzie took the glass and slowly twirled it to move the wine around the circle of the goblet. She shrugged. "That was only a tiny part of the book, I assure you. It's really about the guy whose money built the campus at St. Pat's, and it came out in a *very* small edition." She raised the glass. "Let's drink to Maggie Kelliher," she said.

"The Principessa Della Gonzaga," Jackie added.

"Oh, I'll drink to that!" Rose said with enthusiasm, touching the rim of her glass to those of each of her friends with a satisfying clink. She asked Lizzie why she hadn't spent more time on the daughter than the father in her book. "She sounds much more interesting."

"She may have been," Lizzie said, "but I don't think her story was the happy fairy tale romance of the prince and the commoner that you seem to be seeking in your question. And besides," she added, "I was instructed by the college to write a history of our founder."

Jackie interjected that most colleges had something to be embarrassed about in the sources of wealth that underpinned their founding.

"If it wasn't slave traders, it was industrial magnates with a history of exploiting their workers. Lately it has become popular to pick at those old scabs in public, and our college president isn't the only one to assign to a professor the task of dragging that dark history into the light so that it can be confronted."

"And there was a lot to confront with old Paddy-boy," Lizzie said. "He made his money making buttons and woolens for both sides in the Civil War."

"Did he make a lot at that?" Rose asked.

"More than a million bucks!" Lizzie said, "and all by the time he was twenty-five years old."

Kate defended their long-dead patron. "There is something very impressive in leaving Ireland with nothing at the age of seventeen and making a million dollars before he had even been in America for ten years. I'd say he was the manifestation of the immigrant dream."

Lizzie agreed. "Certainly part of his success was in the timing of his arrival and his having made investments in what we would now call start-up companies just before the war began."

"But you can't deny he had a canny eye for making money," Kate pressed.

"No, I certainly don't deny that."

"Do you condemn him for having supplied both sides in the war?" Rose asked.

"We just condemn him on principle for being a rich guy," Jackie interjected, pouring herself another glass of wine. "And for making his daughter marry a rich foreigner."

"Well that's hardly fair," Rose said insistently. "*He* was a rich foreigner by then—and an Italian prince, I mean, come on, that's no ordinary rich foreigner!"

"And he probably wasn't rich," Jackie said, correcting herself. "He probably needed the Kelliher money to keep up his palazzo."

Lizzie looked at her watch. She had a meeting about the exhibit with Father Lawrence O'Toole, the president of the college, at 2:00 and needed to walk back across the bridge to Charlestown before then.

"Here's what I know of Patrick Malachi Kelliher," she said definitively. "He gave a lot of jobs to Irish immigrants which can be interpreted as either exploiting them or setting them up for success in the New World; he did supply materials for uniforms to both sides in the Civil War, which he justified as not being guns and therefore making him *not* responsible for any deaths; and he founded the college where three of us work, and I'm happy for that." She drained her wineglass and stood up. "And his daughter married into a family that had one of the great collections from the Renaissance. And I can't wait to get my hands on it!"

Chapter 2

Despite the fact that Lizzie considered Rose Geminiani a good friend and had known her for more than a decade, the history of their relationship could be written on a napkin. Almost every meeting had taken place during lunches at Rose's restaurant. Only once, at a Christmas party several years earlier, had Rose been in Lizzie's house. It was consequently a surprise when Rose called Lizzie at home on the Sunday morning following their conversation about Paddy Kelliher, his daughter and the prince.

"My father knew Maggie Kelliher—the Princess Gonzaga!" Rose said enthusiastically after they had exchanged greetings. "She paid for him to go to St. Pat's, and her marriage *was* a love story, just like I hoped."

She slowed down for a moment to explain that it really might have been love at first sight—or at least love at very near to when they first met—then sped up again and chattered on about her father's childhood memories of the old woman. "Apparently she taught many of the local kids in Bologna to speak English, sent several dozen of them to Boston to go to college, and was a leader of revolutionary activity in the Second World War." She finished by saying that Lizzie should write a book about her.

Lizzie thought about this for a moment. "Well I am writing a catalog for the exhibit—it would make sense to work her into the story as the link between the college and the Gonzaga collection."

"My pop wants to talk to you about her."

"I'd love to meet him."

"He wants you to come for dinner tonight. Can you and

Martin do that?"

"Aren't you working?"

"This is a slow time of year. I think I can absent myself from the restaurant for one Sunday dinner, and this conversation sounds too good to miss." From the cadence in Rose's voice Lizzie could almost see the gestures of excitement she was making with her hands on the other end of the line.

"We're going to have dinner with Rose Geminiani's father tonight," Lizzie said to her husband as she hung up the phone. "I hope you don't have other plans."

Martin said that he didn't. "And I'll be glad to see Tony," he added.

Lizzie looked surprised. "You know him?"

"Tony Tessitore," he said. "I've met him several times at Rose's restaurant."

"You're kidding me," she answered. "I've never met him and I go there almost every week for lunch."

"Well I go there several times a week for coffee in the afternoon and that's when the old man hangs around."

"This is part of your secret life, about which you never told me?"

He smiled at her. "I'll drive. I dropped the old guy off at his house once and I even know where he lives."

Boston's North End neighborhood had not changed much in the fifty years that Tony Tessitore had lived there. His row house on North Bennet Street was built early in the nineteenth century; he had moved into the first-floor apartment when he graduated from St. Pat's College, and eventually bought the whole building. There was a small brass plaque above the bell that said "Vito Antonio Tessitore," and Lizzie silently rolled the name over her tongue before she rang.

The door opened almost immediately and Lizzie saw an old man, shorter than herself, with a neatly trimmed beard and eyes that looked like Santa's, as described in the poem about the night before Christmas. He seemed genuinely enthusiastic to see them, as if he hadn't had visitors in years, though that was quickly shown not to be the case as he described how busy he had been in the last several days.

"Martin," he said, holding out his hand, "wonderful to see

you again, and this must be Lizzie, welcome."

Rose stood behind him, waving at Lizzie over her father's shoulder.

"Pop has made you a special Bolognese spread," she said, pointing to a tray of meats, cheeses, olives and bread, "in honor of the Princess Gonzaga."

"Signora Gonzaga," he corrected, turning to his daughter, "she never used the title of Principessa." He rolled his eyes at Lizzie. "Always with the princesses, my Rose."

Lizzie smiled at him. "I know," she said, handing the old man her coat. "Rose and I have had this conversation many times."

"Italians don't want royalty," he continued. "It's bad enough there are the politicians, the mafia, the pope. We don't need another hand in our pockets."

"Well you can tell us the whole story," Rose said, putting her arm around her father and giving him a kiss on the side of the head.

She pointed out chairs to Lizzie and Martin and began to pour wine as her father explained the various cured Bolognese meats and cheeses.

"Most people know us only for baloney," he said, "but there are such great foods from Bologna."

"I can't wait to go there," Lizzie said, happily sampling each piece that was passed her way.

"Where will you stay?" Tony asked her.

"At the Gonzaga family house."

"The palazzo," Rose said enthusiastically.

"The house on Galvani Plaza?" her father asked, ignoring his daughter's commentary.

Lizzie answered that she thought that was the address.

"I was there often in my youth," Tony said wistfully. "My father worked for the Gonzagas in their linen factory and when I was a small child I worked in the house."

Martin asked him what sort of jobs he had done and Tony answered that when he was eight or nine he had held the reigns of horses when vendors came to the door.

"There were still some old guys that used horses then. And after the Second World War there wasn't much gas for cars and they brought them back." He laughed as he thought about it. "Then I went inside and played in the courtyard until the next visitor arrived." He saw the look on Martin's face and turned to him. "Don't worry, this was not any kind of exploitation of child labor. The Signora got us into her house so that she could school us, and she always had seven or eight children of Gonzaga workers there." He explained that she had taught him to read and to speak English, and had used the famous collection in the house to teach about art and science.

"I have just started to read about the collection," Lizzie said. "That's my reason for going there."

"I have some pictures," Tony said, "if you'd like to see them."

"I'd love it," she answered enthusiastically.

During the short time he was out of the room, Lizzie told Rose how much she liked her father, and what a great help it was to her to talk to him.

"Just wait," Rose said. "I told you I think you should write a book about the Princess Gonzaga, and Pop can give you a ton of information."

"I thought he said she never used that title."

Rose shrugged and laughed. "That doesn't mean I can't."

"You are nothing if not persistent," Lizzie said with a smile.

Tony returned with a leather album. On the cover his name was tooled in a fancy script. "This was a gift from the Signora," he said. "She gave one to each of us when we left for America." He opened the book and showed the first pictures, which Maggie Kelliher Gonzaga had placed in the volume. "These are my parents," he said, placing his fingertips lightly on a photo. "Signora Gonzaga had a photographer take this so that I would have it to remember them when I was far from home, and here is a picture of my family and our house."

He pointed to a picture of himself with his sponsor. "This was taken in the courtyard of the Palazzo Gonzaga," he said. "This is me with the Signora."

Lizzie took the album and looked closely at the face of Maggie Kelliher Gonzaga. It was obviously the same woman she had seen in the engagement photo in the *New York Times* from many years earlier, but the expression was quite different. She had a slight smile and her hand rested affectionately on the shoulder of the young man beside her.

"Where was her husband at this time?" Lizzie asked.

"He was dead by then," Tony answered. "He died at the beginning of the war and this is after." He took the book back. "So much happened to her in the war. Her husband gone, her son killed, her daughter executed, and still she was such a kind and steady person. She never turned anyone away who needed help and her house was crowded with people all through the war and long after."

"You told me she was some kind of Resistance fighter," Rose said.

Tony nodded. "She never made any kind of political declaration. It would have been too dangerous for her, but it was known that she supported the Resistance. Her daughter Gianna was executed by the Nazis for spreading partisan propaganda, and her son Pat and son-in-law Archie Cussetti spent much of the war in hiding."

"Her daughter was executed?" Martin said softly. "How terrible that must have been for her."

"It was a horrifying day," Tony said, his voice becoming less steady as he talked. "I was only a kid then, but I remember coming out of the house when I heard a truck drive up to the front door. I saw them throw Gianna's body onto the pavement of the plaza. She was almost unrecognizable, she had been beaten so badly."

There was silence in the room for a time, which Rose finally broke.

"But these awful things are not what Lizzie and Martin came to talk about," she said, putting a hand on her father's arm. "Show some pictures of the collection."

Tony seemed relieved to change the subject and turned over several leaves in his album. "Ah, the famous collection," he said. "I took several pictures of it many years later. These are in color."

Lizzie peered down at the images. Most of them had faded over the forty or so years that they had been pasted in the album. She could not see details well but she recognized an alligator mounted along one wall. "I might like to come look at these again if that's okay," she said.

"Take the album," Tony said. "You can copy any of the pictures you like and get it back to me when it is convenient."

Conversation during dinner turned to more conventional topics, though Tony frequently mentioned Maggie Kelliher Gonzaga and Lizzie found that she wanted to know more about her. The frightened teenager in the newspaper photo was clearly not the whole story.

Chapter 3

The Kelliher family had been generous to St. Patrick's College since its founding, not just with money but by buying books for the library and works of art for the small museum on campus. When Maggie Kelliher married Lorenzo Gonzaga he had given several pieces from his family collection to the college, including a small but magnificent portrait of the Madonna by Guido Reni, and a marble angel carved by Niccolo dell'Arca, artists who had worked in Bologna in the fifteenth and sixteenth centuries. These works were in the campus chapel, but Lizzie had already secured permission to move them to the museum for her exhibit.

Maggie Kelliher had purchased several seventeenth-century books for the campus library that dealt with the Gonzaga collection or others like it in Italy during the Renaissance. Lizzie had a study carrel in the library and she was assembling books for this project so that she could work efficiently with them, and with archival material from the Kelliher and Gonzaga families. When she had written her short biography of Paddy Kelliher a few years earlier, she had surveyed all these collections and she knew there were folders of material related to the Gonzagas that she had not thought pertinent at the time. Now she asked Jackie to bring her all the files related to the Gonzaga family or their collection.

"You won't have room here," Jackie said, standing at the edge of the carrel. "I have a cartful of material and I think it would be best to spread it out on one of the library tables and see what we have; then you can make a plan for the order in which you want to look at it."

"I also have an electronic list of what is currently in the

collection that is in Italian, and I'll need some help going through that."

"Is Father O'Toole giving you money for any assistants on this?" Jackie asked.

"I can hire two student assistants, first for January short-term projects, and then I'm taking the spring term off to work on the exhibit and catalog, and I can keep them through May if they work out. I also have to take on a junior named Justin Carrera as an assistant. I've never met him but he's the great-grandson of Maggie Kelliher Gonzaga."

"The Principessa..."

"Stop saying that!" Lizzie interrupted before Jackie could get out the whole title and name. "Rose's dad, Tony, who knew her, said she never used that title."

"I know," Jackie said. "I just like the way it sounds when I say it."

"You're as bad as Rose," Lizzie complained. "You both love that title, though for different reasons. I have decided to think of her as Maggie. Tony showed me a picture of her last night and I really liked the look of her, very kind and friendly, though she lived a hellish life during the war."

"There are more pictures," Jackie responded, reaching for a folder from the cart and putting it on the table as Lizzie sat down.

"Tony knew Maggie from the time he was a kid. She sent him to St. Pat's to go to college."

She picked up a folder with the title "Gonzaga Family: 1 of 8." Inside were wedding photos of Maggie and Lorenzo Gonzaga and of a growing family; they could be laid out on the table in a chronological order just by the number of children included in the picture.

"I must say this wedding picture makes her look a lot happier than that picture you showed me from the *New York Times*," Jackie said.

"It certainly does," Lizzie said. "Let that be a lesson to us not to judge too hastily from small evidence."

"I'm happy to see they wrote the names on the backs of the pictures. You can't imagine how many old photos we have in this library of people who will never be identified."

They put the wedding pictures at the top left corner of the table.

"These were taken here," Lizzie said, pointing out the stone porch on which the couple stood with their families. "That's the Kelliher house in Brookline. I was there a couple of weeks ago to talk about the exhibit with Jim Kelliher."

"And these are clearly in the courtyard of an Italian house," Jackie said, placing three pictures of the Gonzagas with two little girls on the table. "Eleonora and Margherita, it says on the back."

"And here they are back in Boston, in the yard of the Kelliher house with those girls and a new baby."

"Adino," Jackie said, reading off the back of the picture. "Do you think he was born here?"

"Does it give a date?"

"October 17, 1914.

"Hmm. Paddy-boy died in June 1914. Maybe they came across for his funeral and stayed if she was pregnant."

Jackie was thoughtful. "That was the start of the First World War. When exactly did Paddy-boy die?"

Lizzie opened her computer file on Kelliher and found his death date, June 8, 1914, while Jackie looked online for the starting date of the war.

"'The Archduke Franz Ferdinand was assassinated on June 28, 1914,'" she read to Lizzie. "If I were a mom with a new baby and two little girls, I would not want to take them back into a war zone. Maybe they just stayed here to sit it out. I think the Austro-Hungarians brought their fight into Northern Italy soon after things got started."

Lizzie took more pictures out of the folder. "Well, they were certainly back home by 1918. Here's a picture in the courtyard of the house with four children." She held the picture up to catch the light. "She looks really happy here. Maggie looks really happy. I'm sorry I ever let that first picture I saw of her affect me so much."

"And here is one with five children," Jackie said, reading from the back of the photo. "Eleonora, Margherita, Adino, Cosimo and Patrick."

"Ha!" Lizzie said enthusiastically, "I knew she would have

to get an Irish name in there eventually. I'm surprised they didn't name the first son after her father, especially since he must have been born soon after Paddy's death."

"Some families have a strict naming order. I'll bet Eleonora was his mother's name, and Margherita is the Italian version of Maggie's own name. Adino might have been the name of Lorenzo's father."

"Patrick is still alive," Lizzie told Jackie. "I expect to meet him when I get to Bologna."

"He was born in 1921, so he's getting up there," Jackie said, picking up another picture. "And here is the last child, Giuseppina, born in 1923."

Lizzie took the photo from her. "This must be the one they called Gianna. Rose's dad said she was executed by the Nazis for being in the Resistance." She shuddered as the image came to mind of the broken body of the young woman being tossed onto the pavement in front of her mother's house. "It is so strange to look at this happy family here and think of all the tragedies that beset them over the next twenty years," she said. "Two of them died in the war."

They went quickly through the rest of the family photos, showing the six Gonzaga children at different ages and in different rooms of the house. In several of them Lizzie had glimpses of paintings, sculptures, and even cabinets filled with shells, small statues, china, and other antiques and oddities.

"I wonder how much of what we see here is still in the collection," she said.

Jackie took another large folder from the cart. "This one is labeled Gonzaga Collection." She handed it to Lizzie. "I'm sorry that there is no index for any of this. To my knowledge, no one has ever even looked at it."

Lizzie thought that maybe one of her student assistants could make a start at it. "And if it turns out to be really useful, we could probably get some money from the Kellihers to pay for it."

As Jackie turned to go back to work, Lizzie asked her how the college got this archive. "Did Maggie send it to her family, and they donated it? Or did she send it directly herself?"

"I'll check," Jackie said. "It might have been from one of her children too."

Lizzie went to a new table to spread out the various pages from the file on the Gonzaga collection. There were several dozen photographs in the file—pictures of rooms, of cases of objects, and of individual pieces, from Roman statues and inscribed stones to animals that had been preserved by drying or stuffing; from cameos to an Egyptian sarcophagus. There was also a typed list, mostly in Italian, with several handwritten emendations in English. On the last page of the list was a note that said, "Though the origins of this collection are probably even older, my husband Lorenzo Gonzaga believed it was founded in 1659, inspired by collections in Bologna made by Ulisse Aldrovandi and Ferdinando Cospi." The gift was made in 1959, on the 300th anniversary of the collection.

Lizzie took the page to show to Jackie; she had to seek her friend out in the stacks of the library.

"Here's something cool," she said when she found her. "This material on the collection was given to the college by Maggie in 1959, and there's a note to that effect."

"I know," Jackie said, "We must have discovered that simultaneously—that's when she sent the photographs too. And I found something else in the catalog that I think you might like to see." She was standing on a stepping stool to reach an archival box on the top shelf of the stacks. "This is a file of her letters to her family."

Lizzie stepped forward to take the box as Jackie climbed back down. "I doubt there will be much here that's relevant to my current project, but now I'm intrigued enough by her to want to know her better." She cradled the box under her arm and gave the loose paper she carried to Jackie. "Thanks," she said, "for finding this."

"You have your work cut out for you, Lizzie," Jackie said.

"Yeah, but it has started to take shape here today. I have appointments this afternoon with potential student assistants and if I get some good help I can start assigning some of this organizational stuff to them."

It took a great deal of willpower for Lizzie to resist opening the box of letters first thing, but she left it unopened on the table and returned to an email she had received the day before from Cosimo Gonzaga, who was to be her liaison in Italy. He had, like most of the Gonzaga children, grandchildren and great-grandchildren, lived in Boston for a time and attended St. Patrick's College. His English was perfect and he attached a file that contained "the most current list of the collection" that he could locate. "You must feel free to borrow anything from the cabinet, and when you come to the house can choose other things not on this list." The Gonzaga family was, he wrote, "very eager to support the centennial celebration of the college which was founded by my great-grandfather." He added that he was glad she had agreed to take on his nephew as an assistant, as he thought the experience would be very good for him.

She opened the attachment and saw that it was the same document that was already on the table in front of her, but a much worse copy. Maggie had clearly sent the original to the college, with her own notes on it. The document sent by Cosimo Gonzaga was a scan of a carbon copy that had been made when the original was typed. Lizzie silently thanked Maggie for having sent the better copy, and Jackie for having found it. The fact that the most recent catalog of the collection was more than fifty years old was discouraging, but this would at least give her a chance to make a preliminary list for her exhibit, and then she could see what was in the house when she got to Bologna.

Chapter 4

Justin Carrera was nowhere to be seen when Lizzie arrived at her office promptly at two o'clock, but seven other students were waiting to see her about the possibility of working on the exhibit. The pay was more generous than the usual work-study job, but the hours exceeded what the College allowed for a full-time student, and consequently several people who would have been good candidates were not eligible.

Lizzie finally settled on two students, Jimmy Moe, who was an Italian major and fluent in the language, and Roscoe Wiley, who was a history major and had taken two of her classes. She instantly liked Jimmy, who had an exuberant personality, and she knew that Roscoe was a hard worker.

It was after four o'clock when Justin arrived and his total disinterest in the project was in sharp contrast to the enthusiasm of the students whom she had sent away disappointed.

"What can you tell me about the collection?" she started. "I'm really excited to see it."

Justin looked at her and shrugged. "I haven't ever really looked at it," he said. "I know it's in my Uncle Patrizio's house, but I've only been there a couple of times."

"So you didn't grow up in that house?"

Again he shrugged. "No, I grew up outside of Bologna."

She asked him to explain how he was related to Maggie Kelliher and Lorenzo Gonzaga, and even that he wasn't sure of. "I think they were my mom's grandparents," he said.

"Is there some reason why you want to work on this exhibit?"

"No, not really. My Uncle Cosimo said I should do it because it is about our family." He kicked one shoe against the other as he spoke and concentrated his gaze there, as if looking at Lizzie would be too much work.

"What's your major?" she asked, seeking some way to put him to work that wouldn't waste her time.

He scratched the side of his face and looked up at her. "Don't have one," he said.

"Aren't you a junior?"

He nodded.

"Shouldn't you have declared a major by now?"

Again came the ubiquitous shrug. "Yeah, I guess it's sort of Business, but I'll probably change it."

"Well, you speak good English," she said finally.

"My dad worked in New York for ten years," he said, "and we lived on Long Island."

That explained his completely colloquial American teenage accent, Lizzie thought. She had made a copy of the list of objects in the collection and handed it to him. "Do you think you could start a translation for me of this list?"

He looked at it. "So I just write down like 'alligator' and 'mummy' and stuff?" he asked, looking at the list.

"If that's what it says in Italian, then that is what you write in English. If it isn't clear, look it up or leave it blank."

With another shrug he left her office and closed the door behind him.

"Shit!" she said to herself. It was going to be a lot more difficult to have this kid hanging around than not. If Cosimo Gonzaga hadn't instructed her to hire him for this project she would be done with him right now.

She returned to the library and found that Jackie had piled several more things on the two tables on which she was working, including several ancient books. Lizzie sat down and opened the one on the top of the pile. It was Ulisse Aldrovandi's *Museum Metallicum,* one of several books by a sixteenth-century professor at the University of Bologna who had made a collection that was thought to be the largest in the world at the time. Aldrovandi was a botanist and physician who sought to collect all of nature in his "cabinet," where he could then organize and study it. On the title page was an oval portrait of the author held by angels—an indication that he was dead by the time this book was published in 1611. The central panel contained a lengthy title in Latin, behind which was a hilly landscape dotted with vignettes of mining. Openings into the earth, and cross sections of mineshafts populated by tiny workers, were scattered around the page.

This was only one of the great books by Aldrovandi, who attempted to catalog all things from the mineral, animal and plant worlds. Jackie had put the others on the table as well and Lizzie looked quickly at each, one after the other. These were books she knew well. It was her interest in the history of museums and collecting that had made her the choice to curate the exhibition of the Gonzaga collection. What she had not noticed on any previous reading was the bookplate in each of these copies that indicated it was a gift from Lorenzo and Margaret Gonzaga in honor of Patrick Kelliher.

"I see you have discovered why I thought you might like to look at those again," Jackie said, sitting down next to her.

"Yes, thanks."

"And there is so much more, my friend," Jackie said, obviously excited.

She put a brown folder on the table. "I decided to look up the accession information that was recorded when those books came in as a gift, which was when Paddy-boy died. Maggie and her husband obviously brought these things with them from Italy to make a memorial gift." She pulled a piece of paper from the folder. "This is the letter that Maggie wrote to accompany the gift."

The letter expressed a daughter's loss at the death of her father and her desire to do something to mark the profound change it made in her life. "As I am now the resident of a new country," she wrote, "I want to honor my father's memory with something Italian." She explained that her father had been impressed by the Gonzaga collection when he visited Bologna, and had asked to know more about it. In a brief history of the collection, Maggie credited its founding to Adino and Lorenzo Gonzaga, ancestors of her husband. The father, Adino, had been a student of Aldrovandi at the University of Bologna, and his son Lorenzo had been a colleague of the other great Bolognese collector, Ferdinando Cospi, who lived a generation later. "These books document those important collections," was the last line of the letter.

"There's more," Jackie said as she took the letter from Lizzie. "I can't believe that this was in the correspondence file and was never accessioned into the collection." She opened the folder and slid out a piece of ancient paper. "Here is an illustration of the 'cabinet' in 1677."

Lizzie gasped as she took the piece of paper.

"Oh my God!" she said. "I don't believe it! The College has had this all this time?"

"Since 1959. And I don't think anyone has looked at it since then."

"Oh my God!" Lizzie said again. "It's fabulous!"

The picture was drawn in pen on a thick piece of paper. It was just a bit too big to fit comfortably in the letter-size folder in which it had been hidden for the last fifty years and the edges were frayed along the top and the left side. It showed a room filled with cases that stretched from a few feet above the ground to what she guessed was ten feet or so. There was room both underneath and above the cases for additional display and every square foot of wall space had something stuck to it.

The cases each had five shelves, crammed with birds and small animals, seashells, pieces of coral, scientific instruments, vases and other things that might be ancient pottery, as well as trays of coins or medals. On the wall above the case were marble busts, fantastic arrangements of weapons, and larger animals, including an alligator. Below were elaborate constructions of seashells and coral. Amphora leaned against the wall and other vases with flat bottoms stood in the corners. There was a gigantic foot, apparently from an ancient statue, that stood solidly in the center of the floor. In front of the case was an elegantly dressed man with a pointer, apparently prepared to share information about the collection with visitors. Beside him, at the edge of the case, stood an Egyptian sarcophagus.

"It's wonderful," Lizzie said. "Just wonderful."

"Is it unique, do you think?"

Lizzie shook her head. "No, there are several other illustrations like this." She pulled a book out of the pile in front of her, *Museo Cospiano*. "This was another guy in Bologna who had a collection, and the frontispiece is similar to this image. Maggie mentions him in her letter—Ferdinando Cospi."

She opened the book to the frontispiece and Jackie said, "It's the same picture."

"Not quite," Lizzie said, "though they are clearly by the same artist, and the Gonzagas were probably copying Cospi's collection, or both were copying Aldrovandi's. Both pictures were made in 1677, so the artist might just have transferred some things from one image to the other." She added that she had never seen the Gonzaga image published in any book.

"How are they different?" Jackie asked.

Lizzie looked back and forth between the two pictures. "The most obvious thing is the mummy case. Neither Cospi nor Aldrovandi had one of those that I know of."

"And Cospi doesn't have an alligator," Jackie added, pointing to the one hanging from the ceiling of the Gonzaga collection.

"Which is actually kind of unusual," Lizzie commented. "I've looked at a lot of these kinds of pictures and alligators are strangely common. The collections in Northern Europe usually have a kayak hanging from the ceiling; the ones from Southern Europe have an alligator."

"Where are there alligators?"

"I don't think there are any in Europe," Lizzie said with a laugh, "but by the time these collections were being made lots of stuff was coming from Africa, Asia and the New World. That was part of the reason for making the collections—to put new knowledge into a framework that could be understood."

Lizzie asked if she could commandeer the two tables she was working at, in addition to her study carrel, for the duration of the project. Jackie agreed. "Who knew there was so much stuff here at St. Pat's?" Lizzie said. "I had no idea I would be able to get so much done before leaving for Bologna. Certainly we will want this image in the exhibition; maybe we'll make a photo mural of it and mount some of the surviving objects on it."

"Have you lined up your student assistants?"

"Yes. Two of them are going to be great, but Justin Carrera is a problem. I get the strong feeling he is only doing this because he has been told to do it by his uncle and has no interest whatsoever in the project, even though it is about his own family. I'd jettison him if I could," she said with a sigh of frustration. "Anyway, I'll get them in here next and we'll start parceling out the organizational work."

"I'm glad to see you working on a project that doesn't seem to have any life-threatening aspect to it," Jackie said as they parted company for the day.

"That is a rather new experience for me," Lizzie responded. "But what danger can there be in an old collection?"

Chapter 5

The College was more forthcoming with funds for the exhibit project than was customary in Lizzie's experience. Most of the costs were being underwritten by the heirs of Paddy Kelliher on both sides of the Atlantic. The Boston Kellihers were paying for an exhibit design firm and for a small staff to work with Lizzie, including her two student assistants. The Italian part of the family, the Gonzagas, were not only providing the loan of the collection, but paying all the costs associated with packing and shipping it in both directions. In addition, Cosimo Gonzaga was paying the salary for his nephew to be on the project staff.

Justin Carrera very quickly proved to be the disaster Lizzie anticipated. He didn't show up for the first meeting scheduled to talk about the project and divide up the work with Jimmy Moe and Roscoe Wiley. As she had no confidence that Justin would provide a good translation of the list, she gave a copy of it to Jimmy as well. He had gotten an excellent reference from his Italian instructor and Lizzie asked him where he had learned to speak it so well.

"My family speaks it at home," he said, "and I have been reading the literature since I was a kid."

"I take it that 'Moe' was shortened from something else in the immigration experience of your family?"

Jimmy had very black hair that came to a decided widow's peak, and though it was cut in a way to diminish its prominence, he had a tendency to push his hair straight back when he wasn't thinking. His skin was pale and he had green eyes, so his Italian heritage wasn't obvious.

"Morandzolini," he said with a grin. "My father thought Moe was more American."

Lizzie showed Jimmy and Roscoe the image of the Gonzaga collection from 1677 and made them each a copy to use as a reference. "This will be our inspiration," she said. "The common term in the seventeenth century for a room like this, set up to display a collection, was a 'cabinet,' and I'd like to recreate it as much as we can in our exhibit."

She opened the folder that had photographs of the collection. "These show the collection as it looked more than fifty years ago. They will all need to be scanned and cataloged, and eventually we will want to see what we can identify that is both on the list and in one of the pictures. There are also pictures of the family," she continued, opening that folder as well. "And some of them were taken in rooms in the Gonzaga house in Bologna and have collections in the background." She turned to Roscoe. "I'd like you to start by cataloging the photographs. Scan each of them and note the names on the back. I trust your eye, so give me a brief description of anything interesting in them that has to do with collections."

Roscoe picked up one of the pictures. "So here I would say that the room has four large and eight small paintings and some porcelain vases?"

Lizzie nodded. "Perfect. More detail than that we don't need at this point."

"It's really terrific architectural detail in these rooms," he said, handing the picture to Jimmy. "There are angels in the corners holding up the plaster bits."

One of the angels had his backside to the room, with his legs spread wide and his testicles visible. The boys looked at each other.

"Get used to it, lads," Lizzie said, "there are lots of butts and breasts and other bits plastered around the house."

She put her hand on the box of letters from Maggie Gonzaga to her family back home. "Would one of you mind scanning these for me?" she said. She wanted to have a file that she could peruse at home.

Roscoe agreed, saying it would be no problem to process them while he was working on the photographs.

With pieces of the exhibition beginning to fall into place, Lizzie made a preliminary list of things to be included, so that she could speak to the designer about them. She would have Jimmy and Roscoe full time in January, and part time after the spring term started. She would go to Bologna for three weeks in February, and was glad that she would be able to get such a good handle on the collection in advance of going there. Certainly there would be lots of surprises that weren't included on the list or captured in any of the pictures, but the wonderful image of the cabinet in 1677 was such a strong starting place that she felt confident making a preliminary list that included five things: the Guido Reni Madonna and the Niccolo dell'Arca angel sculpture, which showed the fine arts aspects of the collection; the image of the cabinet, which demonstrated the scientific principles of natural history organization; and the alligator and sarcophagus, which were so prominently illustrated and which were big and had great visual impact.

Smaller things like ancient pottery, sea shells, coral, and animal or fish mounts could be sketched in by deciding how many of each type should be included and then choosing the specific examples when she got to Bologna. The big questions were things like statuary and other works of art. They were all around the house, as a quick glance at the pictures had shown, and Cosimo had said that anything in the house was available for the exhibit.

Lizzie looked again at the 1677 image. There were busts arranged around the top of the cabinet and she thought she would see if those actual pieces could be identified. It occurred to her that since the College had the original image of the cabinet, Cosimo Gonzaga might never have seen it, and she wrote him a short note, telling him how exciting it was to be working on the project and attaching a scanned image of the picture. "It is probably too much to hope that this arrangement is still standing in your house," she wrote, "but I would like to identify as many things as I can that survive from this period."

It was six hours later in Bologna, and she didn't expect any answer this evening, but her thoughts were beginning to turn to her trip and to being in the Gonzaga palazzo on the Piazza Galvani. Even the address had a romantic sound.

Lizzie quickly typed up a similar note for the exhibit designer, and sent him the image as well. "Here is a terrific starting place," she wrote. "Do you think we can enlarge it into a wall-sized mural?"

Her last note of the day was to Justin Carrera. "You missed our meeting today," she wrote bluntly. "Please let me know your schedule and how you are doing on translating the list. Can you stop by my office tomorrow?"

Since Jackie had been finding so many unexpected treasures in the archives, Lizzie decided to stop by the library again before she went home. Roscoe was at the scanner, methodically putting Maggie's letters on the glass plate one at a time, and told her that he would be able to send her a file that evening.

Jackie waved to her from her desk and removed a pile of books from her spare chair so that Lizzie could sit in it.

"Have you found any more unexpected delights for me?" Lizzie asked.

"Haven't I found enough already? I see you have your minions starting to process them."

"I think they'll do a good job," Lizzie responded. "And I'm getting quite excited about it all; it's terrific material to work with."

"How is the background research going?"

"The biggest dilemma before you found that great image of the cabinet, was in distinguishing between two different Gonzaga collections, both famous in their own times, but completely separate. In addition to the 'cabinet of curiosities' that I'm working with, there was a famous collection of fine art made by another branch of the family."

"I've seen in my own dabbling into this that the Gonzagas were a big family, with at least one saint and a bunch of cardinals and bishops."

"They were the Dukes of Mantua for about four hundred years, and sent younger sons across Northern Italy and even into France to form new dynasties. Our branch reached Bologna in the late sixteenth century."

"So where does the 'Prince' title come from? Of what was Lorenzo Gonzaga the prince?"

"I was hoping you could tell me that," Lizzie said. "I haven't found any reference to it except in the engagement announcement in the *New York Times* and in other information that was put out by the Kellihers."

"You don't think Paddy-boy made it up do you? To cash in on some of the notoriety of American heiresses marrying European nobility? It was rather a fad in the early twentieth century."

Lizzie shook her head. "I can't believe he'd make it up out of thin air. There must have been something there to base it on. I think I'll ask Rose's dad. Martin says that he hangs out at her restaurant in the afternoon."

"Let me know when you decide to go. I'd like to meet him and hear what he has to say."

Lizzie assured her that she would let her know when she was going.

"So tell me about the other collection," Jackie said, "so I'll know what I'm looking at if I find anything."

"The Mantua part of the Gonzaga family had one of the great Renaissance art collections; Peter Paul Rubens actually worked for them for a time," Lizzie said. "That collection, which took six generations to assemble, was largely dispersed by 1630, in wars over the succession."

She described to Jackie a large number of paintings that had been acquired by King Charles I of England, including works by Titian, Caravaggio, Tintoretto, Correggio and Guido Reni. "One of the best collections ever sold," she said enthusiastically. "Then after Charles was executed, most of the collection went to Robert Walpole, the Prime Minister, and from him to Catherine the Great of Russia."

"Did any of that collection end up in Bologna?"

"Hard to tell. I haven't found any record of it, but they might have something in the house there. Paintings known to have come from Mantua are scattered around Europe, including in the British Royal collection and at the Louvre. More than thirty of them were in the Hermitage Museum in St. Petersburg until 1930, when the Soviet Government sold them to Andrew Mellon. Some of them were used to start the National Gallery in Washington, and others were purchased by the Metropolitan Museum in New York."

"But no alligators or mummies."

Lizzie smiled. "No, and that is the big difference between the two collections. The Mantua Gonzagas collected fine art; the Bologna Gonzagas made a specimen cabinet, but I have a feeling there was plenty of fine art in the house as well. Look at those two gems in the chapel from their collection."

Roscoe stopped by to say that he had finished scanning the letters and was going to leave for the day. Lizzie thanked him and looked at the clock.

"I've kept you too long again," she said to Jackie.

"I live to serve," her friend answered. She was starting to turn off her computer when she remembered something. "I found two somewhat bizarre articles in a literature search for you. You won't be able to use them, but they show a dark side to human nature."

"I'm all ears," Lizzie answered.

"The first is mostly bizarre because I don't know why anyone would undertake such a project in the first place. It's an article describing how some guy took the skull of a woman purported to be Eleonora Gonzaga, who lived in the early sixteenth century, and superimposed images of it on a portrait of the woman by Titian."

"Yuck," Lizzie said. "Next?"

"This one is much worse. It tells the story of how Vincenzo Gonzaga, the Crown Prince of Mantua, had to prove to the Medicis that he could father a child before they would let him marry their daughter." Jackie gave Lizzie a look of disgust before continuing. "They basically took a girl out of the local convent orphanage and had him rape her to prove he wasn't impotent."

Lizzie was silent for several moments. "Happily, I don't need to process that thought very much, but just out of curiosity, when did this happen?"

"1580."

"So the Mantua family was in their last few decades of power."

"A strange time, obviously."

"And violent."

"Obviously. Once again we see how easily the poor and

powerless get swept up in the politics of the rich and power-ful."

"That is pretty much a constant theme with us, isn't it?"

"Well, Lizzie, if you are going to be a historian, that's what you've got to deal with."

"The eighteenth and nineteenth centuries, where I usual-ly concentrate on British and American mariners, are rather more straightforward I think, but I'm finding these violent, passionate Renaissance Italians rather compelling. I mean how many families can claim a rapist, a saint, and collectors of great art and alligators?"

"I don't think I'd use that on the posters to advertise the exhibit if I were you, but it is a thought to motivate."

"I'll call Rose and see if we can set up coffee with her fa-ther early next week," Lizzie said. "He may be able to give us more insights into the modern parts of the family."

"I look forward to it."

Chapter 6

Since Lizzie was devoting both her January and Spring terms to working on the exhibit, she commandeered a small classroom as a workspace to organize the voluminous materials that needed to be processed. She had a bulletin board installed on the back wall that was five feet high and more than ten feet long, in the center of which she tacked an enlargement of the 1677 drawing of the cabinet. Every time she, Roscoe, or Jimmy identified an object from the drawing, either in a photograph or on the list, they tacked a note or picture around the image. Photographs of rooms in the house sent by Maggie Gonzaga in 1959, which Lizzie assumed must have been taken at that time, each had their own galaxy of accompanying notes and pictures on the board.

The missing piece was a catalog list from before 1959. Lizzie was certain that such passionate collectors as the Gonzagas must have had one at the time they had their cabinet drawn in 1677, and supposed that updates or new editions had been created over the centuries since. But Maggie did not seem to have known of one when she sent her material, and Cosimo Gonzaga hadn't located one either. She wondered if Maggie might actually have inventoried the collection herself and made the list that they were now using. It could have been a project to help her recover from the losses of the war.

Now that she had pictures of rooms in the Gonzaga house up on her board, she could see that there didn't seem to be anything quite like the cabinet shown in the drawing, but there were plenty of glass-fronted cases with shelves filled with rarities and oddities.

When Roscoe and Jimmy arrived she walked them through

the pictures and asked what they had found. It was possible, they discovered, to actually find sections of the list that corresponded to adjacent items in the photographs, which supported Lizzie's theory that Maggie Gonzaga had made the inventory, or had someone do it, at the same time the pictures were taken.

Roscoe and Jimmy were enthusiastic participants. Jimmy got so excited every time he found something on the list in one of the pictures that he was constantly sending Lizzie email messages with connections he had made, and his notations on the board were filled with exclamation points. Even his name was frequently followed by one in his messages:

"Hi Prof. Manning, I found the Etruscan bronze dancing figure described on the list! It is in the case on the left side, third shelf down, three objects over, in picture no. 17! Jimmy!"

Roscoe was quieter than Jimmy, and a steady and careful worker. The photographs were of high quality and he had blown up portions of them so that even small things resting on shelves at the end of a room were identifiable. He had also found an architectural drawing of the palazzo and had placed the photographs of the rooms on it.

"The house is a gigantic square," he explained to Lizzie, using the drawing as a guide, "built around a big open courtyard. The main floor, which they call the *piano nobile,* is up these grand staircases, which are to your right and left when you come through the main door. There's no hallway on this floor, so you go from one room into the next all around the square."

There were six rooms on the *piano nobile,* and there was now a photograph of each of them on the wall in Lizzie's classroom.

"There are names for each room on the back of the photographs," Roscoe said, "and I've added them to this drawing."

"That's great," Lizzie said. "Let's use those names to refer to them from now on and label them on the board."

Up the left staircase from the courtyard, one first reached the Entrance Hall, then proceeded from there through the Yellow Salon, the Chinese Salon, the Dining Room—which was on the far wall of the house opposite the front door—and from there to the Library and Ballroom, which was obviously set atop the other staircase so that visitors could reach it without walking through the rest of the house.

"I'm sorry these pictures aren't in color," Lizzie said. "The Yellow Salon and the Chinese Salon look pretty fabulous." She was sorry that the color in the photos in Tony's album had faded too much to do justice to the rooms.

"There is also a chapel up on the third floor, but we only have one mediocre picture of it," Roscoe added. "There is something lying under the altar that looks like a body."

Lizzie took the picture from him as he pointed to what was clearly a corpse. "Yup, that is a body," she said. "Probably a saint. I've seen them under altars like this before in churches, but never in a private house." She could make out several reliquaries in the picture and commented on them. "These hold body parts of saints for veneration. I'll see if we can't arrange to bring a few of those here for our exhibit."

Her assistants asked if she might bring the whole corpse, but she shook her head. "I think the reliquaries will add to an exhibition on Renaissance collecting, but a desiccated body would only distract museum visitors from the rest of the collection."

The picture reminded Lizzie that she wanted to go again to the chapel on campus and look at the two pieces there that would appear in the exhibit, and when Roscoe and Jimmy had shown her everything they were working on she walked across the campus green, past the statue of Paddy Kelliher. It was only about three o'clock but it was snowing lightly and the sky was dark.

The chapel was unlocked, and Lizzie thought that the time had probably come to do something to better secure the valuable treasures that were kept there. As she pushed open the door she made a mental note to say something about it to Father O'Toole the next time they met.

It was dark inside, with little light being pushed through the dark stained glass windows depicting scenes from the life of St. Patrick. Lizzie found switches near the door and turned on the hanging lamps that lit the front half of the church, and several spotlights aimed at the main altar and at two smaller altars set into niches to its right and left. On the right was a large statue of St. Patrick, surrounded by mementos that had been left there by visitors to the church, including dozens of crosses made of rushes from Ireland. Memorial cards for deceased Irishmen were tacked or taped to boards on either side of the image of the saint, along with notes begging the saint to intercede with higher authorities on their behalf for causes as heart-rending as a child dying of cancer, and as trivial as a good grade on a mid-term exam.

To the left of the main altar was an alcove that had an inscription in stone that said "Gonzaga Chapel." The Guido Reni painting of the Madonna and child was situated in a marble arch at the center of the small altar, surrounded by a golden frame. Lizzie had frequently admired the painting but had never really studied it carefully. She went through the short gate that separated the alcove from the transept of the church and took a few steps to stand at the painting. The Niccolo dell'Arca angel was positioned in front of it to the right, near enough for her to reach out her hand and rest it on the cool marble of its wings. She thought again that there was nothing to prevent either of these pieces from being stolen and resolved again to bring it up with Father O'Toole.

It was an irresistible temptation to step around the altar and put her arms around the angel. It was only about eighteen inches high and she found that she could lift it; there was nothing cementing it to the marble slab on which it sat. It was also, she noted, neither too heavy nor too big for her to put it into a case and carry out of the church.

She lowered it carefully and looked closely at the details of the carving. The face was exquisitely carved, with an expression of such serenity that Lizzie felt calm simply to be in its presence. The angel was depicted as a young boy, with long curls hanging down to his shoulders. He genuflected onto his left knee and rested a large candlestick on his right, keeping it steady with his delicately carved hands; his feet peeped out from under the hem of the gown he wore. Though the statue was carved of hard stone, everything about it looked soft, the folds of drapery that fell from the angel's sleeves and long robe, his curly hair, and the feathers of his wings.

The sculpture and the painting were great works of art and Lizzie felt how lucky she was to be able to include them in her exhibit. She also appreciated that in giving them to the college Lorenzo Gonzaga not only had made a very generous gift, but had separated himself and his family from masterpieces that had been treasured for generations. It seemed to indicate that he had really loved Maggie, and she liked that.

When Lizzie returned to her office she found Justin Carrera sitting on the floor outside her door. She got out her keys and invited him in.

"Where have you been the last few days?" she asked him.

"Sick," he answered. He coughed as he said it, as evidence.

"Why didn't you contact me to let me know?" Lizzie said, barely disguising her irritation.

"I told you, I was sick," he said, coughing once again.

"Were you able to get any work done on the list?"

"Yeah," he said, pulling a notebook from his backpack. "I finished it." He tore two pages out of the notebook and handed them to Lizzie. On them was a scribbled list that looked remarkably similar to the original.

Lizzie sat in the chair behind her desk and gestured to him to sit in another one opposite.

"So what did you find?" she asked, scanning the list.

"It was pretty much just straightforward stuff."

"I see you have a notation here about the mummy," she said. "You say it is from the eighteenth century." She looked up at him and raised an eyebrow. "How is that possible? It appears in a picture of the collection drawn in the seventeenth century."

"That's what it said."

"And what is 'Itrusken,' which you have written here?"

"You know, those guys who lived before the Romans."

"Etruscans?" she asked.

He nodded, but didn't look at her.

"I told you that you would have to look up spellings in English if you didn't know them."

He was silent.

"Well," Lizzie said, folding her hands on top of the papers.

"I'm not quite sure what to do with you. Do you actually want to work on this project?"

"I have to," he answered. "My Uncle Cosimo told me I had to do it."

"Are you interested in the objects in the collection?"

"I guess the alligator is pretty interesting."

"So would you say you are interested in the natural history material, the shells and corals and other animals?"

"No, not really."

"How about paintings or sculpture?"

He shook his head and shrugged. He also started to move his leg up and down in a nervous motion on the other side of her desk, hard enough that Lizzie could feel the floor shake.

"Would you like to do a genealogy of your family, from the time they started the collection to the present? That might be useful." It was almost the only thing she could think of that could keep him out of her hair, and he might even find something that she could use.

"I guess so," he said, still not looking at Lizzie. "I think I've seen one on the wall at my Uncle Cosimo's house, and my mom is kind of interested in that stuff."

"Good!" she said, standing up and going to the door. "So you have a place to start. Why don't you send me a report of what you're finding at the end of every week and we can meet when we need to."

She waited at the open door as he quickly closed his pack and stood up.

"Okay, thank you," he said as he left. He seemed just as relieved to have been assigned a task that would not tax him as Lizzie was to have him sidetracked from the main work at hand.

Chapter 7

Over the weekend, Lizzie had a chance to bring Martin up to date on the work. She appreciated his eye as an artist and wanted to get his opinion on the house and the collection, especially the drawing of the cabinet.

"I really need to see the original," he said, looking at the image on her laptop.

"Come over one day this week," she invited. "In fact, Jackie wants to meet Tony Tessitore and I thought I might try to arrange for us to have coffee with him on Tuesday. Come to the College that day, see the stuff, and then we can all go over to Rose's restaurant."

Martin was making a noise of assent as he forwarded through the pictures on Lizzie's computer. "Nice collection of paintings," he said. "Are you planning to borrow any of them?"

"I don't know," Lizzie said. "What do you see?"

"Nothing quite of the quality of the Reni or the dell'Arca, but there are some very nice Italian things here and a couple of Dutch or Flemish paintings from the seventeenth century." He zoomed in to one landscape painting in the Yellow Salon, until it began to break up into pixels on the screen.

"The photographs are better than the scans," she said. "And one of my students is making some high-resolution enlargements so that we can see things better."

"Well, even without a good image, I recognize this as Jacob van Ruysdael, and there's a dandy naval portrait here that looks to be by Backhuyzen." He turned the screen toward her and pointed out each painting.

"I'm not sure how much they would add to my exhibit,

however nice they might be," Lizzie said. "I really want to concentrate on the specimen cabinet and the exhibition space isn't all that big."

Martin agreed that hard choices would have to be made. "These photographs are just tantalizing enough to hint at unexpected wonders to be discovered when you get to the house."

"Yes, indeed," Lizzie agreed. "I'm getting very excited to see it. I mean, look at this picture of what they call 'The Chinese Salon.' A black and white picture just doesn't do it. Besides all the Chinese porcelains in the room, I think this wallpaper must be from China."

She reached over to advance the pictures on the screen until the chapel appeared. "And here's one you'll really love," she said. "I think there's a corpse stashed under the altar here."

"I have to put my foot down here, Liz. Every time you get yourself involved with an old corpse, someone tries to kill you." He had a half-serious tone in his voice but gave her a meaningful look.

She put her hand on his arm. "Jackie made a similar comment to me. She said she hoped this project was not going to be life-threatening, or something like that, and she didn't even know about the corpse, which must be some saint." She smiled at her husband and got up from the couch where they had been sitting. "Don't worry. Whoever that is lying under the altar is not coming home with me."

Martin closed the computer and stood to embrace his wife. He put his arms around her shoulders and gave her tight hug, before kissing her.

She leaned back to meet his gaze.

"It's funny too, because those two life-threatening experiences were associated with research projects that dealt with good old English families, seemingly the model of civilized behavior. While these guys—the Gonzagas—Whoa! They have a much more checkered past."

"Can I come with you?"

Martin was consulting with an architectural firm in Boston at the moment and when Lizzie had first asked about this more than a month earlier he had said he wouldn't be able to travel with her.

"Do you think you need to come protect me from danger?" she asked.

He laughed and leaned his forehead down to touch hers. "Actually I'm intrigued by the pictures of the house and I'd like to see them with you." He kissed her on the head. "But I can protect you too, in case that corpse turns out to be something other than the saint they think it is."

"I am fairly confident that it is not, in fact, whatever saint they think it is." She rested her cheek against his. "I don't imagine you can come for the whole three weeks."

"No, but I think I'll come for the last week. If Tony is to be believed, the food there is the best in Italy." He released her. "And I would like to come see that sketch of the collection and have coffee with you next week if you and Jackie meet with Tony."

"I'll call Rose today and arrange it."

Lizzie took her computer to the dining room table and opened it again. "I'm glad you're coming to Bologna; you can advise me on the paintings and let me know if there are any treasures that would really make the exhibit."

"If there are, they are likely to be enormously valuable. Do you have a budget to cover the shipping and insurance on a really great work of art? That Ruysdael alone is probably worth a quarter of a million dollars."

"I have been assured that I can take anything in the house, and that the costs will be covered. Both the Kellihers and the Gonzagas are loaded, and they seem to want this exhibit to make a splash, so I don't think that will be a problem." She mentioned that she had stopped into the chapel at St. Patrick's earlier that day to look at the Guido Reni Madonna and the dell'Arca marble angel. "Really, they are so fabulous that they can represent the fine arts all on their own."

"I imagine that some of the things you'll want to borrow will need to be conserved," Martin said. "You have a pretty tight schedule for that, and for the installation if you are going to open in September."

"I know," Lizzie answered. "Cosimo Gonzaga has engaged

a conservator from the University Museum in Bologna, but you're right, it is a short timetable. Once Father O'Toole decided to go forward with this, and the Kellihers agreed to fund it, he was determined to have it open on the actual hundredth anniversary of the founding of the College."

Martin gave her a wry smile. "Maybe you shouldn't have suggested it," he said.

Lizzie returned the look. "I never expected him to take me up on it so quickly!"

When her husband had migrated into his studio, Lizzie called Rose and scheduled coffee with her father for the following Tuesday. Then she opened the calendar on her computer and made a list of people she would need to consult about objects and artworks that would be in the exhibit.

John Haworth was the resident Egyptologist at St. Pat's, and she sent him an email asking if she could talk to him about the sarcophagus, and attached the photograph she had found in the collection file. Unfortunately, it didn't show the whole case, only the part from the chest up as the sarcophagus stood against a wall.

She sent another email to George Tesman, her colleague in the history department, who was a historian of the medieval period. This was mostly just a courtesy. George was a detail man. He had been working for years on a book about the household crafts of Flemish people in the Brabant region and he didn't like to comment on big-picture ideas, or on anything beyond the scope of his own research. Nonetheless, Lizzie thought he might have something to say on the reliquaries in the Gonzaga chapel, and she attached the picture.

Until she had a better list to work with, she would wait to get help with the scientific specimens. Years before, when she was still in graduate school, Lizzie had worked at the Boston Museum of Natural History, and she still had a few old friends there who would love a chance to comment on the rarities in the Gonzaga collection.

Having thought her way through the next steps of her work, Lizzie decided to indulge herself by spending a few hours looking at the letters Maggie Gonzaga had sent to her family in Boston. Roscoe had scanned them all and sent her the file, and Lizzie transferred them from her computer to her e-reader. She settled herself comfortably into the deep cushions of her favorite couch and turned her attention to the woman who had tantalized her in the brief time she had known about her.

The first letter was dated September 13, 1907, which was much earlier than Lizzie had expected. She knew that Maggie had been born on her father's fiftieth birthday in 1892, after five brothers. She married at the age of twenty in 1912 and moved to Italy. This letter was postmarked Rougemont, Switzerland, and as she read it, Lizzie realized that Maggie had gone to school there when she was fifteen.

"I have missed you since you left," the teenager wrote, "but I am finding that I love the mountains, they are incredibly grand and majestic." She described classes in French, German and Italian, and daily sessions with "Madame," where they drank tea and set tables using all the right spoons and forks.

Besides languages and etiquette, the school didn't seem to have much of a curriculum, and Lizzie found herself scanning quickly through three years of correspondence. There were gaps when Maggie came home for holidays and summers, descriptions of Atlantic crossings on ocean liners, and some letters addressed only to her father, when her mother joined her in Europe. They were mostly the sort of chatty letters that girls away from home would write in any century—about teachers, friends, and short trips made with her class. They were unusual only in that Maggie wrote very little about clothes, and never about needing money. Occasionally she wrote about visits to museums and the theater, and in those passages Lizzie could see a budding interest in the arts. Maggie loved Shakespeare and convinced her parents to let her spend an additional year in England in order to study the plays and see as many productions as she could.

"What are you reading?" Martin asked, as he passed through the room to refill his coffee cup.

"Letters sent by Maggie Kelliher Gonzaga to her parents from a finishing school in Switzerland."

"Are they interesting?"

"They start to get more interesting toward the end when she leaves there and goes off to get a real education in England."

"What was it they were hoping to 'finish' at those places anyway?" he asked.

"I think they wanted to put a polish on girls so that they could marry well and be good hostesses."

"Did it work?"

"In Maggie's case I'd say that most people would think she married very well."

"How did she meet her prince?"

Lizzie said she didn't know, but hoped she would find out as she read on. Martin offered to pour her a cup of coffee and when she had the hot mug in her hand she turned back to Maggie's letters.

May 29, 1910

Dear Mama and Papa,

Pascale Bourdin, my friend from school, has joined me in London. Thank you for engaging the house for us, but please instruct the landlady that she is not to act like either our mother or our teacher. I don't know what you possibly could have written to her to make her be so bossy with us, but she isn't knowledgeable about plays or music, and so if you told her that she should act like a governess please write back and tell her to stop.

If you insist that I must have an older companion than Pascale, I suggest we engage Miss Philippa Reeves, who taught at my school for several years. She is an Englishwoman who returned home to tend to her mother, who recently died. Miss Reeves hasn't decided if she will go back to Rougemont in the fall, but is in any case looking for employment through the summer. I will enclose her address and references with this letter.

Maggie clearly got her way, as the next several letters described visits to the theater and concerts with Pascale Bourdin and Miss Reeves. They took a trip to Stratford-upon-Avon to visit the Shakespeare sights, and then went to Scotland for several weeks when the weather got too hot in London. They met Scotsmen named Duncan and Macbeth, which thrilled all three women, but Maggie was very discreet in her descriptions of those adventures.

In the fall of 1910, Maggie Kelliher and her companions decided to travel to Switzerland to visit their old school, and when Miss Reeves decided that she liked traveling with her two charges better than teaching twenty often less-agreeable girls for a salary lower than what Paddy Kelliher was paying her, they decided to have a grand tour of Europe. They took the train from Zurich to Milan and then developed an itinerary that took them to all the places in northern Italy where Shakespeare had set a play: Verona, Padua, Mantua, and Venice.

Maggie wrote effusively about the food, pledging to learn how to cook while she was in Italy. She was also becoming increasingly interested in Roman art and architecture, especially after a close reading of "Julius Caesar" with her companions. Italian sites were constantly described in Shakespearean terms and she regretted that the Bard had not, like herself, ever visited the country. In Bologna, Maggie and Pascale took a course on Roman archaeology at the university, and traveled with the lecturer Lorenzo Gonzaga into the hills south of the city on several short trips.

Knowing that Maggie would marry Lorenzo Gonzaga, Lizzie paid special attention to her descriptions of her teacher, and wondered if her parents had seen in their daughter's prose that she was falling in love with him. To Lizzie it seemed obvious. She went from calling him "Prof. Gonzaga," to "Lorenzo" and then "Renzo." He was brilliant and had an unfailing eye for discerning ancient sites lying beneath perfectly ordinary landscapes; he had read everything, even Shakespeare in English, and his manners were impeccable.

"I have become quite the Archaeologist," she wrote on November 8, 1910. "I wish I had studied Latin more seriously.

Some of the things we find go to the University Museum, but Prof. Gonzaga has a wonderful collection at his house of Roman and Etruscan carvings of various kinds."

At Christmas, Maggie was invited to stay at the house on the Piazza Galvani and to meet Signora Gonzaga, Lorenzo's mother. The letters no longer contained descriptions of activities with either Pascale or Miss Reeves, and Maggie was finally forced to admit, in answer to a direct question from her mother in a telegram, that they had each gone home more than a month earlier.

"I assure you that there is nothing the least bit inappropriate going on," Maggie wrote on January 26, 1911. "Certainly Signora Gonzaga, a woman with a sterling reputation, can do the job of chaperone just as well as Philippa Reeves."

When Martin passed through the room on his way to the kitchen, Lizzie quickly brought him up to date on the adventures of Maggie Kelliher. "The plot thickens!" she said gleefully. "Not unlike Elizabeth Bennet seeing Pemberley for the first time, Maggie is at the Gonzaga Palazzo in Bologna and falling for the young master!"

"She stayed with him before they were married?" Martin asked, surprised at the notion.

"Not quite," Lizzie admitted. "His mother is there and she sounds like a devout Catholic, so I don't think they are having sex or anything."

"The plot thins," Martin joked. "What happens next?"

"I read on to see," Lizzie said, turning back to the letters.

February 19, 1911

Dear Mother and Father,

I am mortified that you sent Tom here to get me. Do you really think that I cannot be trusted to behave correctly? Do you think that I am not modest, chaste and moral? Nothing, nothing has gone on in this house that is the least bit unseemly and I am bitterly disappointed in you for thinking that I cannot, at the age of 18, make responsible decisions.

The Gonzagas are an ancient noble family, extremely well positioned in the community; Signora
Gonzaga is a devout Catholic, Lorenzo is a heredi-
tary prince...

The words came blistering off the page as the angry young
woman defended herself. The next letter was from her brother Tom, who at twenty was two years older than his sister.
He had taken a leave of absence from college to follow her to
Italy.

February 20, 1911

Dear Mom and Dad,

Maggie is awfully mad at me for coming here
and she greeted me with the angriest words she has
ever thrust my way. She says I have embarrassed
her with the Gonzaga family by treating her like a
child, but frankly I think both the mother and the
son respect you for sending me.
She went from barbs to tears late in the night,
telling me that she loves Lorenzo Gonzaga but is
confused because he has never declared his love
back. Frankly, he is a nice guy, but he must be close
to forty. He was married once, widowed and has no
children. I think he would like a young and spirit-
ed wife, but he is clearly too old for Maggie, and I
can't believe she would really leave us all behind to
live in Italy, but she insists she is in love with him.
She also says she won't come back with me.
I asked Signora Gonzaga what sort of invitation
she had issued to Maggie and it doesn't seem that
it was ever the old lady's intention that Maggie
should move into their house. She came for dinner
one night and never left. This is not to say that they
don't seem to love having her. We all know that
Maggie can be a real charmer and she has gone
all out to win these two over, so I can't see either

Signora Gonzaga or her son asking her to leave.
I'll write more when I know more.

Your loving son,

Tom

There were no more letters in the collection from before the wedding of Maggie and Lorenzo, so Lizzie was left not knowing if her brother had dragged Maggie back to Boston and the Italian archaeologist had followed, or if she stayed on as the lingering guest in the house on Galvani Plaza until a beleaguered Lorenzo proposed marriage. The former was more likely than the latter, as it seemed improbable that Maggie had ceased communicating with her family; whoever saved the letters had been thorough about it.

Lizzie wished that she had the letters Maggie's parents had written to her. "But that is the curse of the historian," she said to herself as she closed the reader, "you don't get to be the one to choose what's saved."

Chapter 8

Cosimo Gonzaga took several days to answer Lizzie's email, and then he reported that he had never seen the 1677 image before, and that he didn't live in the house on Galvani Plaza, but was pretty sure that there was no such organization of cases in any room there as was pictured. "My uncle Patrick Gonzaga lives in the house," he said, "but he is rather infirm at age ninety-two. The collection has been his hobby for most of his life and though his memory of current events is shaky, I think you'll find he has a lot of information for you." He added that there was another image from 1677, probably by the same artist, that showed the chapel in the house, and he attached a scan of it. "My grandmother gave the original to my father around the time I was born," he explained.

"I hope my nephew Beppe is working hard for you. My niece Pina Corelli will be available to help you when you are in Bologna next month, and of course Beppe will be here to help prepare the collection to be shipped in May."

"Beppe," Lizzie said softly. "Beppe, how did you become Justin?"

As if to answer her question, Justin Carrere appeared at her door.

"I got a copy of a genealogy," he said. "But it only goes up to 1940."

"Can you add the rest of the names up to the present?"

"How?"

"Don't you at least know the names of your aunts, uncles and first cousins?"

He said that he did.

"Show me what you have," she said.

He asked if he could use her computer to check his email, as it was in an attachment from his mother.

Lizzie let him use the office computer and then printed out the five-page attachment. It was a genealogy of the Gonzaga family from 1407, showing the Dukes of Mantua, Dukes of Nevers in France, and several cardinals and bishops. The Bologna branch divided off in 1590 when one Adino Gonzaga moved there and married into the powerful Bentivoglio family. Adino was the student of Aldrovandi and his son Lorenzo, born in 1608, was the founder of the cabinet and the one who had the picture drawn in 1677. There was a clear line of eldest sons down to Lorenzo Gonzaga, born in 1874, who married Maggie Kelliher in 1912. Their children were listed, and familiar to Lizzie from the family photographs she had looked at with Jackie: Eleonora, born in 1913; Margherita, born in 1914; Adino, born in 1915; Cosimo, born in 1918; Patrick, born in 1921; and Giuseppina, born in 1923, whom Tony Tessitore had called Gianna.

"Your great-aunt Giuseppina died in the war," Lizzie said to Justin, "though since this document was made before the war it doesn't show her death date."

"I know." Justin said. "She was some sort of resistance fighter. I'm named after her."

"Your name is Giuseppe?" she asked.

He gave his familiar almost noncommittal nod.

"Your uncle, Cosimo, referred to you as Beppe in a message to me; is that what your family calls you?"

Same nod, accompanied by chin scratching.

"When did you start calling yourself Justin?"

"When I came here. It just sounded better."

Lizzie returned to the family tree. "So which of the people on here are your grandparents?"

Justin pointed to the name Margherita and said, "I think she was my grandmother. I barely knew her. She died when I was just a kid."

"Maybe you can get more information from your mother," Lizzie said hopefully. "And there is a file in the library with pictures of the last generation listed here. You might like to take a look at them."

He said he would do that and left quickly without taking the papers.

"What a dope," Lizzie said under her breath.

In need of an antidote to Justin, Lizzie walked across campus to meet with John Haworth, St. Pat's only Egyptologist. She didn't know him well, but he always injected a welcome humor into faculty meetings and what she knew of him she liked.

He greeted her like an old friend, even kissing her on the cheek when she entered his office. He was a big man, with a shock of white hair and piercing blue eyes. "Love that picture you sent me," he said instantly, "and can't wait to see the sarcophagus. Am I right in thinking that you're bringing it here for the exhibit you're working on?"

"If it's in good enough shape to travel I absolutely will."

"When will you know?"

"I'm heading to Bologna in a few weeks and will go over the whole collection with a conservator from the University Museum to see what can travel, but it is at the top of my list." She pulled a copy of the 1677 image out of her bag and showed it to him. "The sarcophagus was already in the collection in the seventeenth century, and I'd like to try to assemble as many things as I can that are in this drawing."

He took off his glasses to look more closely. "I can almost see some additional details here," he said. "But as soon as you can, send me pictures of the whole case and I will translate the hieroglyphs for you."

"Can you tell me anything from the picture I sent you?"

"A fair amount, actually," he answered, bringing the picture up on his computer screen. "It's a classic Eighteenth Dynasty piece," he said.

"Ah!" Lizzie interrupted. "My ineffective student assistant translated that as eighteenth century, which I knew wasn't correct since we have it here in a seventeenth-century image."

"It's from the age of King Tut," John continued. "A very good sarcophagus for a well-placed functionary in the court. Since I can't yet see the whole of the inscription, I can't tell you exactly what he did, but it is consistent with several other pieces in museum collections here and abroad. The fact that it is illustrated in that early drawing makes it very special."

"I'll have better pictures for you in a few weeks," she said. "Is there a mummy in the case?"

"I have no idea," she said, surprised that it had not yet occurred to her to ask that question. "Should there be?"

"I doubt it," he answered. "Most of the mummies that came into Europe in the Renaissance were cannibalized for medicinal purposes."

This was a statement for which Lizzie was unprepared.

"Are you serious?" she asked, her voice expressing her surprise.

"I am," he answered, unfazed. "It was a common cure-all in the Renaissance and appears in a number of medical texts."

John Haworth then began to rattle off early references to "mummy" or "mumia" as a medicinal agent.

"The tenth-century Arab doctor Avicenna was the first to mention it. He was pretty enthusiastic in prescribing mummy for bruises and wounds especially, but also for almost everything else that could go wrong in a human body: broken bones, palsy, congestion of the lungs or throat, problems with the heart, spleen, stomach, liver, and it could even be used as an antidote to many poisons. There were few things it wouldn't cure, and because he was an important figure in the medical world, doctors all over Europe and the Middle East began to demand it."

"For how long?" Lizzie asked.

"*The New Jewel of Health,* from around 1560, was still prescribing mummy for everything from the grandest problems of all, plague, poison, and arrow wounds, to the most mundane things—headaches, eye problems, gout and worms." He pulled a book off the shelf, speaking all the time. "Amboise Paré, who was one of the great scientific thinkers of the late sixteenth century, and clearly a doubter of the efficacy of mummy, said it was 'the very first and last medicine of almost all our practitioners' to treat severe bruising at that time."

He opened the book. "This is one of my favorites," he said gleefully. "William Bullein's *Bulwark of Defense Against All*

Sickness, from 1562. I think Bullein was probably considered something of a quack even in his own day, but he was a great proponent of the curative power of ground-up mummy parts." He read aloud a recipe that included mummy, honey, poppy juice, carrots and fennel to treat epilepsy as well as a number of other less serious ailments. He looked up at Lizzie with a sly smile. "If anything worked it was probably the poppy juice."

"I have heard that Julius Caesar was epileptic and that one of the Roman treatments was to drink the blood of young gladiators killed in the games at the Coliseum," Lizzie said. "At an intuitive level, I kind of understand the idea that fresh blood from a young healthy athlete might make you stronger."

John chuckled. "Though of course from a medical perspective drinking blood does you no good at all. It goes into your digestive system, not your circulatory system. Of course Bullein also thought that you should squirt some of his mixture up your nose."

"Of course," Lizzie said quickly. "I'm only saying that I understand the *idea* of drinking fresh blood. What I don't get is why anyone would have thought that ingesting parts of a thousand-year-old desiccated corpse would be good for you."

"For an answer to that, let me give you a quote from Bullein. He writes that mummies are made of the dead bodies of 'noble people, because the said dead are richly embalmed with precious ointments and spices, chiefly myrrh, saffron, and aloes.'"

"So he thought that the preservatives that kept the corpse from deteriorating would somehow keep the living person preserved as well?"

John Haworth clasped his hands on the book in front of him. "It might be that," he mused. "Or it might be the notion of immortality, which was clearly so important to the ancient Egyptians. Maybe those later Europeans were inspired by that and wanted to capture something of the effort that went into it." He closed the book. "Our friend Bullein went too far, of course, as is in the nature of quacks. A later recipe in the book calls for a mixture of mummy and dragon's blood as a cure for bruising."

"Maybe the dark color of the preserved mummy's skin was the connection to bruising," Lizzie ventured.

"That's not a bad notion," John answered. "Certainly that was one of the most commonly mentioned reasons for using it. The king of France in the early sixteenth century is said to have carried a purse full of ground mummy with him at all times in case he fell off his horse."

Lizzie stood and walked to the window as she thought about the unexpected education she was getting.

"Most of the examples you are giving me are from the sixteenth century," she said. "How long do you think the Gonzaga mummy was in Italy before this picture was made?"

"Impossible to say," John answered. "There was a guy, da Carpi, who reported seeing numerous mummies in Venice before 1518, so certainly there was a trade in them from Egypt across the Mediterranean very early in the sixteenth century. The oddest thing about the Gonzaga piece is that it has a sarcophagus, which was *not* common."

"It seems very consistent with the seventeenth-century notion of collecting exotic rarities, however," Lizzie responded.

John nodded. "Even so, it's a very early example in Europe."

"And I haven't seen one illustrated in other collections of the time." She paused and thought about this for a moment. "Venice isn't all that far from Bologna, however," she said slowly, "and the Gonzagas in Bologna made their fortune in trade, so *how* they got it isn't too hard to imagine. I just wonder *when* they got it."

Her companion asked her if there was a catalog of the collection.

"Sadly, the earliest one I've seen so far is from 1959. But I'm hopeful when I get there I might find an earlier one."

"Well keep me in the loop on this," he said. "More pictures when you get them, of the sarcophagus, certainly, and of any mummy parts you might find in it."

"Mummy parts?"

"Oh sure," he said. "If you're going to make medicine out of a mummy you need to pull it apart and grind it up. And I should warn you that by the end of the Renaissance there were a lot of false mummies on the market, mostly recent corpses that had been either buried in the desert sands or baked in an oven to dry them out."

"How absolutely astonishingly gross," Lizzie said. "If I find a finger or toe lying around in the sarcophagus and bring it back, would you be able to tell the nature of the mummification process and give me a date on when it was done?"

"I would," John said. "But be warned that shipping any human remains as part of your exhibit will require some special paperwork. I wouldn't worry about it," he said with a grin. "I'll be surprised if there is anything of the mummy left at this point."

"This has been a real education," Lizzie said, stretching out her hand to shake his, but he came around his desk and hugged her.

"I look forward to more pictures," he said. "Maybe I'll even write something about this if it doesn't tread on your work."

Lizzie was inspired by the idea. "How about an essay for the catalog?" she asked. "I'm sorry the timeframe is short, since we need to wrap up everything in the next eight months, so we'd need to be ready to go to print by May."

He told her that if she could get him good pictures within a month, he could turn something around for her by the end of the spring term, and she left his office feeling she had made a great stride forward on the work.

The information on the cannibalization of mummies as medicine was too interesting not to share immediately with Jackie, and Lizzie made her way quickly to the library. To her surprise, Justin Carrera was sitting at the table with the Gonzaga folders spread out around him and he was looking at pictures. She pulled out a chair and sat next to him.

"Are you finding it interesting, looking at these pictures of your family?" she asked.

"Yeah," he answered. "My mom sent me some more information and I'm trying to put it all together."

"Excellent," Lizzie said. "I look forward to seeing what you find."

Jackie was sitting at her usual desk and Lizzie approached her with a broad smile on her face.

"What are you up to?" Jackie asked.

"I've been talking about mummies with John Haworth."

"And?"

"And did you know they used to eat them in the Renaissance as medicine?"

Jackie raised an eyebrow. "I seem to remember reading something about that."

"Dammit, Jackie! How come I can never surprise you even with the most unusual and gruesome information?"

"Because I'm a librarian and I sit here looking at information all day. Besides," she added, "I saw a mummified hand once in a pharmaceutical jar at a museum in London and it has stayed with me."

"Anything else about mummies you want to share?"

"They are mentioned a couple of times in Shakespeare."

"They are? In what plays?"

"*Macbeth,* of course. The witches put some mummy in the cauldron that they 'boil, boil, toil and trouble,' etcetera, and I think there is a reference in *Othello* as well, which I will look up for you right now."

Lizzie walked around the desk so she could look at Jackie's computer screen.

"See," Jackie said, pointing, "Othello had a handkerchief that his mother dyed with mummy, which must have given it some curative powers." She continued to type as she talked and with a Google search of "mummy powder" brought up a witches' supply store in Manhattan that had it on their inventory list. "Oh my God, Lizzie, look at this," she said with a groan. "You can order some if you want it."

"No thank you," Lizzie said. "I wonder what it is. It can't actually be ground up mummy."

"They claim it is, but how would you ever test it?"

"I guess you'd have to see if it cured your bruise," she said with a laugh. She looked up to find Justin staring at them, but he quickly looked away. She put a hand on Jackie's shoulder. "Enough of this unseemly talk, madam. We both have real work to do."

"This is real enough for me," responded Jackie. "And I have an excuse, because I'm helping you with your exhibit."

Lizzie reminded her that they had a date the following day with Rose and her father for coffee.

"Ah yes, to speak about the Principessa della Gonzaga."

"I told you not to call her that," Lizzie whispered. She looked again at Justin, who was staring intently at the pictures on the table in front of him, but she had the feeling that for once he was paying close attention.

Chapter 9

Martin's opinion on matters of art was always influential to Lizzie, and when he had a chance to look at the original drawing of the Gonzaga cabinet he noticed many things that she and Jackie had overlooked. He was interested in how the artist had used line to create perspective and give dimension to the vaulted corners of the ceiling, and how both the cases on the wall and the tiles on the floor drew the eye to the collection.

They sat with Jackie in the library and Lizzie opened the book on the Cospi collection to show him the print that covered the two center pages. It had been drawn the same year and Martin not only agreed it was by the same artist, but argued that he had used the same template for both pictures.

"This isn't so strange for an artist who did this kind of work," he said. "But it means that you can't consider this drawing like you would a photograph. The artist was trying to capture the essence of the collection and it might not reflect the actual architecture of the room."

"There are differences in the collections, though," Lizzie said, hoping that this new information would not scuttle her plans to try to recreate the drawing in her exhibit. "Look especially at the alligator and the mummy. They are really key elements in the Gonzaga picture, and the family still had those in the 50s."

"Don't worry, my dear," Martin reassured her. "There's enough difference in these assemblages of weapons along the top wall, and of the vases along the bottom to make me think that having created a general template, the artist then put in the specific details to reflect what the customer actually had in his house. Otherwise there would be no reason to hire him."

"Who knows how many collections in Bologna might have been drawn by this guy that we don't know about," Jackie added. "Because they don't survive or they are lost in some archive, filed in the wrong drawer."

She took the picture when Martin had finished looking at it and slipped it into a Mylar sleeve that she had made to protect it. "I assume you'll have this framed for your exhibit, Lizzie," she said. "And when you're done with it, I think I'll transfer it to the museum collection rather than keep it in the library."

"The same artist made a sketch of the Gonzaga family's private chapel as well," Lizzie said. She had printed a copy of the scanned image sent to her by Cosimo Gonzaga and now she pulled it out. "In this case we can compare it to a photograph of the same room from the 50s, and see that the drawing here is more realistic and less emblematic than the drawing of the cabinet."

She had already spent some time comparing the two images and she quickly pointed out the important differences. "Our Guido Reni Madonna is the central feature of the altar," she said, "just like it is in our campus chapel. And here is the dell'Arca angel—again in much the same position in our chapel today as in this old picture of the Gonzaga chapel."

"There is a pair of angels on the altar in this drawing, though," Jackie said. "And I don't see any in the photo from 1959."

"And they aren't an exact pair," Martin said. He had taken out a magnifying loop and was looking closely at the drawing. "They each have a candlestick on one knee and they are the same size, but they certainly aren't identical."

"Is there a way to tell which one is here at St. Pat's?" Jackie asked.

"It's the one on the right," Lizzie answered. "You can see that they are right- and left-handed candle holders. If you switched them, the candlesticks would obscure the faces of the angels."

"Where is the second one?" Martin asked. "I don't see it anywhere in this photograph of the chapel."

"I haven't found it yet," Lizzie answered. "It isn't listed on the inventory, but neither are any of the relics in the chapel. I have my assistants on the lookout for it in our current sources and will ask about it when I get to Bologna. It would be very cool to unite the pair in the exhibit."

The three of them spent another hour looking at the original photos of collections in the rooms of the Gonzaga Palazzo in Bologna, with Martin using his magnifying loop to see more detail of paintings. He was impressed with the collection and told Lizzie he couldn't believe that with so many important painters represented there wouldn't be a catalog of it somewhere.

"I've thought there might be a list of paintings, which Cosimo Gonzaga would not have considered part of the specimen cabinet, and consequently not sent to me," Lizzie said. "But I'm also starting to get the feeling that Cosimo is not the one who really knows about the collection anyway. He doesn't live in the house."

"Is there someone else who knows more?" Jackie and Martin asked simultaneously.

"One of Maggie's sons is still living in the house, Patrick or Patrizio, and he is apparently the expert on the collection."

"He must be ancient!" Martin said.

"He's in his nineties," Lizzie responded. "And Cosimo says that his memory about the collection is good, but don't ask him what happened yesterday."

As they walked across the bridge from Charlestown to the North End to meet Rose and her father at Geminiani's Restaurant, they spoke more about Lizzie's upcoming trip to Bologna, and a jealous Jackie learned for the first time that Martin would join her there for a week.

"Not fair," she said with real sense of disappointment in her voice. "I was hoping to go."

"You joined Lizzie on her last adventure in England," Martin countered. "It's my turn!"

Lizzie linked an arm with each of them until the sidewalks narrowed where plows had pushed snow up onto the curb, and they had to walk single file. "As you have both acknowledged to me in the last week that my history projects are really dangerous, I hope your desire to accompany me is based on a need to keep me safe."

"That is certainly my intention," Martin said, taking her arm again. "I am here to protect you."

"Well I'm not!" Jackie said emphatically. "I'm looking for adventure, and you seem to find a hell of a lot more of it out on the road than I find behind my desk. I have to live vicariously through you."

"Interesting," Lizzie said, "since I often feel that I am living vicariously through the people I'm studying."

They reached the door of the restaurant. "And Maggie Gonzaga's life was filled with real danger, as you shall soon hear."

Even though they had come for coffee, Tony Tessitore had insisted on laying out a spread for them and showed them to a table where he pointed out a mousse made of ham, a soft cheese, and herb crackers, all of which he had made himself.

"How wonderful," Martin said, putting a hand on Tony's shoulder.

Jackie was quickly introduced and Rose provided them with both wine and coffee and promised that she had fresh cannoli when they finished the appetizers.

"She must always compete with me," Tony said in a loud whisper.

"I heard that," Rose said, halfway to the kitchen.

The conversation began pleasantly, with Tony describing his childhood in Bologna and his relationship with the Gonzagas. Lizzie had brought copies of the pictures of the rooms in the house and he was enthusiastic in pointing out small details of things he remembered.

"Do you know anything about the art?" Martin asked.

Tony replied that he had left there as a teenager and had only been back for short visits since. "I'm sorry I didn't pay attention to those things."

His information was interesting but anecdotal, and there was nothing that Lizzie would be able to use for her research. He didn't remember any parts of the cabinet beyond the alligator, the mummy, some preserved fishes, and something that was called a "dragon," but was only about the size of his hand.

She steered the conversation back to the family. "When Maggie Kelliher married Lorenzo Gonzaga, the American papers said he was a prince, but you said that she never used any title."

"No," he said, shaking his head slowly. "I remember when her husband died, I was maybe eight years old. He was quite a bit older than she was," he explained. "But there was a crown on his coffin when they took it through the town, and the Gonzaga chapel at St. Paulo Maggiore church is full of crowns. But she never called herself anything but Signora Gonzaga, and her children never used any sort of title. I don't think she would have let them, especially after the war."

"So what was he the prince of?" Jackie asked. "He clearly wasn't the prince of Italy."

"Oh no," Tony said. "Italy isn't like Britain, where there is only one royal family. Before the unification in 1861, every city-state had its own nobility. The Gonzagas are most famous for having been the dukes of Mantua, but sons went to other places, like Bologna, and brought titles with them— even if there wasn't any land or power associated with them. I think at some point all or most of the so-called noblemen in northern Italy were allowed to take the title 'Prince of the Holy Roman Empire.'"

"But surely there was a king of Italy during the war," Lizzie said. She had been reading about the topic as background, but still felt very ignorant about the details.

"When the city-states were unified to make Italy, one of the noble families, the Savoys, were made kings of Italy, because their leader, Victor Emmanuel, had been rampaging around the country fighting for it, but before that there hadn't been a monarch over the whole territory since the Romans."

Jackie made a comment about Napoleon giving it a try, but her comment passed quickly under the wheels of Rose's demanding inquiry of her father: "Why don't we have a king today?"

"Because we got rid of the whole business in 1946," her father said. "We voted on it, and for once an election did something good in Italy. The Savoys were ordered out of the country and we became a republic."

"I'm pretty sure that I saw a prince from that family on the European version of 'Dancing with the Stars,'" Jackie said.

Rose instantly wanted more information but her father gave her a look that silenced her.

"Last week at your house you said that Italians would never want a monarchy again—that with the politicians, the mafia and the church there were already enough hands in your pockets." Martin turned his chair as he spoke, so that he was facing the old man.

"I think that is exactly the reason why Signora Gonzaga found the whole idea so distasteful," Tony answered. He made a motion with his hands. "The time for kings and princes had passed. We live in a modern world now."

Rose sighed audibly and they all laughed.

"A modern world with corrupt politicians, organized crime and a powerful church!" Jackie said slyly. "It sounds very medieval to me."

Tony gave her a surprised look that turned to an expression of sadness or disappointment. "You're right, Jackie," he said. His Italian accent, which had largely disappeared, came through again as he spoke and for the first time that afternoon he showed his age. "When it comes right down to it," he said, "I guess we Italians are not really all that good at governance." He chose his next words carefully. "And for that reason we have to be especially wary. It was a vacuum of power in the 1920s that allowed the Fascists to take over."

Jackie leaned toward him and said something softly in Italian. He smiled and responded in the same language.

Rose put two cannoli on Jackie's plate, so whatever she had said to Tony must have been good, Lizzie thought. Jackie had such a tendency to be a smartass that her thoughtful nature was not always visible, especially to strangers.

"So how come that guy on 'Dancing with the Stars' is still called a prince?" Rose asked. "And I think I've heard of other Italian princes in recent years who were married to American actresses."

"There's really nothing to prevent anyone from calling themselves anything they want," Martin said. "I could call myself a prince."

"And I would love you even more if you did," Lizzie said. She leaned over and kissed him, accompanied by moans of disgust from Jackie.

"Your claim, Martin, would be more convincing if your father and grandfather had also called themselves princes," Rose said. "It is the heritage of it that is important."

Martin made a joke about his father, "a noble gardener" who was one of the Mexican kings.

"Do you mean the Salsa band?" Jackie asked.

Rose put her hand up. "I'm serious," she said. "If your ancestors were kings, can you continue to call yourself a prince when the title is no longer tied to an actual position of power?"

"Of course not!" Jackie responded instantly. "It is meaningless to say you are the prince of Italy if the Italian people voted not to have a monarchy and kicked your grandfather out of the country."

"There are still a number of families in Italy that use those old titles, even though they are now meaningless," Tony said. "But the Gonzagas are not one of them."

Lizzie remembered this the next day when Jimmy and Roscoe told her that Justin Carrere had told several students that he was a prince.

Chapter 10

In the hundred-year history of St. Patrick's College, there had been only five presidents, all Jesuits. The first was William O'Brien, who had immigrated on the same ship with Paddy Kelliher and become his lifelong friend. The most recent was Father Lawrence O'Toole, who had held the post for thirty-two years.

Lizzie sat in his outer office and looked at the five photographs on the wall opposite her. O'Brien, who had been called "Willie" by Kelliher, had a big smile on his face. The closer you got to the present, the sterner the presidents looked until O'Toole, who glowered in his photograph with such ferociousness that Lizzie thought the picture could only have been chosen to keep people, especially students, from visiting him.

He was not a mean man, but he had an arrogant assuredness that left no room for alternative opinions and Lizzie always found herself holding her tongue in his presence. She had, however, nothing to complain of in his treatment of her. On the contrary, he had not infrequently taken notice of her over the fifteen years that she had taught at the college. His training had been as a historian and he liked to talk about history with her. He had assigned her the task of writing the biography of Kelliher, and he had sought her advice on how to celebrate the centenary of the College.

It had been his original thought to have some sort of exhibit about Paddy and his family, and it was Lizzie who first mentioned the "cabinet of curiosities" of the Gonzagas. She had come across several mentions of it in her earlier research, and thought there might be an opportunity for her to study it if Father O'Toole liked the idea. In fact, Father O'Toole *loved* the idea. It was an opportunity for him to raise money from both sides of the family and he gave an immediate green light to the project with Lizzie as curator.

In the months since then, Lizzie had corresponded principally with two family members, one on each side of the Atlantic. Jim Kelliher, Paddy's great-grandson in Boston, who had inherited both the estate and financial acumen of his ancestor, had helped Lizzie with the biography and was willing to underwrite the local expenses of the exhibition. Cosimo Gonzaga, another great-grandson, gave a sizable contribution to the College every year, but was persuaded to increase his gift and become a patron of this project.

Lizzie had met once with both men, in this office with Father O'Toole. Though the two were distant cousins, they knew each other well. They had been undergraduates at St. Pat's at the same time and Cosimo had frequently been a guest at the Kelliher home. Both the Kellihers and the Gonzagas had fortunes that were built on textiles but had diversified over the years, and the Italian branch had long been involved in trade as well.

Lizzie liked both men. They were in their late fifties, smart and energetic. Neither wanted to have an active role in the project, which suited her just fine. Each had agreed to open his home to Lizzie in case she might find useable material, and she had spent a day at Jim Kelliher's house in Brookline looking at the family papers there, though it turned out that the things the Kellihers had already donated to the college library were more valuable to her.

"Father O'Toole will see you now, Liza."

The voice of the president's secretary broke Lizzie's reverie.

"Thanks Loretta," she said. As many times as she had told the woman her name, she never got it right.

The priest gave her a warm welcome. "Lizzie," he said. "I think you are leaving for Bologna next week and I wanted to get an update before you go."

"Your timing is perfect!" she said in response. "I would have contacted you in the next few days to ask for a meeting because there are some questions where I could use your advice." She had brought her laptop to talk him through the work and she took it out of her book bag.

He gestured to the conference table in the room and they sat side-by-side to look at her computer screen.

"First," she said, "I have to tell you that it turns out that the College has a wonderful archive about this collection that nobody has looked at in years." She had the 1677 drawing of the cabinet as the screen saver on her computer, but she quickly opened a higher-resolution photograph of the image. "This is the central image around which I hope to build the exhibit," she said, pointing to several of the now-familiar objects and identifying them.

"How do you know they still survive?" Father O'Toole asked.

"They were still in the house in 1959," she said. "Cosimo Gonzaga sent me a scan of an inventory, and I found the original in our archive here."

"So the collection survived the two world wars," the priest said. "Bologna was occupied by the Nazis in the Second World War, and bombed many times by the Allies. I wouldn't have been surprised if much of the collection was lost, and once when I was in Rome I heard that they had lost at least one important work of art to Nazi looting in the war."

This was the first time Lizzie had heard this and she waited for him to elaborate, but he only said, "It was decades ago that I heard it and I don't remember any details."

"I'll try to find out more about that when I get to Bologna," Lizzie said. "For now, I wanted to familiarize myself as much as I could in advance with what I might find in the collection."

"There will be surprises of course."

"Of course! I look forward to them!"

Father O'Toole had lived in Italy, spoke the language fluently, and knew the history of the country better than Lizzie did. She knew more about the history of collecting and had a better sense of the ethnographic and natural history items in the collection, and that gave her confidence that she might otherwise have lacked in the situation.

He asked her about several of the things that were visible in the pictures and she told him what she had learned.

"Have you ever been in this house?" she asked.

He told her that he hadn't. "In all the times I've met Cosimo Gonzaga it has either been here or in Rome. I've never been in Bologna." He spent some time looking closely at the photos. "There look to be some interesting paintings," he said.

"I haven't seen any list of pictures, yet," she said. "But I will ask when I am there."

"Will you borrow works of art for the exhibit?"

"I'm not planning to at this time, though of course the Guido Reni Madonna and the dell'Arca statue will be highlights."

He nodded. "In those I think they might have given us the best of the lot."

She agreed. "When the exhibit closes and they go back into the chapel, the college should look into better security for them," she added, and he told her he had already had that thought as well.

"Did you say you had some specific questions for me?"

Lizzie showed him the picture of the chapel in the Gonzaga Palazzo. "There are some wonderful reliquaries in their private chapel. They aren't part of the cabinet, but if it isn't sacrilegious to put them into the secular setting of the museum, I'd like to include three or four of them."

Again he looked closely at the picture, and Lizzie zoomed in to show him details of the reliquaries, which held remnants of bones from various saints.

"Do they still have the holy relics in them?" he asked.

"I'm certain they do."

"Can they be removed?"

"I'm not sure," she said. "I think in some cases you might have to break the reliquary to open it."

"Well, we certainly don't want to do that. Let me ask the cardinal about this. As it happens, I'm going to be dining with him tonight." He added that there were plenty of relics visible in reliquaries in museums. "I saw a tooth purported to have come from the mouth of Mary Magdalene at the Metropolitan Museum in New York," he said, "and other reliquaries with bones visible at other museums. Of course nothing like the churches in Italy; it is really quite astonishing what they have there."

Lizzie wondered if she should mention that many of them were probably fakes, but he surprised her and said it first. "Of course, I've seen enough fingers of our own patron St. Patrick to give him four or five hands." He paused. "I don't see anything sacrilegious in showing those things in a museum at a Catholic college," he said. "Still I will ask the cardinal."

"There is also a sarcophagus and I don't know if it still contains a mummy, but Professor Haworth has told me that human body parts need a special license for international transfer."

"Will you bring the mummy?"

"No," she said, shaking her head. "John Haworth thinks there probably isn't one in the case, but I don't want to get into the paperwork required for it and our space is fairly small. I'm just wondering if a single finger in a reliquary would require a license."

Father O'Toole assured her that he thought whatever needed to be done in this case could be done through the cardinal's office in Boston, and his own connections in Rome. "When you are in Bologna, make your choices and send me pictures and descriptions as soon as you can."

"You are absolutely on the top of my list," Lizzie assured him.

"By the way," he said as she packed up her bag, "how is Giuseppe Gonzaga, or Carrera I think, working out as an assistant?"

"Terribly," she said honestly. "He is lazy and unreliable for most tasks, and my latest attempt to get some work out of him has had a surprising twist."

He gave a look indicating he wanted details.

"I asked him to work on the Gonzaga genealogy and just this morning heard a report that he is now telling people he is a prince."

Father O'Toole laughed hard at that. "I should have warned you. Cosimo told me he was good for very little and that it would be a real favor to put him to work. I wonder how his family will greet this news?" He smiled at Lizzie and continued, "They were once a very powerful family, the Gonzagas, the Dukes of Mantua. I'm not sure how the one that married the Kelliher daughter came to be described as a prince, but I seem to remember that he was."

"Patrick Kelliher certainly described him that way when his daughter married him," Lizzie said.

"Well, Italians were always very free with their use of titles. I have had some correspondence with the president of the University of Bologna and he is called the 'Rector Magnificent.' Now *there* is a title."

Lizzie was quite satisfied with the course of the meeting and shook hands warmly with Father O'Toole. "Thanks for giving me this project," she said. "The collection is really interesting."

"Just make me a good exhibit," he said. "And safe home God speed you."

It was an old Irish blessing for the road, which Lizzie's father had often said to her when she was traveling. No one had said it to her in a long time and she found herself leaving with warm thoughts about Father O'Toole.

The information that any part of the Gonzaga collection might have been looted by Nazis during the Second World War was new to Lizzie, and she sat on a chair in the hallway outside Father O'Toole's office to see if she could verify it. She started with the website of the International Foundation for Art Research, which maintained a list of stolen art, and from there went to the Commission for Art Recovery, but couldn't find anything listed on either site that identified any works stolen from or repatriated to the Gonzagas.

The Nazis had stolen tens of thousands of works of art during the war, and though many were discovered at the end of the war and returned to the original owners, the process of discovering and repatriating others was still going on sixty years later. The systematic looting of museums, libraries and private homes, especially of wealthy Jews, had been done in a very thorough manner and the Nazis had kept good records of those things that were destined for Hitler's planned "Führermuseum," or for the private collections of high-ranking officers like Herman Göring. But there must have been individual soldiers who took things without reporting them, and if the family that was victimized didn't report the things they lost it would be difficult or impossible to find them.

Lizzie returned to the classroom where Roscoe and Jimmy were continuing to identify objects from the list and photographs and connecting them to the seventeenth-century drawing of the collection. Justin was nowhere to be found.

Walking along the length of the board, Lizzie put her hand up and traced connections with her finger. "Wow," she said, "you guys have done terrific work. Thank you."

Jimmy was excited to show her the list, which he had printed in anticipation of their meeting. "There is so much great stuff here," he said enthusiastically, "dragons, unicorn horns, magical stones and mirrors, along with these terrific wind-up machines that move up and down the dinner table dispensing salt." He pointed to where he had identified several of these things in the drawing. "Here," he said, pointing to a long spiral tusk, "if I hadn't read the description of the unicorn horn I never would have recognized it."

"It's a narwhal tusk," Roscoe said bluntly.

"I know," Jimmy returned. "Geez, let me have my moment."

Roscoe seemed contrite as he apologized, but nonetheless took over the conversation, turning it to the things he had found.

"I'm working on the Natural History list," he said. "I've found two tortoise shells, several blowfish, and a bunch of eggs, from ostriches, emus and dozens of other birds."

"I have found several pictures of these big clay vases called *kraters*," Jimmy said, taking control of the exchange again. "And the subjects depicted on them are pretty hilarious: lots of sports, lots of animals, and a fair amount of sex."

He handed Lizzie a picture of a shelf laden with large ceramic jars. Using the magnifying glass that Jimmy had at the ready, she looked at wonderfully vivid illustrations of chariots, musicians with pan pipes and lyres, a woman with a dove on her outstretched hand, and, as Jimmy had pointed out, sports, animals, and a fair amount of sex.

"If you were to choose one of these to be in our exhibit, which would it be?" she asked.

"This one is the biggest," Jimmy said. "It is almost a meter high, but the repairs on it are really obvious." He pointed to another one. "This is in the best condition, and I think the wrestlers are awesome, but they are maybe too realistically rendered in the wrong parts for us to exhibit, if you know what I mean."

Lizzie could tell that he was blushing and she was careful not to look at him. "I don't think you need to worry about it if this is your favorite," she said collegially.

"It's not my favorite," he said. "It's just in the best condition. My favorite is the one next to it, which is smaller and has some repairs, but is really beautiful."

Peering through the magnifying glass, Lizzie could see five young women standing side-by-side, each holding a lyre. In a black and white photo it was impossible to see the colors, but the women were lighter than the background of the pot.

"It's sweet," Jimmy said softly. "I read that the painter had to work on the vase while it was still wet, before it was fired, and that he couldn't really see the image he was creating because the slip is close to the same color as the clay. It's just impressive that he could make something so perfect under those circumstances."

"You're right, it has a wonderful sweetness and an impressive artistry."

"And it's more than two thousand years old!" Roscoe added.

"I'll put it on the list," Lizzie said, "and unless it's too fragile to travel, I will make sure it is included in the exhibit." She asked the two young men if there was anything else they would like to see included.

"There is a little dragon," Jimmy said, showing a picture to Lizzie and Roscoe. "Of course it isn't a real dragon, it is pretty tiny and on the list it is called a *Draco dandinii*, some kind of a salamander, but it has wing-like appendages and a reptile's face, so it is very dragon-like."

"The mounting of it is great," Lizzie said, looking at the small animal, its mouth open and spread in a grin, clinging to a branch and looking up with its large glass eyes. "All it needs is a little flame coming out of its mouth."

"We can add that when it gets here," Roscoe offered.

Lizzie laughed. "And what would you choose to include?"

Roscoe said he would like to include the unicorn horn. "The narwhal's tusk," he said, nodding at Jimmy. "And the alligator, of course. But I imagine that both those things are already on your list."

"They are," Lizzie said. She asked if either of them had seen anything of the angel candleholder that was shown in the early sketch of the chapel, but neither had.

Chapter 11

Cosimo Gonzaga did not write to Lizzie often. Usually it was to answer a question about arrangements for her upcoming trip, or give details of family history, but he never sent a message that did not include thanks for taking on his nephew as an assistant. It had been understood early in the project that Justin would work with her in Bologna as well as Boston and as the time of her departure neared Lizzie felt she needed to clarify the situation. She sent Carmine an email asking to make an appointment to speak on the phone, and brought the subject up with Justin on one of his rare visits to her office.

"Are you going to Bologna this winter?" she asked, tossing the question off casually so that he would not think she expected him to help her there.

"I dunno," he said. "I think my uncle is expecting me to help you there in May."

Lizzie took a breath and held it. "I'm not going there in May," she said, exhaling slowly. "I'm going next week."

"So what's happening in May?"

"The collection will be packed and shipped then," she said. "But we have hired a conservator and a professional art-packing firm to do the job."

"So what am I supposed to do?"

"I don't know," she answered. "But I'm sure it will be nice to have a visit with your family."

The next morning she got up at four o'clock to talk to Cosimo. He had listed several times that were convenient for her to call him, and though the time difference made this an awkward time for Lizzie, the next opportunity he gave her was not for two days. She wasn't in a mood to exchange pleasantries at that hour so she got quickly to the point.

"I'd like to know what your expectations are for Justin on this project?" she asked. "Beppe," she clarified.

"Isn't he your assistant on the project?"

"Not quite," Lizzie responded. "He's one of three student assistants."

When she paused for a moment, Carmine said, "I know he isn't a hard worker, but I hoped he might learn something about his family that would inspire him, and the fact that he is going to your school while you work on this project made it seem a natural association."

"I think he has found interesting family information," she said, unwilling to go further into detail. "But he tells me he is planning to work on this project in Bologna in May and I wondered if you have specific plans for him then."

"Isn't that when the collection will be packed and shipped?"

Lizzie said that it was.

"Well, our family firm will manage the shipping and I think he can learn something about it. Don't worry," he laughed. "I don't expect him to be doing the heavy lifting, but certainly he can help with the paperwork."

"Thanks," Lizzie said, maintaining a cheery voice. "That helps. I'll be sure to design the project in a way that takes advantage of his strengths."

"Oh Gawd," she said as she climbed back into bed. Martin woke slightly and asked her if anything was wrong. "The curse of the Gonzagas," she whispered, kissing him.

"Ah, the little prince," he said, rolling over and returning to sleep.

Lizzie pulled the covers up to her chin. "If only he was on his own planet," she thought.

There was plenty of work to do in organizing and cataloging the Gonzaga archival material and Lizzie set up all three assistants with tasks to do while she was away. Since she now knew that Justin would actually be in Bologna when the collection was shipped, she went over the current list of what she hoped would be in the exhibit, stressing that more would be added after she saw the contents of the house.

The whole process of creating the exhibit was going so well that Lizzie thought nothing could impede its success. Armed with a computer full of images and a preliminary list that included an extraordinary selection of artifacts, she boarded a plane for Bologna with the highest expectations. She had no doubts that the exhibit and the accompanying catalog would take a very interesting and eccentric collection and give it a serious analysis without losing the whimsy that made it so charming in the first place.

Pina Corelli, another of the great-grandchildren of Maggie and Lorenzo Gonzaga, met her at Marconi Airport and drove her into Bologna. She had a degree from M.I.T. and worked for the family company.

"My Uncle Cosimo, whom you will meet tonight, has put me at your service this week," Pina told Lizzie.

She was obviously a very bright young woman and she wasn't exactly unfriendly, but there was nothing warm about her. They drove very fast into the city, and past many of the important monuments, without a word on Pina's part. Lizzie asked where they were going.

"To the Gonzaga Palazzo on the Piazza Galvani," Pina said. "That's where the collection is and where you'll be staying."

"Do you live there?"

"Oh God no! It's my Uncle Patrizio's house. He lives there with a caretaker." As she spoke, Pina came to an abrupt stop and turned off the busy Via Farini onto the Piazza Galvani. There was an electric gate that required an entry code, and after Pina had punched the numbers into the pad, the gate lifted and a garage door opened in the building on their left.

"You might want to get out here," Pina said. "It's a more impressive view to come into the house through the courtyard than the garage. I'll come open the door for you."

Lizzie got out of the car and stood in the plaza. It was her first chance to look at the big stone face of the Palazzo Gonzaga, about which she had read and heard so much. It didn't look like other palaces she had seen in England and France. It was not ostentatious. It sat on a regular street in Bologna and did not stand out in any way; it was more elegant than opulent.

The house had three floors and they were distinguished

on the front by the shape of the windows. The ground floor, made of dressed stone, had a large central door topped by a rounded stone archway. On either side of the door were five windows that mimicked the shape of the doorway; in each arch a perfect stone scallop shell had been carved. All the windows on this floor were closed by shutters on the inside and covered with iron grates on the outside.

The floor above was faced with stucco, which here and there was worn away to show the bricks behind it. At one time it must have been an earthy red, but it had long ago faded to a dark coral pink. Unlike the windows below them, those on this floor were rectangular. The casements were carved into pillars holding up curve-topped pediments.

The top floor of the house obviously had a lower ceiling than the floors below it. The smaller windows echoed those below, but the pediments were pointed rather than curved. Above them was an eave that bowed out from the wall of the house. Small round windows alternated with carved alligators, dragons, and other fanciful figures that might have been in the cabinet.

Looking around the square, which was dominated on one side by the Gonzaga house, Lizzie saw a statue of a man trying to balance a tumbling pile of books on a pedestal—a kindred spirit. She walked over and read the name on the pedestal: Galvani. She didn't know who Galvani was but she liked him, and she liked the fact that the sculptor had captured him in an awkward moment of juggling research and ideas.

When she returned to the front door of the house, she saw that the big double doors each had an alligator-shaped knocker. She had just reached out to touch one of them when the door opened behind it and Pina welcomed her inside.

Stepping through the doorway, Lizzie entered an unexpected world. She did not pass from the outside of the house to the inside, but from the street to the courtyard, an expansive open space where sunlight picked out and illuminated architectural details, even on a winter day. On this level was a series of open archways that remained in darkness, but above were balconies and windows thrown open to receive the light and air.

"It's marvelous," Lizzie said to Pina.

"Have you never been in an Italian house?"

Lizzie said she hadn't. "Are there many like this?"

Pina told her that there were hundreds of houses like this in Bologna, perhaps thousands. "Most don't have just a single family anymore, though. A lot of them have been turned into apartment flats or offices."

"You would never know from the street."

"Come upstairs," Pina said. "I'll bring your luggage up later in the elevator." In response to Lizzie's querying look, Pina said that they had put the elevator in for her Uncle Patrizio many years before. "He just couldn't handle all the stairs," she said. She gestured as she spoke to the curving stone staircase beside them that led up to the main floor of the house. There was an identical one on the other side of the door.

There were several pediments along the staircase and each had a Roman statue on it. Male and female, and draped with swirls of fabric, the figures had been captured in motion. Two of them made grand gestures with their arms, as if to point the way to the entrance of the first grand room.

Lizzie had seen black and white photos of the rooms in the house, taken in the late 50s, and the faded color pictures of Tony Tessitore, but they had not prepared her for her first entry to the *piano nobile,* the main floor of the house. As she stepped into the entry hall she could see through a series of doors the full length of the house, and every surface was covered with color. Paintings, plasterwork, carvings and carpets brought together designs on floors, walls and ceilings that would seem incongruous in another setting. Unlike the simplicity that she had admired in the courtyard, with its plain stone floor and stucco walls, here the patterns were meant to impress, and they did.

"Whoa!" Lizzie said, her neck bent back so she could look at the carved ceiling high above her. The scale of the room had not been captured at all in the photographs. It was not quite twice the height of a room in an American house, but it seemed at least that high.

"If Uncle Patrizio is clear in his head today, he's the best one to give you a tour," she said. "If he isn't, Uncle Cosimo said he would show you around the house when he comes to pick you up later."

There was a fresco on the wall of the entrance hall that showed the genealogy of the Gonzagas and Lizzie asked Pina if she was on it.

For the first time, Lizzie heard Pina laugh. "No," she said, "I think that thing is something like two hundred years old." There was a small framed document on the table in front of it to which she pointed. "Even this one, which brings us into the middle of the twentieth century, doesn't include the most recent generation."

Maggie Kelliher's children were the last full generation on the updated family tree, with just a few grandchildren, including Cosimo Gonzaga, who was the son of Maggie's son Cosimo, and three children of Maggie's daughter Margherita. All the other family members had been born after it was made.

"That's my mother," Pina said, pointing to the name of Margherita's daughter Anna.

"So is Justin your first cousin?" Lizzie asked, remembering that he was also a grandchild of Margherita.

"Justin?"

"Giuseppe," Lizzie corrected. "Giuseppe Carrera."

Pina laughed again. "Beppe?" she asked, then answered her own question. "Yes, his mother and mine are sisters."

Lizzie was tempted to tell Pina about Beppe's adoption of the title of prince, but held her tongue. She didn't know her well enough to know if she would find it amusing or not. She looked at all the crowns across the top of the fresco, alternating with the mitres of bishops.

"You have an impressive family," she said.

"Many dukes, cardinals and bishops," Pina said. "But none of that is worth much now."

Again Lizzie thought about "Prince Beppe."

They went quickly through what Lizzie had seen referenced as the "Yellow Salon"—which might better have been called the Gold Room for the amount of gold leaf on the furniture and on the plasterwork that was scrolled in great loops around the framed pictures on the walls. Pina strode so quickly that there was no time for Lizzie to see if she could identify any of the paintings for which Martin had given her a preliminary identification from the old black and white photographs.

From there they went to the "Chinese Salon," on the back left corner of the house. Again, Pina didn't pause, so Lizzie had to take in the hand painted wallpaper and the porcelain without being able to look closely at anything. The dining room had the balcony that had charmed Lizzie from the courtyard. It had three large archways that looked down onto the courtyard from the wall opposite the main door.

Beyond the dining room was the library, also called the "Cabinet," where they found Patrick Gonzaga sitting at a large table with a book.

Pina introduced them in English. "Uncle Patrizio," she said, "this is Professor Manning from St. Patrick's College."

He turned and smiled. "My grandfather founded St. Patrick's College," he said. He extended his hand, which Lizzie took, and he invited her to sit at the table with him.

It took some effort to concentrate on her host and not let her eyes wander around the room, where all the treasures she sought were kept, but Lizzie looked into his eyes, dark and filmy and set into deep lids that drooped at the edges. His face was soft and lined and, Lizzie thought, sad.

"My grandfather founded St. Patrick's College," he said again, still holding Lizzie's hand.

She squeezed it. "I know," she said. "I know about your grandfather." She pulled her hand away and opened her book bag. "Here is a copy of a small book I wrote about him," she said, handing him a copy of *Patrick Kelliher, Immigrant Industrialist*. "I sent you a copy when it came out, but I am happy to give you one in person."

He leafed through the book and Lizzie took her first opportunity to scan the room. There was the famous alligator, hanging from the ceiling, though this room was clearly not the room in the 1677 picture. The library had a mezzanine, approached by a narrow staircase at one end, and had shelves from floor to ceiling. Some were filled with books, but others clearly had specimens from the old cabinet.

The old man followed where her eyes were going. "This is the Wonder Chamber," he said.

"The Wunder Kammer," Lizzie said, repeating the phrase in its original German.

"Exactly," he said. "You are the first person to know that. No one else calls it that, they call it the 'library,' as if that will somehow dissipate its power." He then said something in Italian and Lizzie looked up to see if Pina would translate, but she just shook her head. Stopping abruptly he looked suspiciously at Lizzie and demanded in Italian that she identify herself.

"I'm Lizzie Manning," she said. "I teach at St. Patrick's College."

"My grandfather founded St. Patrick's College."

"I know," she said. "Paddy-boy Kelliher." She was instantly sorry that she had used the nickname by which she and Jackie spoke of their college founder, but Patrizio responded positively.

"Paddy-boy," he said. "My mother sometimes called me that. I'm named after him."

"Of course," Lizzie said. "May I call you Patrizio?" she asked, "or would you prefer I be more formal?"

"You may call me Pat," he said. "That is what Americans call me, it's what they called me at St. Patrick's College."

"Have you been there in recent years?"

"No, not since 1974. I went there just after my mother died, but not since."

"Your English is still very good."

He told her that he had grown up speaking it with his mother, but that he didn't have a chance to speak it very often now, and for several minutes they spoke of Boston and of the college. He had first gone there in 1938 and remembered details of the city and of the campus that were long changed. She eventually turned the conversation to the collection by asking about the alligator on the ceiling.

"He came from America too, you know. He was captured in Florida by an early traveler and brought back to the Mediterranean on a Spanish ship."

"It must have been a very early traveler indeed," Lizzie

said, "because I know it was in this collection by 1677."

"How do you know that?" Patrizio asked.

Lizzie took a copy of the original image out of her book bag and laid it on the table in front of him. It was an excellent reproduction, a high-resolution photograph printed on an expensive matte paper. Lizzie had had five copies made especially to give to members of the Gonzaga family.

"Where did you get this?" Patrizio demanded and then spoke rapidly in Italian.

Pina finally stepped into the conversation. "He wants to know how you have this sketch," she said. "He says it has been missing for years, that he has been looking for it."

Lizzie was flustered and embarrassed. She tried to explain, with Pina translating, that the image had been given to the College by his mother in 1959, and that this was a copy of it.

"Tell him that this will be the centerpiece of our exhibit," Lizzie said.

"What exhibit?" he asked angrily.

"The exhibit at St. Pat's of your collection," Lizzie explained, "to celebrate the one hundredth anniversary of your grandfather founding the college."

Patrizio turned to Pina and spoke rapidly for several minutes. He was obviously upset.

"He says no one has told him about this, that he will not let anything leave the house," she translated. As she said it, Pina held her hand up slightly, as if to indicate to Lizzie that she should not be too worried about this alarming news. The two continued back and forth in Italian for several minutes. "I have told him that he knew about this, but has forgotten," Pina explained. "But I'm going to call Uncle Cosimo and ask him to come over now if he can." She put a hand on her uncle's shoulder, which he shrugged off.

A tiny woman came into the room and Pina turned to her. "Graziella is Uncle Patrizio's housekeeper," she said first to Lizzie, and then she spoke to the woman in Italian.

Graziella put her arms around Patrizio and with a strength that impressed Lizzie, lifting him out of his chair and into a standing position. She could not have been much more than five feet tall and he was two heads taller than she, but he put himself meekly into her small hands and was positioned onto his walker. As he shuffled from the room, Pina said softly, "Uncle Patrizio will sleep for a while, and when he gets up will probably not remember any of this."

"I feel awful about this," Lizzie said. She had stood up when Graziella brought Patrizio to a standing position, but now she sat down again and rested her hands on the table in front of her. She was angry with Cosimo that he hadn't been more forthcoming with information about his uncle's condition—she certainly didn't want to have to face this situation every day that she was here. "How can we do the exhibit if he doesn't want anything to leave this house?" she said to Pina, the frustration clear in her tone.

"I'll call Cosimo," Pina said, pulling a cell phone from her purse. "In the meantime, you should look around at the collection."

While Pina spoke into her phone in rapid Italian, Lizzie took her first walk around the room. From what she could see from the main level, the open shelves of the mezzanine were entirely filled with books, and despite the large number of things hanging from the ceiling in the Renaissance drawing, today there was only the alligator.

Pina closed her phone and said that Cosimo would join them within the hour. "Can I get you a cup of coffee?" she asked.

"I'd love one," Lizzie said thankfully. "Can I drink it here?"

"Of course," Pina answered, "I'll just get it and come back."

When she had gone, Lizzie began a slow stroll around the room, looking in every case. Most of them had glass doors, though some that contained only books had doors made of a decorative screen and others were just open shelves. Lying in the cases were oddities and wonders in equal numbers. Some things had dried and shriveled until they were no longer recognizable; even if they could be identified, they were mostly just grey lumps that would not be suitable for exhibition. Other things crossed over the wonderful line between "natural" and "artificial" curiosities. There were trees of coral that had been worked into wonderful miniature landscapes, where plants and animals from the sea were transformed into their counterparts on shore. Bits of ancient pottery were sometimes hard to distinguish from samples of minerals, and small dried sea horses lay on a shelf among small bronze figures, dancing, playing instruments and engaged in battle, like some ancient Etruscan toy soldiers. It was as if a child had played with them at one time and organized them into an imaginative world.

Lizzie saw the automaton that Jimmy had identified from one of the photographs. Wrought of silver into a marvelous tabletop model of the solar system, this orrery could roll under its wind-up power down a dining table dispensing salt. There were ancient bottles with unidentifiable animals inside them and Lizzie considered that a few of the bottles exhibited together would capture the essence of this early collection and be visually interesting.

Of dried animals there was no shortage. A few hundred bugs, lizards, fish and birds looked back at her with glass eyes or no eyes, their skin or feathers covered with a layer of dust. While the rest of the house looked quite clean, the shelves in this room had clearly gone a long time without a dusting. She assumed that Patrick would not let anyone touch the things but himself.

Picking up the 1677 image of the "cabinet" that Patrizio had left on the table, Lizzie held it up against each wall of the room. It was clear that if the image represented this collection, it had not been located in this room when the sketch was made. Because of the architecture of the house, with the courtyard in the center, each of the large rooms was much longer than it was wide. The width of the library was reduced even more by the shelves that covered the walls. The furniture was limited to a very long table that ran almost the length of it, surrounded by chairs. On the table were two large globes, one representing the earth and the other the celestial sphere of the sky.

The shorter walls of the room were dominated by a large double door at one end, which was currently closed, and the staircase up to the mezzanine on the other. There was a small window there built into the wall of the stairs, and Lizzie climbed up to look out. Below her trucks were unloading in the street behind the house.

When Pina returned, Lizzie was examining the globe of the earth and wondering if she could have it in her exhibit. She sighed at the thought. Would she be able to have any of this? Had Patrizio not responded as he had, she would be making a list right now of marvelous things to go to Boston.

"I'm sorry that I didn't know more about Patrick's condition before I started all this," she said to Pina.

"Why? What difference does it make? He just doesn't remember things."

"I'm not talking about his short term memory," Lizzie said. "I meant that he lives with these things and cares about them and will be deprived of some of them at a time when he is otherwise confused. If they are the familiar things in his life, it might even hurt him." What if he died while his collection was on the other side of the Atlantic? she thought. "Oh God," she prayed silently, "please don't let that happen."

Pina gave Lizzie a cup of coffee. It was a tiny cup, very strong and bitter, which Lizzie sipped slowly.

The image of the old collection was still on the table and Pina picked it up. "Is this really what all this looked like three hundred years ago?"

"I'm not sure," Lizzie explained. She told her about the Cospi image and the similarities between the two. "It's possible that the artist laid down a template and then drew the individual collections onto it. But certain identifiable things are still here, obviously." She pointed up. "Our friend the alligator and the sarcophagus." As she said it she realized that she had not seen the sarcophagus in the room.

"I hope so, anyway," she said. "Is the Egyptian mummy case still in the house?"

"It's in the ballroom," Pina said, leading Lizzie to the closed doors at the far end of the room. "For some reason, it started to really upset Uncle Patrizio, so my Uncle Cosimo moved it into the ballroom, where he never goes."

She pushed open one door and they stepped into a dark room. Some light filtered in from the courtyard windows, which had shutters that leaked light along the edges and between the lattices. A dim light showed up the stairs at the far end, where the second staircase from the courtyard emerged into this room.

Pina found a switch and turned on the nearest of three gigantic chandeliers. The room was filled with furniture covered with sheets or other covers to keep the voluminous dust from ruining upholstery.

"No balls or parties anymore," Pina explained, "so this has mostly just become a dumping ground for the overflow from the house." She turned on the other two chandeliers. Each of the great lamps was made of pale ivory-colored blown glass that twisted like snakes up and around the glass plates that had originally held candles. Decades before they had been replaced with candle-shaped bulbs, and many of those were now burned out. For good measure, Pina also opened one of the floor-to-ceiling shutters onto the courtyard, releasing a cloud of dust. She swore in Italian, a word that Lizzie had often heard Jackie use.

The stream of light that burst in from the courtyard turned the ghosts around the room into chairs and tables, whose forms could now be seen beneath their coverings. The shape of the sarcophagus was unmistakable under an incongruous linen tablecloth patterned with green vines and yellow flowers. It lay on its back against the wall opposite the courtyard window and as Lizzie walked over to it, Pina joined her.

"I assume you have seen it before," Lizzie said.

"Once," Pina said. "I was just a little girl and it was still in the library. I put my hand on it and Uncle Patrizio screamed at me not to touch it and I never did again."

They pulled back one end to reveal the face, carved and painted on the lid of the sarcophagus. The eyes were large, with big black pupils against the bright whites of the eyes. A black line surrounded each eye and fine eyebrows were painted above them. The face was beautifully carved; all the features but the eyes and eyebrows were left unpainted and the wood was of a color that could represent the skin of an Egyptian, light brown with a golden undertone. Across the forehead and tucked behind the ears a wig of tiny braids was carved to cover the head. The protective wings of Isis came down around the face and three lotus blossoms hung like a crown, painted in gold, green and red over the dark black plaits of the hair.

They pulled the cloth down further to expose ornaments in the hair, and painted clothing in multi-colored geometric shapes. The hands lay across the lower part of the chest, crossed and pointing in opposite directions.

"They are very finely carved, aren't they?" Lizzie said, pointing to the hands.

"The whole thing is quite beautiful," Pina said.

They had only pulled the covering back to the waist of the sarcophagus when they heard a voice in the library and Pina walked quickly back to the door. "I'll make sure Uncle Patrizio hasn't come back," she whispered to Lizzie.

It was Cosimo Gonzaga who came through the door just as Pina reached it.

"Uncle Cosimo," she said, "here is Professor Manning from Boston." She said something more to him in Italian, and Lizzie sensed that she was telling him about Patrizio's behavior earlier.

He seemed not to hear. "Professor Manning," he said, extending his hand, "how very nice to see you again."

"Please call me Lizzie," she said, taking his hand and shaking it.

"And you must call me Cosimo," he said politely.

She remembered him from their brief meeting in Boston as a friendly man who cultivated a common touch, and he seemed sincere in his welcome to the house.

"Ah, my old friend!" he said enthusiastically when he saw the sarcophagus. "I once tried to open it to see if there was a mummy inside and I got such a beating from Uncle Pat!"

"Did you ever find out?" Lizzie asked curiously.

"No," he said, taking her arm and leading her back to the library. "But I don't think there is."

Lizzie told him that the Egyptologist at St. Pat's said that any mummy acquired in the Renaissance had probably been cannibalized as medicine and Cosimo laughed hard in response.

He asked Pina to get them more coffee and indicated a chair for Lizzie, and then sat at one at a right angle to it at the end of the table.

"Pina tells me that Pat gave you some trouble about the collection," he said, getting right to the point.

"He says he doesn't know anything about the exhibit, or the College borrowing things for it."

"Of course he has been told many times," Cosimo said, "but he has the dementia of old age and frequently doesn't remember things."

"I'm worried about removing the most familiar things in the house," Lizzie said. "Don't you think it could make his situation worse?"

"Unfortunately, he is completely unpredictable. Some days he has mental clarity and thinks this is a wonderful idea, other days he is confused and doesn't know what I am talking about."

Lizzie reached for the picture of the cabinet and handed it to Cosimo. "He practically accused me of stealing this," she said.

Cosimo took the picture. "Thank you for sending me this before," he said, "though this one is a much better quality image. Did you say that my grandmother gave it to the College?"

"Along with photographs of the house and the original of the list of which you sent me a copy." She paused and thought about this. "Did you know your grandmother?"

"Very well," he answered. "She didn't die until I went to America to go to St. Pat's. Though my family didn't live in this house, I spent some part of almost every day here when I was young. She taught me English, among other things, but she had been very scarred by the war. I had both an aunt and an uncle who died then."

"I heard about your aunt Gianna," Lizzie said, "and remember that there was also a son who died, but never heard the circumstances."

"That's because he was a Fascist and we never speak about him. I think my grandmother may have sent some things to America for safekeeping after the war, fearing what might happen to them here in the future." He picked up the picture again as he spoke and looked at it closely. "Old friends," he said, "the mummy, the alligator."

"You know of course that those are the most interesting things to me, and consequently important to include in an exhibit."

"Of course," he said, "I want this exhibit to be one that captures the spirit of this collection. I told you before you can take anything you like and I meant it."

"And I don't need to be worrying about Patrizio?"

"Leave Pat to me," he said.

Chapter 12

The room where Lizzie was to live while she was in the Gonzaga house was on the third floor above the ballroom. Unlike the rooms on the main floor, these rooms were provided with privacy by a corridor that ran along the outside wall of the house. Her window, consequently, faced the courtyard and the windows of the bedrooms on the opposite side of the house, in one of which she could see Patrizio sitting in a chair staring at her.

Graziella was in the room with Patrizio. Pina had told her that the two had adjoining rooms so that the housekeeper could respond quickly in case the old man had an emergency during the night. Lizzie was very sorry that her room was situated in such an awkward position and she closed the shutters. She had no idea if she was free to move about the house at night or if she was expected to stay in her own room. When Pina showed her the way, she had pointed into the chapel, which was on this floor, and Lizzie wanted to look at it more closely, but didn't know when that would be possible.

The house had a decidedly sinister aspect at night and Lizzie found herself looking at the lock on the door and wishing it were not such an ancient keyless thing.

It was six hours earlier in Boston and she called Martin to hear the reassurance of his voice.

"Hello, my love," he said. "How is Bologna?"

"Somewhat weird, actually." She explained the situation with Patrizio.

"Is this going to keep you from being able to put the exhibit together?"

"I don't think so," she said, "his nephew, Cosimo, is keen on it, but the old man was pretty upset."

"How's the house?"

"Fabulous, but slightly creepy at night." She explained the setup of the rooms. "There are only three people in this big house," she said. "Me, the old guy, and his caretaker, who is named Graziella and looks like her parents waited until she grew up to see what she would look like before they named her."

"Ha! You say that because you don't actually know the meaning of the name."

"Even I can see the 'grace' in it, but it is such a stereotypical name for the cruel stepsister."

"Not like Hengemont, then," Martin said, referring to a house in England where Lizzie had worked on another family collection under very different circumstances.

"Not at all," she said, "nor like Alison Kent's house which *might* have been creepy, but never was."

Those two projects in England, both of which had put Lizzie into what seemed like safe havens, had each proved dangerous, but Lizzie had met some of her own distant family through the first, and a close friend and colleague on the second. While Cosimo Gonzaga might be a good collaborator, Lizzie didn't see him ever becoming a close friend, and Pina was keeping her distance. If only she had met Patrizio when he still had all his marbles, she thought.

When she had said goodnight to Martin, she turned off the lights and peeked through the shutters. There was still a light on in Patrizio's room, though shades had been drawn. She could see no other light on in the house and she turned on the bedside lamp before she pulled back the covers and got into bed. Despite the traveling and time change, she was too restless to sleep so she took her e-reader and returned to Maggie Gonzaga's letters. She had read so far about her time at school in Switzerland and about her meeting with Lorenzo Gonzaga. The next set of letters was written after her marriage and described the house in which Lizzie found herself, but it was a very different place seen through Maggie's eyes.

September 9, 1912

Dear Mama and Papa,

I loved this house the first time I saw it, and while I don't think that I began to love Renzo because of it, he is such a part of the house and it of him. They call it a "palazzo," but it turns out that all the big houses in Bologna are called that. There is a central courtyard and all the rooms in the house face it—several have balconies that allow you to sit outside without the noise and activity of the street, which is very pleasant and peaceful. Renzo and his father, as avid archaeologists, have filled up much of the courtyard with pieces they have found in the countryside around here. There are a number of Etruscan sarcophagi, small and lovely with the familial relationships carved into the stones. One has a couple holding hands and looking so lovingly at each other. Another has a mother with a little girl and there is what appears to be a doll carved near her. It is strange that these people, who lived here almost three thousand years ago, should seem so familiar to me in these stones. I wept when I first saw them and Renzo told me that he did too, when he and his father first uncovered them.

There are also Roman ruins, including a number of fragments of statues and columns, and that is only what is in the courtyard! When I first saw the space I told Renzo that he should host a production of "Romeo and Juliet" here, as it could accommodate all the scenes in the courtyard, and the balcony scene would work perfectly on the landing of one of the staircases. He has now challenged me to produce it and I am looking for young actors among the students at the University.

I am very happy here, as I told you I would be. My mother-in-law and I share much in common, despite our very different backgrounds. There is a small chapel here in the house where a mass is celebrated every morning, which is a way for us to begin our days together. She is patient with my Italian, and has even learned a few words in English.

Except for missing you, my darlings, which I do every minute, I feel that mine is a very fortunate life. Come visit me! Or at least send Tommy.

Very much love from your daughter,

Maggie

The next letter was written a few days later.

September 13, 1912

Dear Mama and Papa,

I had just begun to tell you about the house in my last letter, and I didn't even get inside. Renzo describes the entrance hall as the place where "the Gonzagas first seek to impress visitors with their importance." One wall is covered with a family tree that is painted directly on the wall. This is a marvelous work of art, full of detail and color. The background is an actual tree, with expansive branches that hold several hundred names on small scrolls unrolling among the leaves. Across the top are small portraits of the most famous and important Gonzagas, men who were the Dukes of Mantua and other places, as well as twelve cardinals, fourteen bishops and St. Aloysius Gonzaga, who has a special place among the branches of the tree.

The ceiling of this room is like a Chinese puzzle of wood pieces fit together to form an intricate pattern, and it is painted in colors that you would not think appropriate for a ceiling, and yet seem quite right in this room: pink and green and brick red

and gold. Every other wall surface is covered with
paintings of ancient Gonzagas, many with crowns
carved into the frames above their heads. There are
also busts of three of the cardinals, so I think that
the objective of impressing a visitor works very well.

The next several letters described Maggie's life in Bologna. When the weather was fine enough, furniture was set up in the courtyard and the family spent much of their time outside. The two salons were where the majority of time inside was spent. In each of them were groups of chairs with small tables arranged for conversation, and a large table with chairs where a meal could be served. These rooms were where the women gathered to do needlepoint, have tea or coffee, and gossip; they had light from both the street and the courtyard, and a good cross draft of ventilation.

The details of the gilded plaster filigree of the Yellow Salon were in Lizzie's head as she drifted off to sleep and when she woke the next morning she found that Pina was waiting for her in that very room. Her hostess had brought fresh rolls, cold cuts and cheese and was arranging them on a platter when Lizzie came into the room.

"Graziella won't prepare anything for anyone but Uncle Patrizio," Pina said, "so I'm afraid that you will mostly be eating out."

"Not a problem," Lizzie said. "I've heard the food in Bologna is the best in Italy."

She asked Pina if she would get a key to the house and Pina took one from her purse and gave it to her. "Uncle Cosimo asked me to have this made for you."

"Am I free to wander in the house?" Lizzie asked. "Or should I wait for an escort?"

"Where do you want to go?"

"I just want to look at the collections."

"I'll ask Uncle Cosimo. My only concern is that it might frighten or upset Uncle Patrizio if he were to come upon you unexpectedly."

A few minutes later the old man came into the room, moving quickly behind his walker and seemingly in good spirits.

"Miss Kenney," he said, stretching out his hand to Lizzie. "This is such a pleasure. I'm so glad you're still here."

Lizzie gave him her hand, which he kissed. "I'm glad to see you, Pat," she said.

Pina pulled out a chair for him and he sat down.

"Would you please bring us some coffee?" Patrizio said to Pina, as if she was a waitress and he was in a café.

Unsure whether he thought she was someone else, whom he actually liked and was happy to see, or if he had simply forgotten her name, Lizzie made no attempt to correct Patrizio about her identity.

He asked her about Boston and about life at St. Pat's, which made her think that he did remember her, but as he rambled on about walks along the Charles River and riding in the swan boats on the lake in the Public Garden, Lizzie thought that he might have mistaken her for some other American woman he had known decades before. Her knowledge of Boston and of the campus allowed her to participate in the conversation, even without knowing precisely what was in the convoluted circuitry of Pat Gonzaga's demented brain.

"Do you remember when you came to visit here with your mother before the war?" he asked at one point. Fortunately he answered his own question and Lizzie was not forced into either an outright lie or exposure of her real identity.

"Those were such good times, Theresa," he said, smiling shyly. "You don't mind if I call you Theresa, like the old days?"

Lizzie mumbled something that could sound like an assent. She was wondering how much she could take advantage of this bizarre situation before the bubble burst.

"This is such a lovely room," she said, hoping he would tell her more about it. It really was an extraordinary space. There were paintings that went from the chair rail right up to the ceiling molding, and each of them was surrounded by elaborate gilded plasterwork. The walls were also painted directly with *tromp l'oeil* images that looked like carved molding, recesses in the wall, and extensions of frames. Only the ceiling molding was really three-dimensional, the rest just looked like it was.

"I guess that once the walls were painted and plastered, you couldn't move the paintings," she said.

"My mother used to make that comment all the time," he said jovially. "Maybe she said it to you."

"Perhaps she did," Lizzie said cautiously. It occurred to her that she might, in fact, have read that in one of Maggie's letters the night before. "When was the room set up like this?"

"I'm not sure exactly," he said. "But there were some Americans here just after the Revolution who described this room in a letter dated 1789, and it seems to have been just as you see it now."

"It's a fine collection of paintings," Lizzie said. She looked for the Ruysdael that Martin had pointed out from the 1959 photograph, but couldn't find it.

"I have a catalogue of all the paintings in the house if you are interested," Patrizio said, and Lizzie was astonished when he offered to show it to her.

Pina had delivered the coffee and stood in the background. She moved forward to help her uncle stand, but he brushed her away. "Miss Kenney," he said. "Can I take your arm?"

"Of course," Lizzie said and watched as he put his hands on the arms of the chair and pushed himself up. He seemed years younger than he had the day before.

There was a cane on the walker and Patrizio used that with one hand and leaned heavily on Lizzie as they walked from the Yellow Salon into the Chinese Salon. He pointed out the hand-painted wallpaper, imported from China in the eighteenth century, and the several pieces of porcelain, from vases big enough to hide in to small delicate plates.

"The Gonzaga fortune was largely made from trade," he said, pointing out a few special pieces, "and many of these things travelled great distances to come here."

Walking through the long dining room, they paused to step out onto the balcony and look into the courtyard. Lizzie identified the window to her room on the floor above and then turned her attention to the two staircases that rose on the wall opposite her on either side of the main doorway. She thought of Maggie's impulse to see a production of Romeo and Juliet using the landing of one of the staircases as the famous balcony.

"Did your mother ever get to produce her Shakespeare?" Lizzie asked, and then immediately regretted that she had let the veil slip, but Patrizio didn't notice.

"She did," he said, still smiling simply. "How did you know?"

"She mentioned it," Lizzie said cagily.

"'Merchant of Venice,' 'Two Gentlemen of Verona,' 'Romeo and Juliet,' anything that was set in Italy she considered fair game for her courtyard. She loved Shakespeare."

It was a very different entrance into the "Wonder Chamber" today. While she had been greeted with indifference by Pina and hostility by Patrizio the day before, now she was warmly welcomed. Patrizio gave her a history of the collection and pulled several pieces out to show her.

"This box is from Mexico," he said, setting one of the artifacts carefully on the table. "It is from the sixteenth century, and look at how different it is on the two sides. On one is a tree, the source of life, and springing around it are animals of many kinds, and flowers that have grown to a gigantic size, and here," he said, turning it around, "is the priest, holding up his cross." He looked up at Lizzie. "It is capturing that moment of confusion when the old ways are supplanted by the new." He turned the end to face her and pointed out the figure of the traditional god, symbolically depicted as a jaguar.

He pushed the box toward her and Lizzie picked it up. It was made of a light wood and had once had an arched top that was now missing. The shape of it was indicated in the tall rounded side walls of the box, and there were still old hinges and a keyhole present. The colors of the pigments were remarkably vibrant and, like Patrizio, Lizzie was struck by the incongruous presence of the black-robed priest among the colorful foliage.

Patrizio was clearly tired from walking and standing, and Lizzie helped him into a chair.

"You said there was a catalogue that I might see?" she said hesitantly.

"Of course," he said. He pointed to one of the bookcases that was covered with a screen and told Lizzie that if she put a finger through the screen on the lower right shelf she would find a key. Once the door was open, Pat had Lizzie run her hand along the volumes until she touched a big ledger book, bursting with extra papers. She pulled it carefully from the shelf and put it on the table in front of him.

"This is it," he said. "All the records of the collections in the house."

Lizzie had known that records would have been kept since the collection was first started—those early founders of the collections were men of science, who would have documented everything they had. She quickly began to see that Patrizio's ledger book was filled with earlier inventories and descriptions than the one she had seen, as well as later typed lists. Cosimo had obviously known nothing about this when he sent her the inventory from the 1950s.

"Some things were lost over time," he explained, "and many items went missing during the war, when we had so many people in the house, including Nazi soldiers who had no respect for the property of any Italian. We hid as much of the cabinet as we could, under the stones of the courtyard and behind walls in the cellar, but we had to hide so much and there wasn't room for everything. We had a Michelangelo candlestick that was stolen then."

She wondered if he could possibly be correct about this. Had Michelangelo even made candlesticks? She wondered if he might have translated the word incorrectly.

"There was a Michelangelo in the collection that was stolen?" she asked.

Patrick nodded. "My mother kept it in her bedroom and loved looking at it so much that she didn't want it to go into hiding during the war, and a Nazi officer stole it." He suddenly saw the photograph of the 1677 drawing of the cabinet lying on the table and said, "Oh here this is! I have been looking for it." He slid the photo into the ledger as he pulled out a printed list for Lizzie. "Here is a catalogue of the paintings," he said, "made by someone from the Art Museum after the war. At that time, my mother and I went through the house and tried to see what had been lost and damaged, and we also made a new list of what survived from the cabinet, but I haven't been able to find that list either."

"Perhaps she put it somewhere for safekeeping," Lizzie said gently, thinking of the original of that list sitting in the library at St. Pat's, and the copy of it that was on her computer.

He nodded thoughtfully. "Yes, perhaps she did."

He was obviously very tired and though Lizzie tried to direct the conversation back to Michelangelo, he would not follow. She thought she should try to find either Pina or Graziella, but had no idea where they might be or how to contact them. She went to the door into the dining room and then through it to look into the Chinese Salon, but neither woman was in either room. When she returned to ask Patrizio about this, she found him asleep in his chair.

Had she not had Cosimo Gonzaga's blessing to "take anything in the house" for her exhibit, and the expectations of Father O'Toole and others that she would return from Bologna with a plan to proceed, she would have felt a lot more guilty about sneaking around Patrizio, pretending to be someone else and taking advantage of his nap to copy the documents from his ledger book. But her time was limited and the demands were real.

Taking her cell phone from her bag, Lizzie used the camera on it to photograph all the loose papers from the ledger. She wanted to capture images of the pages in the book as well, but she feared waking Patrizio by taking it, and so she simply pulled the separate sheets out quickly but silently and went about the job. When she had photographed those, she went systematically around the room, photographing every shelf. Most of the cabinets were unlocked, but where they weren't she found that the same key would open all.

Here were the ostrich eggs, the tortoise shells, the blowfish, and the small *Draco dandinii,* the dragon-like salamander that had delighted Jimmy. On a shelf near it she located the other item on Jimmy's wish list, the ceramic *krater* with its five lyre-playing sisters, surrounded by ceramic cups, plates, and shallow bowls with handles. There were bronze or copper bells, keys, pails, plates, spoons and ladles that had all turned green over the centuries, and many small decorations for clothing in the same metal: pins, beads and toggles that would have held cloaks together.

On a long bottom shelf she found the six-foot narwhal tusk lying side-by-side with a Marquesan club. They were the only things in this particular cubical of the cabinetry and Lizzie was very happy to see them. She was on her knees and had stretched out her hand to move the club to see the details of it when she felt a hard blow on her shoulder.

She turned quickly and saw Patrizio standing above her, his cane raised to strike her again. She managed to deflect the blow from her head with her arm, but had some difficulty getting to her feet and wrestling for the cane at the same time.

"Thief!" he screamed. "Thief!"

"I am not a thief!" she called, hoping Pina or Graziella would hear them and respond.

It did not take long for her to disarm him. At 93, he was much weaker than she, and though he had hurt her, she didn't want to hurt him; she was alarmed when he stumbled backwards and fell.

"Help!" she cried. "We need help!"

Pina came rushing into the room and Lizzie could see that Graziella was not far behind her. The conversation between them and Patrizio as they helped him to his feet was in fast-paced Italian, with many gesticulations. The only word that Lizzie could recognize was "Thief!" which Patrizio repeated several times in English, always pointing at her.

"What happened?" Pina finally asked, turning to Lizzie.

"He was asleep at the table and I was looking at artifacts on this low shelf when he started hitting me with his cane," she said breathlessly.

Graziella asked Pina for a translation and then shook her head in disbelief. Lizzie thought she was telling Pina that it simply wasn't possible.

"He stood up on his own and crossed the room and hit you?" Pina asked incredulously.

Lizzie held up her arm, where an ugly bruise was forming.

"Before he fell asleep, we were having a very friendly conversation," she said. "This was entirely unexpected."

Graziella guided Patrizio into a chair and then left to retrieve his walker, mumbling something that Lizzie was certain was aimed at her. He seemed such a pathetic old man, but she was his constant companion; wouldn't she know that he was capable of occasional feats of strength?

"Are you injured?" Pina whispered. She gestured at Patrizio, who had once again fallen asleep in his chair.

"No," Lizzie answered, rubbing her arm and reaching around to touch the place on her shoulder that had received the first blow. "Nothing is broken. It all just took me so completely by surprise."

When Graziella returned, Pina asked Lizzie if she would mind going through into the ballroom while they took Patrizio away. "I'm not sure what sort of a response he might have to your presence."

Lizzie agreed and went through the door, closing it all but a crack. She watched as Graziella woke her charge and told him it was time to go back to his room. He was a docile shadow of what he had been earlier, first as a charming host and companion, and later in his savage rage. The two women helped him put his hands on his walker and practically moved his feet for him as he left the room.

It was with some satisfaction that Lizzie saw that the ledger and its contents were left on the table and as soon as the room was empty she went back and resumed her plan to photograph everything. She started with the narwhal tusk and Marquesan club, which she pulled from their place near the floor and arranged on the long table to get better pictures. Page-by-page she photographed the entire ledger. She laid on her back on the table and photographed the alligator from several angles.

When Pina returned she was putting the ledger and its contents back together.

"I'm really sorry about this," Pina said. "He is so unpredictable now."

"There is nothing you could have done," Lizzie said. "I will have to be more careful in how I approach him and the collection."

"You're staying then?"

"Yes, of course. Now that I have seen what's here I know what a terrific exhibit it will make in Boston."

"And the regrets you voiced yesterday, about depriving him of his familiar surroundings?"

It seemed too crass to say that Patrizio's cane had relieved her of any concern she might have felt for the old man, but she realized that, in fact, it had. She knew Patrick was loony, and she felt sorry for him, but she had a job to do and she was going to do it.

"Everything will be returned when the exhibit ends," Lizzie said. She didn't think that she owed more of an explanation to Pina. She took the ledger book and put it back in the bookcase where it belonged, but didn't lock the case or return the key. If Pina didn't know about the key, Lizzie would not be the one to inform her of it.

Chapter 13

The packing and shipping of such an old and valuable collection as that belonging to the Gonzagas required expertise. Cosimo was involved in a shipping company and would handle the actual transportation, and a company that specialized in moving works of art would pack the collection. Before any piece could be approved to travel, however, it needed to be examined by a professional conservator, and possibly either repaired, or scheduled to be repaired in Boston. The conservator would also determine what sort of exhibit mounts might be required, so that the designer and fabricator in Boston could begin their work. Lizzie had been told while she was still at home that one of the conservators from the Museum of the University of Bologna, Carmine Moreale, would take on the work for this project and she had an appointment to meet him for coffee at the end of his workday.

She was particularly anxious to get out of the house after her extraordinary morning. Once Patrizio was taken off to his room she had accomplished a lot. Worried that she might not have another chance, she had photographed all the documentation of the collection, and every object that might possibly be included in the exhibit. As she walked to the University Museum to meet Carmine, she stopped at an office store and had printouts made of all the various versions of the catalogue lists.

She also sent a quick email to Jackie: "Some very nutty stuff going on here, about which I will write more later. Can you check and see if there was a student at St. Pat's in the late 30s or early 40s named Theresa Kenney, and if so, where she went from there? Thanks, Lizzie."

Arriving early so that she could look at the University of Bologna Museum, Lizzie wandered from room to room, interested in how the oldest collections were presented, and wondering if she should use modern cases in her own exhibit—ones that might seem to disappear around the objects—or old-style cases that would make their own statement and establish a sense of another time. This museum had what was left of the collections of Ulisse Aldrovandi and Ferdinando Cospi, as well as other scientific collections that had been amassed during the nine-hundred-year history of the University.

As the first two Gonzaga collectors had been a student of Aldrovandi and a collaborator of Cospi, it was not surprising that there were many similarities in the collections. Here were the alligators, the narwhal tusks, the blowfish, ostrich eggs, and elephant tusks. There were also ethnographic objects, and the range represented the same locations and potentially the same sources as did things in the Gonzaga collection: travelers who had gone to the New World, to Africa and Asia as traders and missionaries when Europeans were expanding their networks of commerce and colonization to distant locations.

Interpretive labels in both Italian and English provided Lizzie with information on a number of objects that had analogs in the Gonzaga collection, and she took many notes and pictures for her file. There were other systematic collections that were still among the oldest of their kind in the world, though none so old as Aldrovandi's. There were minerals, shells and corals, and a fascinating anatomical museum. Several different anatomists and artists had begun work in the eighteenth century on making models of human fetuses in different stages of development, then moved on to fashioning human musculature in wax attached to actual skeletons, and finally made straightforward full-size wax models of organs.

The exhibit culminated in a full-length figure of a nude woman, neatly dissected to show the embryo in her womb. Her back was supported on a pillow, but her neck was arched, exposing the strands of a bead necklace. Her legs were crossed casually, her lifelike hand gently touched one thigh. Real hair had been attached both to her pubic area and her head, where it was arranged in a long plait over her shoulder.

A nearby label described the development of scientific obstetrics in eighteenth-century Bologna, and mentioned Luigi Galvani, a professor at the University who was the first to make a connection between neurophysiological circuitry that went from the brain to the uterus to start contractions. Lizzie was thinking that he must be the man juggling books in front of the Gonzaga house, and was pondering the difference between that memorable memorial statue and the wax model of a woman being autopsied in front of her when a man's voice interrupted her thoughts.

"Are you Professor Manning?"

"I am," she said, turning to see a man coming toward her, his hand extended.

"I'm Carmine Moreale," he said. "I know we were supposed to meet outside the museum, but I suspected that you might be here in advance."

Lizzie had been given his resume when he was hired for the project and she knew that he was thirty-four years old, born in Rome, educated in Bologna and Florence, and had studied art restoration in London and New York. He spoke English with more of an Italian accent than anyone she had met so far. From the time Maggie Kelliher became part of their family, all of the Gonzagas had learned English as children and had spent significant time in the U.S.; most of them had gone to St. Patrick's College. They spoke English with almost imperceptible inflections of their native tongue, but Carmine's accent was so extreme that at times he sounded like a comedian mocking an Italian. He added a vowel to the end of every word, whether it had one or not.

"Letsa getta summa coffee," he said to Lizzie after they exchanged their first pleasantries.

He asked her how mucha she hadda seena of Bologna and when she said she seen nothing so far, insisted that they walk down the Via Zamboni from the University, past the two famous towers that were the symbol of the city, and along the Via Rizzoli to the Piazza Maggiore, the central square. Carmine was a knowledgeable and funny guide and knew the city and its history very well; as an art historian and conservator he also had inside information on works of art and their various restorations.

"I love to walk here," he said, pointing out the porticoes that covered the sidewalks on all the major streets and most of the minor ones. Some of them were more than a thousand years old, he explained. "You can walk for miles and miles along Bologna's streets and never be exposed to the rain or sun."

When they reached the great fountain topped by a gigantic statue of Neptune, he explained to Lizzie how the Bolognese people had dismantled it during World War II, when the city was occupied by the Germans and bombed repeatedly by the Allies. Neptune was surrounded by mermaids who shot water out of their nipples and even in the midst of his serious explanation, Carmine could not help laughing, and Lizzie was relieved because she had been desperately trying not to crack up as she looked at them.

They sat at one of the many small cafes that surrounded the square and looked across it at the unfinished front face of St. Petronio's, the principal church in a city that had a church on almost every block. Marble panels had been placed along the bottom third of the red-brick wall and there had obviously been an intention in the distant past to cover the entire surface.

"Is it being restored?" Lizzie asked.

"No," Carmine said with a wonderful gesture of his hand. "This is a very Italian story. Construction started in the fourteenth century and continued for about two hundred and fifty years, at which time, according to some sources, there was a fight with the church authorities in Rome and they just stopped building." He pointed to either side of the edifice. "It was supposed to have the side wings that would give it the required cruciform shape, but neither they, nor the front surface, were ever completed."

"I find that rather astonishing," Lizzie said. "No one ever thought to try to finish it in the last three hundred years?"

Carmine shrugged in that way that she had now come to accept as a peculiarly Italian gesture. "Oh I think there were attempts, but you see the results before you. You must go inside sometime, though. Among other things it has a meridian line, a brass marker in the floor that runs almost the length of the church. Go at noon," he continued. "The sun comes in through a lens in the roof and hits the line, marking the date."

They talked comfortably for more than an hour about Bologna and things to see. Carmine was a wealth of information and had such a musical voice that Lizzie loved listening to him. He told her of a project he was working on to compare as many images of St. Petronio as he could identify. The saint, he explained, was always shown holding a model of the city in his arms.

"He is the patron saint of Bologna," he said, "the bishop in the fifth century. When various artists either painted or sculpted him, they never tried to capture what the city looked like in the time of St. Petronio, but rather depicted the city as it looked in their own time. It is always enclosed within its medieval walls, but the configuration of the towers changes over time and I think I can see and describe the built history of the city in this way."

"When were the towers built?" Lizzie asked.

"In the twelfth and thirteenth centuries. Come," he said, laying some money on the table and leading her across the square to the front of the church. In the carving of the saint above the door he pointed out the features he had been describing.

Lizzie asked him about the brick towers, which were a defining feature of Bologna, and he told her that they had been built by the principal families, for defense against Germanic invaders.

"There were probably 180 of them in the thirteenth century," he said. "I think less than twenty survive and the most famous are the two we passed on the Via Zamboni." He pointed out those two towers in the model held by the saint above the door. They were recognizable by their close juxtaposition, and by the decided incline of one of them.

They passed a wall with a series of portrait photographs printed onto ceramic tiles. "It's a memorial to resistance fighters in the war," Carmine explained.

Lizzie thought of Gianna Gonzaga, who had been in the Resistance and was executed by the Nazis. She stepped over to see if there was a picture of her and found herself disappointed when she didn't find it.

"Are you looking for someone particular?" Carmine asked.

Lizzie described what she had learned of Gianna.

"Was she married?" he asked.

"Yes," Lizzie answered, struggling to remember back to the conversation at Tony Tessitore's house when he had described the trio of Patrizio, Gianna, and Gianna's husband Archie working for the Resistance. "Her husband's name was Archie," she said, pressing three fingers against her forehead, as if it might make her brain work more efficiently. "Archie, something that starts with a C."

She walked a few steps backwards along the wall and scanned the photographs of people with surnames starting with the letter C. "Giuseppina Cussetti," she said softly. "Here she is."

Looking back at her was a young woman with large dark eyes. Her hair was parted in the middle and hung to her shoulders. She had a slight smile on her face, almost like the expression on the face of the Mona Lisa that had inspired so much discussion over the centuries.

"How very very sad," Lizzie said. She turned to Carmine and explained the little she knew about Gianna. "I was told that her body was thrown out of a truck onto the plaza in front of her house. That she had been raped and beaten to death."

Carmine put a sympathetic hand on her shoulder. "Such terrible things happened during the war," he said. He suggested they have a drink and then asked what her plans were for dinner.

"I think I'm supposed to get my meals on my own," she said. "It is a strange situation at the house."

"And we haven't even talked about the collection yet," he said. "Let us have a glass of wine and then dinner."

"I won't be keeping you from your family?"

"No, only from my cats, and sometimes they have to be reminded that I am the boss and my world does not actually revolve around them."

He had pronounced it "I amma da bose," and Lizzie found it completely charming. By the end of the evening they each felt they had found a friend, and Lizzie looked forward to working with Carmine both here in Bologna, and in Boston, where he expressed a desire to go when the exhibit was mounted.

"It is my impression that Cosimo Gonzaga can be persuaded to pay for almost anything having to do with this exhibit," Lizzie said. "Though I'm not exactly sure what his motives are."

"Well I can tell you that there is no shortage of money there." Though they had become friendly, Lizzie didn't push him to say more about their sponsor.

It was a short walk from the restaurant to the Piazza Galvani, which was directly behind the church of St. Petronio.

Lizzie asked Carmine about the statue of Galvani and was told that the building across the square from the Gonzaga house was the original home of the University of Bologna. "Galvani taught there," he said.

"I love the statue, with him trying to balance this pile of books."

He said that he had always liked it too.

"The building is now the Archiginnasio Library," he continued. "You should go in there too. It was damaged by a bomb in the war, but they have done a great restoration, and it has the original autopsy theatre where I think Galvani probably worked. He was a physician."

Lizzie said that she knew that from reading a label about him in the museum.

The logical next step for them was to schedule a time to look at the collection. As they stood in front of the Palazzo Gonzaga Lizzie repeated what she had told Carmine at dinner, that Patrizio's dementia made him very unpredictable. "Unfortunately," she said, "we have to be prepared for him to object to having any part of the collection moved to Boston for the exhibit."

"Is he ever out of the house?" Carmine asked.

"So far no, but this is only my second day here. I'll ask Pina or Cosimo about it tomorrow."

They exchanged phone numbers and as Lizzie entered
Carmine's number in her cell phone she realized that it was
after eleven o'clock. "I should have called Pina this evening,"
she said. "I never told anyone where I was going or when I
would return."

"Do you have a key to the house?"

"I do," she said. "I know I would never be able to get Patrizio's attention from the front door, and frankly his housekeeper Graziella scares me."

He walked her to the door and waited until she opened it,
then kissed her on both cheeks.

"I look forward to making a plan tomorrow," he said, and
Lizzie said that she did too.

The key moved easily in the lock and she stepped into the
courtyard. There was a light on in the dining room, which
sent a diffuse yellow light across the space, and a few smaller
lights on in other rooms, which Lizzie thought either Pina or
Graziella must have left for her to find her way around. She
thought again that she should have called Pina. If Patrizio, or
even Graziella, found her sneaking around the dark house she
might get another blow.

She used the flashlight on her cell phone to find her way
up the stairs to the *piano nobile* and found a lamp on in the
Entrance Hall. There was a smaller staircase that continued
up to the next floor of the house, but it was not the one that
Pina had originally used to show her to her room, and Lizzie
did not want to be finding a new route in the dark. There was
another lamp on in the Chinese Salon, and that was enough
to guide her through the Yellow Salon to the back corner of
the house where there was another staircase. This was also
where the small elevator had been installed for Patrizio, who
no longer had the ability to climb stairs.

The staircase had a silk rope rather than a railing and Lizzie felt along the length of it as she followed the curve of the
stairs and reached the top floor. Her room was down the long
hall that ran the length of the dining room on the floor below,
around the corner and halfway down another long hallway.

She walked as quietly as she could. There was a soft light
from the doorway of the small chapel, which Pina had pointed

out to her the afternoon before, but then the door was closed. Now it was open slightly and she heard Patrizio's voice in prayer. Lizzie put her eye to the opening and looked in. There was a lovely altar surrounded by a marble railing and lit by several dozen candles. A small chandelier of angels held up a crown filled with some gentle light source, which glowed above the bowed head of the old man.

There were no pews. Instead there were eight individual bench seats, built into small cabinets with attached kneelers. Patrizio occupied one that was in the back row and neither in the center nor on the end. It must have been his accustomed spot when there were more people who used the chapel regularly. Lizzie remembered reading in one of Maggie's letters that she had attended daily mass there with her mother-in-law. Perhaps she had continued that tradition with her children.

There was something sadly poignant in seeing the old man alone in the chapel, and Lizzie was again struck with concern about the impact that taking the collection away, even for a few months, might have on him.

Walking softly to her room, she thought about what this house must have been like when Patrizio was a child. Lizzie had already fallen in love with Maggie Gonzaga and was convinced she must have been a wonderful mother. With six children in the house it would have been an active place, full of life; how different from the situation now.

When she was comfortably in bed, she took up Maggie's letters again. From 1912 to 1914 they were filled with news of her growing family, and her increasing familiarity with and love for the house, which she described in wonderful detail. In a letter from June 1914 to her mother, Maggie acknowledged the receipt of the telegram that informed her of the death of her father, and stated her plans to return to Boston for the funeral with Lorenzo and her two small daughters. There was a gap in the correspondence for more than a year after that. Lizzie knew that she had stayed in the U.S. for the birth of her oldest son, Adino.

She turned off her light and got out of bed. Standing at the window she looked into the courtyard. The lights were still on where she had left them around the *piano nobile*. Opposite her, a light came on in Patrick's room and Lizzie saw Graziella guiding the old man to his bed. She got back under her covers and opened her computer. In the file of family photos she looked for images of Gianna, first as a child, then as a little girl with a pageboy haircut, and then as a young woman. There were several pictures of Gianna and Patrizio, who had been handsome in his youth. One of the two always had an arm wrapped around the other. Eventually another young man appeared in the photos and at some point he was in every picture of Gianna. Jimmy had been careful to attach a caption to each picture from the notations on the back, and the second young man was identified first as Arcangelo Cussetti and then simply as Archie.

There was a picture of Gianna sitting on the railing of the courtyard staircase in an outfit that might have been a costume to play Juliet. Her mother stood beside her with an arm around her shoulders. Archie and Patrizio were both wearing doublets and tights and had swords with which they pretended to threaten each other as they fought their way up the stairs. Maggie and Gianna looked at them with great smiles of amusement.

Lizzie placed her computer on the bedside table and looked at that picture until she drifted off, at which point the machine also went to sleep.

Chapter 14

Theresa Kenney was an undergraduate at St. Pat's 1938-42. After she graduated, she became a teacher at St. Pat's Prep and worked there until she retired in 1986 and then she moved to Florida. She died in '96. I can't find any evidence that she was married or had children."

Lizzie was still in her room as she read the email from Jackie, which had been sent the previous day. It was eight o'clock and the house was silent. Once again she didn't know if there was a time when she might begin her work, or if Patrizio was again going to be a problem. She decided to call Pina.

"I'm confused," she began, "with how I am to proceed with my work here. I met with Carmine Moreale yesterday and we'd like to start assessing the condition of the pieces that might be traveling to Boston."

Pina answered that she had spoken to her Uncle Cosimo after yesterday's incident and that he suggested that maybe Patrizio should be taken out of the house while Lizzie worked. He wanted her to feel free to do what she needed to do, and didn't want her to worry about being in any danger if Patrizio were to have another violent outburst.

"How will you proceed today?" Pina asked.

"I'll play things as they come," Lizzie answered. "If Patrizio is willing to work with me I'll do that this morning; if he isn't I'll go out and do some research at the University Museum."

She hung up the phone and answered Jackie's message. "Can you find a picture of Theresa Kenney and tell me if she looks anything like me?"

It was a dangerous game to pretend to be someone else,

especially someone about whom she knew nothing, but if Patrizio once again confused her with Theresa Kenney, Lizzie would use it to communicate with the old man.

As she walked past the chapel door to the stairs, Lizzie once again heard Patrizio at prayer. She took a deep breath, pushed open the door and went in. Moving slowly and with as little sound as she could, she sat on one of the seats and bowed her head.

The light this morning came from three stained-glass windows that caught the morning sun and sent a few rays into the room. In some places the colors held their individual intensity, and a beam of blue or gold picked out the details in wood and marble carvings around the altar. Mostly the colors were diffused into the air, in a heady mixture that left Lizzie breathless.

It was several minutes before the old man turned and looked at her. She nodded and whispered, "Hello, Pat."

He looked confused for a moment, and then said in English. "Who are you?"

Her voice caught for a moment in her throat as she reconsidered the lie she was about to tell. "Theresa Kenney," she whispered hoarsely. "Your friend from St. Pat's."

Patrizio put his hands on the railing of the kneeler and pushed himself up; she immediately stood and went to help him. He took her hand and kissed it. "Have you forgiven me?" he asked.

Lizzie gave a confused nod. Clearly there was a more complex story here than just classmates in college.

"I made such a terrible mistake," he said. His next words were in Italian and then he seemed to catch himself and returned to English. "I'm glad you're here."

Embarrassed at the game she was playing, Lizzie found she could not look at him and her eyes instead moved around the chapel. The night before when she had looked in, the altar was covered with candles, but they had all burnt out, leaving wax dangling from the tall silver candlesticks in slender teardrops, and laying in hardened disks on the marble of the altar. Nothing on the surface of it looked like what she remembered from the seventeenth-century sketch, but under the altar the corpse looked just as it had in that sketch, and in the photo from the 1950s. It lay behind a panel of glass.

Patrizio saw where Lizzie's gaze was focused and said something about the man being a martyred Crusader knight. "He was killed on his way to Venice."

"Was he a member of your family?"

"Oh no. We claim only one saint, Aloysius. This man died here in Bologna and was buried in our parish church, St. Paolo Maggiore. When this chapel was built, relics were needed and St. Paolo's wanted more room than it had, so he was transferred here."

Lizzie continued to look around and Patrizio pointed out columns brought from Constantinople during the fourth crusade that had also been moved here from St. Paolo Maggiore. There were a number of reliquaries, mostly in niches on either side of the altar. Lizzie had always thought that a few of these would add to her exhibit and now that she actually saw them she was even more convinced.

"May I look at the reliquaries?" she asked tentatively, ready to back away instantly if Patrizio showed any misgivings.

He opened the door in the marble railing as an answer and gestured to the inner part of the altar. There were at least forty large reliquaries and dozens of small ones visible there; the largest were more than two feet tall and some had full arm or leg bones visible. Many were in the shape of the saintly body parts that they held, including arms and heads. Lizzie had seen many reliquaries before, but still found the juxtaposition of human body parts, precious metals and gemstones somewhat jarring. The artistry and expense that had gone into the creation of the container, compared to the morbid earthiness of the contents, was simultaneously fascinating and repellent.

If she could choose three of these for her exhibit, they would be a huge hit in Boston, and Father O'Toole had already said that he would arrange with the cardinal to transport them if there was any problem. She began to make a mental list of the ones that would have the most visual impact, by either the impressiveness of the artistry and materials, or the shock of the bones.

"They do inspire," Patrizio said beside her. His mind had

obviously been going in a very different direction and after that he was silent for more than a minute. "If you like old things," he continued, "may I show you our archaeological collection?"

Lizzie was surprised and pleased by the offer and readily assented. She looked around for Patrizio's walker and saw Graziella at the door. Patrick spoke to her in Italian and she rolled the walker into the room. He apologized to Lizzie for having to use it and led her to the elevator adjacent to the chapel. The housekeeper glared at Lizzie, as if challenging her not to excite, confuse or hurt her charge.

"You must find me very decrepit," Patrizio said as the elevator took them to the courtyard. "You have aged very little and yet I have become an old man, but thirty years is a long time."

Lizzie didn't have the heart to tell him that it was more than seventy years since he had met Theresa Kenney at St. Pat's. She opened the elevator door and the old machine creaked its way down to the courtyard.

"When you were last here," he said, "it was 1939, the summer before the war started." He sighed. "That was the last happy summer in this house."

"But after the war," Lizzie said, wanting to cheer him up, "you said that you and your mother worked together on the collection. That must have given you both some joy, to work together on a shared project."

"It was the way we survived. Honestly, just to get through each day was a struggle for us; the loss of Gianna, Adino, and the situation with Greta, it all left such a scar."

Greta was a new name to Lizzie and she probed carefully. "Greta," she said, "was she..."

Before she could continue, Patrizio put his hand gently on her mouth. "Don't speak of her," he said. "I'm sorry to have mentioned her name in your presence." He turned to fragments of a Roman column that lay near them and changed the subject.

The recesses of the courtyard were filled with archaeological fragments that Lizzie had not noticed previously. Even in daytime the sun did not reach into the spaces behind the arches and she had not walked into or around the courtyard in the few days she had been here.

There were hundreds of carved stones, some cemented to the wall and others lying on the ground. They had to navigate around a gigantic foot, long separated from its marble body, to get to the objects Patrick sought, two Etruscan tomb chests.

"My grandfather found these to the south on the road to Marzabotto," he said. "He was an enthusiastic archaeologist and he inspired my father to love the subject." He described tramping through the hills south of the city looking for Etruscan and Roman sites. "The Etruscans were in this region almost three thousand years ago," he said. He put his hand on one of the carved stone burial boxes. "My mother always loved these two sarcophagi because they captured something so essentially human."

"I remember them," Lizzie said, thinking of the letter Maggie had written to her parents in which she described them—on one a loving couple, on the other a mother and child. Maggie had said that both she and Lorenzo wept when they first saw them, and Lizzie felt the tears well up in her own eyes.

"I'm glad you remember," Patrizio said, and Lizzie could see that there were tears in his eyes as well.

She felt that she might be getting into dangerous territory with Patrizio, playing in this way with his faltering memory and questionable mental health, and was somewhat relieved when Pina appeared on the stairs, having just come up from the garage.

"I'm astonished to see you here," she said. "Uncle Patrizio, aren't you tired with all this walking?"

"I am actually getting quite tired," he said, "but Miss Kenney is such a delightful companion and she is interested in our fragments of the ancient civilizations."

"I don't want to keep you from your rest," Lizzie said, "or from anything else that you might need to do."

Pina was rather firm in insisting that he should go back upstairs, and led him into the elevator. As there wasn't room for three, Lizzie stayed behind and was glad for the additional time to look at the archaeological collection.

It was spread around all four sides of the courtyard. Some of the flat plaques were mounted onto the walls and there were numerous inscriptions in Latin that challenged Lizzie's limited knowledge. Once again her thoughts turned to her exhibit and she wondered if the two Etruscan sarcophagi could be included. They weren't especially large, but they were made of stone and she expected they were enormously heavy. Each was less than four feet long and two to three feet across, and each had both a carved stone lid and a stone mortuary box, which was about three feet deep. She made a note to put these and the giant foot on her list and ask Carmine about them when he came.

"What were you doing down here with Uncle Patrizio?" Pina asked. She was walking down the back staircase to the courtyard.

"We were talking about the archaeological collection," Lizzie said.

"He called you Miss Kenney," she said.

"I know," Lizzie lied. "I tried to correct him, but he just can't seem to remember my name."

"Does he think you are someone else?" Pina asked.

Lizzie mimicked the Italian shrug. "I don't know," she said. "But I was happy that he was interested in talking to me about any part of the collection."

"Uncle Cosimo will come this afternoon and talk to you about how the work is going."

"Good," Lizzie said. "Has your Uncle Patrizio gone back to his room?"

Pina said he had.

"Then I'd like to spend some time in the library," Lizzie said, "while I can."

"I'm sorry I can't stay," Pina said, "as I have correspondence that must go out today from my office, but you can call me if you need me."

Lizzie thanked her and waited until she had gone down the steps to the garage before proceeding across the courtyard and up the stairs to the ballroom. She wanted to take pictures of the sarcophagus while she had the chance. She made sure that the doors into the library were closed and opened two of the shuttered windows to get the daylight from the courtyard. Having learned from Pina's experience, she moved very slowly to keep a pile of dust from falling on her. She also turned on the three chandeliers.

"All right Mr. Well-placed Functionary in the Court," she said, looking at the painted face on the mummy case. "John Haworth wants some pictures of you and I'm going to take them."

She pulled the rest of the cloth off the case and found that it was in beautiful condition. There was no way, however, to get good photos of it where it lay against the wall, so with some effort she pulled out first the feet of the case and then the head and inched it across the floor to the center of the room. The wood floor of the ballroom was a smooth surface to move across, though Lizzie estimated that the sarcophagus must weigh several hundred pounds.

When it was finally in a clear space, Lizzie walked around it and took pictures from every angle. She concentrated especially on any place that had hieroglyphs, as John Haworth had said he would use those to identify the original occupant.

Putting her camera on the floor, she got down on her hands and knees to look more closely at the seam where the lid met the bottom of the box. She was curious if there was a mummy inside and wondered if she could open the coffin by herself without damaging it. The weight of the thing was no good in assessing this, as she didn't know what sort of wood it was or how thick the sides were. Running a fingernail along the seam she found that it was sealed tightly, apparently with some sort of glue, which seeped out of the seam in several places.

As she stood up, a horrific scream rang out across the courtyard, a long, loud piercing cry that reverberated against the stones and was repeated several times before it ended in a pathetic strangling yell. She went to the window and saw Patrizio at his window on the floor above, pointing at her and screaming with all the strength he had. Graziella quickly appeared behind him, pulling him away from the window, though Lizzie continued to hear him cry out pitifully for several more minutes.

She pulled out her phone and was going to call Pina, or Martin, or Jackie, or anyone who might take her ears away from the horrible sound, when she saw Cosimo Gonzaga emerge into the courtyard from the garage stairs and, hearing the sound of his uncle, run up the steps to Patrizio's room.

Lizzie didn't know what she should do or where she should go. There was no question that seeing her with the sarcophagus had instigated this attack of fury or extreme agitation or whatever it was. She saw Graziella and Cosimo come to the window of Patrizio's room so that the former could point at her, and within a few minutes Cosimo had come to join her.

"I'm so sorry!" she said, with real concern. "This must have been caused by my moving the sarcophagus. It didn't even occur to me that he would be able to see into this room."

"I told you he once beat me for touching the thing," Cosimo said.

"How am I to proceed here?" she asked. "I have such a short time to get the work done..." She didn't want to sound unsympathetic, and she wasn't, but she was frustrated. The exhibit and catalog were too important to her to be abandoned and they couldn't be delayed. They were the centerpieces of the college's centennial plans.

Cosimo was very businesslike. "First, let me assure you that Patrizio is not your responsibility. The Gonzaga family has a contract with St. Pat's for an exhibit and I plan to honor that. Obviously, my uncle cannot stay in the house while you are working here, or when the pieces you want are removed for shipping."

Lizzie agreed. "But where is he to go?"

"I will take care of that," Cosimo responded. "As I said, Patrizio is not your responsibility."

A half hour later the back doors of the courtyard opened and an ambulance drove in. Patrizio was taken down the main staircase on a gurney, loaded into it, and it drove out again. Both Cosimo and Graziella disappeared with the ambulance and Lizzie found herself alone in the house.

Chapter 15

Carmine Moreale's phone voice proved to be just as charming as his voice in person and Lizzie was relieved to talk to him. She explained the strange circumstances that had transpired at the Gonzaga house and asked if she could take him to lunch.

"If you are alone in the house let me come there," he said enthusiastically. "I'll bring lunch. I am so anxious to see the collection."

Lizzie agreed and he said he would be there in an hour. She returned to the library, which she had not been in since the morning when she had done a rushed survey and made more than 100 quick photographs. Now she felt relaxed for the first time in this room and had a chance to look more slowly. There were several things that she had not seen on that first furious glance, and now she began to notice details and to consider what things might work well in the exhibit. There were ceramic items, and artifacts made of bronze and glass, about which she knew too little to make a judgment.

When Carmine arrived, she rushed him through the entrance hall and salons, where he would have lingered to look at the artworks and the architectural details. "It is so wonderful," he said. "They have hardly changed anything in the last two hundred years!"

In the dining room he planted his heels and would not be rushed. Lizzie had only used this room as a passageway and had only lingered that one time, when she and Patrizio stood at the balcony and looked into the courtyard, but Carmine found the light switch and turned on a series of wall sconces that illuminated a painted ceiling that Lizzie hadn't even noticed before.

High above them a battle was played out within the walls of a medieval city. A seacoast lay just outside one portion of the painted stone wall and ships were lined up along it. In the central part of the ceiling, individual soldiers were painted with ferocious expressions, women held their torn clothes to their breasts, and horses picked their way across fallen corpses, some in armor. Along the edge of the painting, where the ceiling met the walls of the room, angels worked to keep a faux cloth from falling to the floor. These were the angels that Lizzie's student assistants had found so amusing in one of the photographs they had studied, and seeing it here it was impossible not to be amused. Some of the angels peeked out from under the cloth, and one of them was in the process of falling—keeping himself aloft only by clinging to the cornice.

"Good heavens!" Lizzie said. "I have walked through here every day and never looked up."

"This is actually a work that appears frequently in the literature on the Bolognese school of art," Carmine said, "but hardly anyone ever gets to see it. It is by Annibale Carracci."

"That can't be Bologna," Lizzie said. "It has the walls, but Bologna doesn't have the sea coast."

"It's Constantinople, now Istanbul," Carmine responded, pointing to the ships, "and those are the vessels that arrived from Venice in 1204 during the Fourth Crusade."

Lizzie studied the details. There were at least two hundred people depicted in the foreground, and all had individual features and attributes. Behind them stretched an army of thousands. Now that Lizzie recognized the subject matter, she could distinguish the Moorish characteristics of the architecture, and the difference between the curved blades of the Easterners and the straight swords of the Europeans.

"There are some things from this event in the chapel upstairs," Lizzie told her companion. "Maybe that is why the Gonzagas were inspired to have this painting done."

"Maybe. What kind of things?"

"A corpse, for one," Lizzie said, smiling. "Though he was apparently killed here before he even got to Venice, and there are some columns that Patrizio told me came from Constantinople."

"Any idea how they got them? This house was clearly not built until late in the sixteenth century."

"According to Patrizio they were in the church of St. Paolo Maggiore, and were moved here when the Gonzagas built their family chapel."

Carmine nodded. "That makes sense. I'd like to see them when we're done here."

Lizzie agreed. "I can't wait for my husband to see this," she said. "He's a muralist and the frescoes here are going to wow him!"

"I believe your husband is Martin Sanchez. Is that correct?"

"He is," Lizzie said, turning to look at her companion. "How did you know?"

"I Googled you, of course. It says so in the biography on your college's website. I'm a fan of your husband's work," he continued.

"You'll get a chance to meet him. He's coming here in two weeks."

They talked as they walked from the dining room into the library, and Lizzie felt that with Carmine as a companion she was seeing it with fresh eyes. She certainly felt her enthusiasm for the collection returning. She quickly pulled the ledger out of the bookshelf and put it on the table.

"Here is a seventeenth-century drawing of the cabinet," she said, speaking quickly to cover as much information as possible, "and here are the various lists." As Carmine studied the image, she talked about how similar it was to the drawing of Ferdinando Cospi's collection made the same year, and explained Martin's theory that the artist had used a similar template for both and then filled in specific items from each collection. Before Carmine had a chance to respond, Lizzie went on to describe her plan to base the exhibit on this picture and to identify as many surviving things from it as she could.

"I have a preliminary list," she said, opening her computer.

As Carmine digested all of the information she had flung

his way, Lizzie asked if they might get the food out. "They don't feed me here and I have had nothing to eat yet today."

Carmine handed her a package and told her to take it to the far end of the table. "We must keep some professional standards," he said. "Keep the food away from any objects, artworks or papers."

Lizzie opened packages of rolls, cheese, prepared meats and olives. "It's a good thing I love this Bolognese food," she said, "because you all seem to eat the same things for every meal."

"Well, for breakfast, lunch and snacks, anyway. For dinner we go for pasta. Do you have any plates?"

"I don't even know where the kitchen is in this house." She remembered seeing a sideboard in the dining room and she went to find not only plates, but also silverware, goblets and linen napkins, which she brought back and put on the table.

"I also have a bottle of wine in my backpack," Carmine said, gesturing to where it lay on the floor behind him. He looked as Lizzie set two places on the table. "You do realize that you have about $10,000 worth of tableware here?"

Lizzie smiled sweetly. "It was made to be used, and nobody else is using it."

Carmine opened the wine with a corkscrew on his pocketknife and moved down to Lizzie's end of the table.

"That seventeenth-century image is certainly a great place to start for an exhibit, especially in America, where I think people are less familiar with them."

"I know. Pictures of similar collections are all over the museums here in Bologna, but no one I showed this to at home had ever seen anything like it."

Carmine took a slice of cheese and one of mortadella and placed them on one half of a roll. "Where is the mummy?" he asked as he began eating. "I don't see it here."

"It's in the ballroom next door," Lizzie answered, "and I definitely want you to see it today."

She talked through the list of things she hoped they would be able to send to Boston, starting with the alligator, and when they finished eating, they went up the staircase to the mezzanine that ran around the upper part of the library. The ceiling was quite low here and while Lizzie could just walk under it without stooping, Carmine was required to keep his head bent as he moved around first one side and then the other looking at the alligator and the way it was mounted. He had a good camera and as he took pictures he explained what he was looking at to Lizzie.

"You can see that the whole thing has been mounted on a metal rod, with some sort of straps around the neck, waist and tail to hold it up." The straps were the same dark brown color as the beast and invisible from the floor below. "It looks to be in pretty good shape, but we'll have to get it down to be sure." He took a tape measure from his pocket and asked Lizzie to hold one end of it opposite the tip of the animal's nose, while he walked down to the end of the tail to measure its length.

"Is there a good working space here?" he asked.

"I think the ballroom could be turned into a very good workroom. There is certainly plenty of space and it is right next door." She led the way back to the main floor of the library and on through the double doors to the ballroom. The shutters were still open from when she had moved them that morning, and the chandeliers were still on. Several chairs and small tables that she had pushed aside to accommodate the mummy case were scattered around the room, still covered in their protective cloths.

Carmine was enthusiastic about the space. "This will be a great place to work," he said. "Do you think Cosimo will approve?"

Lizzie was confident that he would, but said she would call him later to confirm; she wanted to find out where Patrizio had been sent as well.

The mummy case was where Lizzie had left it and Carmine was already on his knees examining it closely. He took a pair of latex gloves out of his pocket and a case of small instruments. He ran his gloved hand along the line where the top of the sarcophagus closed over the bottom, and when he came to one of the places where Lizzie had thought excess glue had squeezed out of the tight seam, he took a small metal pick, like a dentist's probe, and got a sample of it. Putting it into a small plastic sample bag he said that the glue had certainly been added at some much later stage, but he would take it back to his lab to test it and see what it was made of and when it was made.

The two of them stood on either side of the sarcophagus and discussed its condition. "Except for some flakes here and there to the paint, which is completely normal given its age, this piece is in remarkably good shape," Carmine said. "I know this is high on your list of desirable pieces and I don't see any reason why it can't travel."

Lizzie clapped her hands together. "Great," she said. "The day is looking better. Alligator, check; mummy, check."

"Do you think there is a mummy inside?" Carmine asked.

Lizzie said she didn't. "I have a colleague at St. Pat's, an Egyptologist, who told me that most of the mummies that came to Italy in the Renaissance were consumed for medicine."

Carmine accepted the comment as if he heard about cannibalism every day. "It seems strange that someone glued it closed," he said. "Especially if the coffin is empty. It's obvious the lid was well-made, to fit tightly."

"Maybe there *is* a mummy inside and someone was trying to protect it from being eaten!"

Her companion smiled politely at her humor and asked what else was on her list. They returned to the library and Lizzie took the remains of their lunch into the dining room. Then she wiped off the library table and pulled out the narwhal tusk and the Marquesan club and placed them on it.

"I see they have the ubiquitous unicorn horn," Carmine said, "to go along with the alligator."

"But this is a real find," Lizzie said, pointing to the club. She found the 1677 image and placed it next to it. "I only noticed this late last night, but do you think that this club is the center item in this fan of weapons?" She pointed to a decorative arrangement above the case in the center of the picture.

Carmine looked hard from one to the other. "I think it is clearly this club."

Lizzie clapped her hand on the table in excitement. "I thought so, but I was almost afraid to believe it. If this club was in this house in 1677 then it can only have been collected on a Spanish expedition from Peru to the Philippines in 1595. After that, the next European visitor was Captain Cook in 1774. This is probably the oldest Polynesian artifact in any collection that wasn't taken from an archaeological dig."

Carmine carefully took the club from Lizzie and examined it. It had an arched top with two large eyes carved into it, giving it the appearance of a head. "Certainly this is in excellent condition and can travel. The Gonzagas were prolific traders and must have had connections with Spanish counterparts."

"Patrizio, when he was in one of his good moods, showed me this box from Mexico, which must have come from a similar source." Lizzie put the painted box on the table with the other items.

"There is a lot of Etruscan and Roman material here," Carmine said, opening doors of cabinets to look at the contents.

"Lorenzo Gonzaga, Patrizio's father, was an archeologist."

"A professional or an amateur?"

Lizzie said she didn't know, but that Maggie Kelliher had apparently taken some sort of course from him at the University. "And his father introduced him to the field. There are a lot of stone pieces down in the courtyard and I'd like you to look at some of them, especially two Etruscan burial boxes."

"This is very nice," Carmine said, putting a delicate bracelet on the table. It was made of twisted blue glass and he said it might be as much as two thousand years old. "And here's another piece I would use if I were you." He brought out a bronze jug, about eight inches tall; the handle was made of a young man dancing, his arms held up joyfully. It had, over more than a millennium, turned a lovely blue-green color.

"Done!" Lizzie said. "It's lovely. I'll put both these things on the list." She looked at the inventory she had first brought to Bologna, and at the list she was making now and was happy to find that the best things from the pictures and the typed catalog were all still here in the collection. "I want to give a good representation of both natural and artificial curiosities," she said to Carmine. "So we must include a tortoise shell, an ostrich egg, one or more of the blowfishes, and there is a wonderful chameleon, mounted on a stick, in a beautiful case in the cabinet to your left."

"I think you might also consider a piece of furniture in that room with the Chinese wallpaper. We rushed through there, but I noticed a beautiful old-style curio cabinet there, of the type used by people who didn't have a whole room for their collection like the Gonzagas."

"Show me," Lizzie said, proceeding through the dining room to the Chinese Salon. She hadn't spent any time looking at the details of this room, and it had always been poorly lit when she passed through. Now she noticed not only the piece of furniture to which Carmine had referred but also a beautifully painted harpsichord. Above it were paintings of two young people, a boy and a girl, sitting at that very instrument.

Carmine called to her. "Look at this. The cabinet is filled with medals, coins, cameos, all kinds of beautiful small stuff. You might just be able to take the whole thing and highlight what is already in it."

As Lizzie went to join him, they heard footsteps on the back stairs and Cosimo Gonzaga soon after appeared in the room. He began immediately to apologize to Lizzie for the events of the morning.

"I'm so sorry I left without saying goodbye, but I'm sure you must understand that I was concerned about my uncle."

"Of course," Lizzie said. She introduced Carmine, whom Cosimo had never met. Someone from his office had contacted the Director of the University Museum after Lizzie had said the project would need a conservator, and Carmine had been hired on his recommendation.

"I'm very impressed that you've been able to move forward on the project so quickly," Cosimo said.

"We were just considering whether we might be able to bring this cabinet and its contents to Boston," Lizzie said, explaining why they were not in the library.

"Of course. I told you that you may choose anything in the house and I meant it." There was a group of chairs near them, facing the windows into the courtyard, and Cosimo gestured to them to sit while he opened the shutters to let in the afternoon light. "How do you plan to proceed?" he asked as he sat down and took out a cigarette. "Sorry about this," he said as he lit it, "I'm always trying to quit."

"There is so much wonderful material to work with here that the only challenges I can see to selecting a final list for the exhibit loan will be the condition of individual pieces, and the difficulty of limiting ourselves to what will fit in the space in Boston."

"Will you be able to complete the work you planned in the three weeks you are scheduled to be here?" Cosimo asked.

Lizzie said she would. "I think a solid preliminary list will be ready in the next three or four days, then Carmine and I will go over every piece taking measurements, making photographs, and assessing condition."

Cosimo turned to Carmine at this point and in a mixture of English and Italian they spoke about his availability and whether or not Cosimo would need to talk with anyone at the University Museum to make special arrangements for Carmine's work time.

"And after you go back to Boston?" he asked Lizzie.

"Then Carmine can supervise any restoration that needs to be done, make special mounts for objects that need them, and supervise the packing of the collection for shipment. We've scheduled three months for that part of the work."

Cosimo reminded her that his nephew Beppe would be available to help for some part of that time. Lizzie silently thanked her stars that Carmine was so competent, since Justin was so incompetent.

"Everything should be ready to ship by the middle of May and then we will spend the summer installing," she continued. "The exhibit will open on September ninth, the hundredth anniversary of the arrival of the first class of St. Patrick's College."

"Very good," Cosimo said. "And the book to accompany it?"

"I am working on the research now and will devote the spring to writing."

He took a long drag from his cigarette and put it out in an ashtray on the table. It was the only modern piece Lizzie could see in the room and it explained why he had chosen to sit here. "Will you be bringing in anybody else to work with you while you are in the house?"

Carmine said that he would need some help removing the alligator from the ceiling, and that he would like to set up a workspace in the ballroom, which would require a few additional hands with the labor.

"Then my only concern now," Cosimo said, "is the security of the house and the collections. I trust you two, of course, but if you are going to bring in any other help I'd like to have a guard stationed here, and I'd like to do a quick security check of anyone who will be coming into the house. You can call me with the names and I'll have someone in my office take care of it."

"Would you like me to arrange for the collection to be appraised for insurance purposes?" Carmine asked. "I know art and antiquities dealers who would be able to do the job well."

Cosimo agreed and thanked him. "Pina will be around the rest of this week, and after that I hope you will call me and let me know how the project is going. Will you need Graziella?" he asked as a final thought.

"I'm sorry that her English and my Italian are equally bad," Lizzie said honestly, "so I don't think that I will personally need her help, but I assume she is still living in the house, even with your uncle away." It was almost a disappointment to learn that she would still be here.

Cosimo nodded.

"May I ask about your uncle?" Lizzie said as they all stood. "How is he? And where is he?"

"He's in a very good small hospital, and he seems to be doing fine," Cosimo answered. "We'll keep him there while the work goes on here in the house."

Lizzie thought about Patrizio returning to his library to find the best parts of the collection missing. It was a sad thought and she determined to visit him in the next few days. He was still the best source of information on the collection. A visit from her might not be the best prescription for his recovery, but a chat with his old friend Theresa Kenney would probably cheer him up.

Chapter 16

With Cosimo gone, Lizzie and Carmine returned to work and moved quickly through every item on the shelves in the library. Lizzie was astonished when the clock in the room rang ten o'clock.

"I can't believe it has gotten so late," she said, looking at the table, which was now covered with artifacts of all sorts. "But we have gotten so much done."

"Without another table, we can't really pull anything more out," Carmine said. "Dinner?"

"Isn't it too late?"

"Not at all. We eat late around here. There is a restaurant on Via Farina that makes a very good tagliatelle Bolognese."

Lizzie knew the signature dish of the city because Rose and Tony had each made it for her in Boston, but she hadn't eaten it since she'd arrived and was glad to accept the offer.

Over dinner they talked about a schedule for the next two weeks. Carmine could come the next morning and they decided to walk through the ballroom and figure out how to best set it up for the work they needed to do. He had other obligations in the afternoon and for the whole of the next day, but Lizzie wanted to devote that time to going through the various collection records to see what more she could find out about individual objects. She also decided to call Pina and see if it would be possible for her to visit with Patrizio the next afternoon.

When she returned to the house she remembered the dishes she had left on the dining room table and wondered where she would wash them. There was a small bathroom off the library and she thought there might be some sort of pantry or small kitchen off the dining room. She hadn't really gone exploring in the house before, but she was willing to now that she was alone.

When she got to the dining room the dishes and the food scraps were gone. In their place were two plain white ceramic dishes and appropriate cutlery, cups and glasses. The table-ware she had taken from the sideboard had been washed and returned. It was a reminder that she was not, in fact, alone in the house; Graziella was also here.

Though it was past midnight, Lizzie wasn't tired and she opened her computer, which was still lying on the table in the library.

"Theresa Kenney looked just like you," Jackie wrote in an email, "in that you both share human features. She had hair in the 1939 St. Pat's yearbook, but the picture is black and white and I can't tell what color it is. Why do you want to know this? It's not like there is an astonishing likeness or any-thing. She's a nice-looking enough girl, but she's also eigh-teen or something, so you have quite a few years on her as she looks in this picture."

She attached a scan of the photograph and Lizzie had to admit that it wasn't because there was some remarkable re-semblance between Theresa Kenney and herself that Patrizio had mistaken her. Maybe it was her voice and American ac-cent. Plus, Jackie was right, Patrizio had known Theresa in her twenties, not her forties.

Jackie added another picture from the yearbook that had the title "The Bologna Boys." In it were five young men, including Arcangelo Cussetti, the man who had married Gianna, and Pa-trizio Gonzaga and his brother Cosimo, the father of Lizzie's host of the same name.

When she returned to her own room, Lizzie once again took out Maggie's letters. She had already gone quickly through the 1920s and 30s, which were mostly reports to her mother and later her brother Tom about life in Bologna with a growing family. Lizzie was sorry that since she was looking at scans of manuscript pages there was no way for her to search for Theresa Kenney's name to see if she appeared in any of Maggie's messages.

She went to the window and looked across at the other side of the house. There were no lights visible anywhere, even where she had left some burning when she came upstairs. As much as it bothered her to have Graziella following around cleaning up after her, Lizzie thought the housekeeper must be even more disturbed to have her bothersome presence in the house.

Filled with a restless energy and an enthusiasm for her exhibit project, Lizzie climbed into bed. She had no doubt at this point that the exhibition would be fabulous and she looked forward to devoting the next seven months to working on it. Though there was always the potential for glitches along the way, Cosimo was a committed supporter and Carmine was a terrific collaborator for this stage of the work.

She scrolled through Maggie's letters until she came to 1938, the year that seventeen-year-old Patrizio had gone to Boston to attend St. Pat's College. Her mother had died by then, and Maggie's primary correspondent was her brother Tom, the youngest of the five Kelliher sons and the closest in age to herself. Maggie had apparently brought Patrizio to Boston and stayed in the family home, now occupied by her oldest brother Frank, and his family.

"Dear Tommy," she wrote on November 1, 1938. "We have arrived home safely and many thanks for seeing us off at the ship. It was a comfortable enough passage and Gianna is a born sailor. Pat was very sad to see us go, but I know that you will look out for him and make sure he always feels that he is still surrounded by family. I'm glad he is there right now, and also my protégé Archie Cussetti, because we are being bombarded with anti-Fascist literature and radio broadcasts from Spain. Numbers of our young men are headed to fight the Fascists there, since there is no opportunity at this time to fight them here. I know that Archie would join them if he could, and while I don't think Pat's political convictions are quite so strong, I'm afraid he might follow his friend."

In her next letter, she announced that she had taken Gianna to Switzerland to go to the same school she had attended as a teenager. "I hope she'll still go to St. Pat's as well when her time comes," she wrote, "but Renzo feels that girls need socializing in a somewhat different way." Several words were then crossed out before the text continued. "I don't want to give you the sense that Renzo thinks Gianna any less intelligent or accomplished than her brothers, and in many ways she is clearly more advanced than any of them. Languages come wonderfully naturally to her (a talent I envy), and she reads prodigiously. But she has a wild streak that worries her father. Obviously he thinks I turned out delightfully, and hopes that Rougemont will work the same magic on her. Kiss my dear Pat for me."

Gianna came home for Christmas, but Pat stayed with his Boston relations and Maggie felt keenly the absence of her grown children. As 1938 turned to 1939, the letters included references to small presents enclosed for Pat, and news of Gianna's progress as a young woman. On July 21, 1939, Maggie finally wrote the letter that had the information Lizzie sought.

"We have a visitor, one of Pat's Boston classmates who is traveling in Italy with her mother. Apparently he invited them to stay here for a week, but he never told me and it put me in a bit of an awkward position when they arrived. Accommodating them was no problem, of course, with the children moved out, but I'm sorry I wasn't prepared to greet them with something more special than our usual dinner fare on their arrival."

Another letter gave more details about the Kenneys. "Do you know them?" Maggie wrote her brother. "Pat says they are a prominent Irish-Catholic family in Boston and that the father is a friend of Frank's. I can't quite tell if he is smitten with the girl, Theresa, because he is so awkward around her. My God, you'd think he hadn't been speaking English from infancy—sometimes his words come out all broken and accented. Renzo likes her and the mother is nice enough. She is very interested in the family tree in the Entrance Hall—it's hard to tell which of them, mother or daughter, would most promote a match."

At the end of the summer, Maggie wrote again to her brother about her son Patrick.

August 28, 1939

Dear Tommy,

Pat is headed back your way and I hope you will once again take him under your wing while he is in Boston. I want this to be a year that he concentrates on his studies, but his mind has certainly taken a romantic turn this summer. First there was that girl Theresa Kenney from Boston, and after she left he fell madly in love with a German girl who came home from school with Gianna. The second candidate for Pat's affections, Greta Winkler, has the advantage of speaking Italian, which Renzo appreciates, but Germans are not altogether popular in this house right now, with the rise of the Nazis.

I have written you many times of Renzo's dislike of Mussolini and his Fascist movement, and I'm sorry to tell you that Adino and Cosimo are both interested in the advantages that could come to them by throwing their lots in with the Fascists. They try to convince Renzo and me that Mussolini and the King will prove to be the best allies for anyone in business, and they don't understand their father's strong philosophical objections.

The next letter, written in late September, announced the start of the war and the fear that Mussolini would ally Italy to the Nazis. "Switzerland's neutrality makes it a safe place for Gianna," Maggie wrote, "and I hope that as things develop, you and Frank will try to convince Pat to stay in Boston during any period of conflict. I appreciate your offer to put us all up for the near future, but Renzo won't leave Bologna now, and consequently, neither will I."

Chapter 17

Pina was not entirely comfortable with the idea of Lizzie visiting Patrizio. "I thought he was a problem for you," she said irritably.

"Maybe in different surroundings, where he is not suspicious of my interest in his collection, he'll be more willing to talk to me," Lizzie explained.

"But what do you want to talk about?"

"He's still the most knowledgeable person about the collection, and I want to get as much information as I can."

"I'll call my Uncle Cosimo and see what he thinks," Pina said.

Lizzie had tried to call him at his office just a few minutes before to leave the names of the workers that Carmine would bring into the house in two days, and she knew that he was not in.

A frustrated Pina snapped her cell phone shut and said, "Okay, I'll drop you off at the hospital, but I can't stay and you'll have to find your own ride back."

"Thanks," said Lizzie. "I'll take a taxi."

They took the steps down to the garage, which Lizzie had not yet been in. It was part of the old cellar of the house, where Patrizio said they had hidden part of the collection from the Nazis during the war. Pina spoke as little as possible during the twenty-minute drive and Lizzie was unreasonably eager to make her talk by asking questions about various city sites that they passed, all of which were answered tersely.

The hospital of St. Columba of Bobbio was located on a hillside above the city, with a long curved drive lined with olive trees. Pina pulled to a stop in front and informed Lizzie that Patrizio was in a room on the main floor. "You'll need to check in with the nurses." The young woman was clearly conflicted between wanting to get away fast and thinking that her presence might be necessary to keep her great-uncle from embarrassing the family. The former impulse was greater though, and she sped away as soon as her passenger was out of the car.

Lizzie stood for a few minutes on the stone steps of the hospital and looked down the valley toward Bologna. Even on a winter day it was a landscape filled with color. The olive trees had dry silvery leaves that rattled together as the breeze passed through them, a sound that, when she closed her eyes, might have come from a stream passing over stones, or a fire crackling in a hearth.

There were dark brown fields of earth waiting for a new crop in the spring, and patches of grass that had turned from green to golden brown. The red tile roofs of houses made a line down the hill and in the distance she could see the towers that rose above the old core of the city.

A receptionist inside the building had seen Lizzie standing on the porch, opened the door and now greeted her in Italian. With her limited knowledge of the language, Lizzie managed to convey her desire to see Patrizio Gonzaga and the woman showed her into the building. She pointed Lizzie to a seat and went off down the hall.

The building was unlike any other that Lizzie had seen in Italy. There was a courtyard, but it was enclosed in glass and accessed by hallways that ran around each side. The rooms were designed to look at the outside view rather than the interior one. A sign on the wall just inside the door acknowledged the patronage of Margaret and Lorenzo Gonzaga in memory of Patrick Malachi Kelleher in 1915, with a list of subsequent donors that included two different generations of Cosimo Gonzagas. It explained how Cosimo was able to make the arrangements for Patrizio so quickly.

The purposeful click of high-heeled shoes on the stone floor brought Lizzie's attention to the tall well-dressed woman who walked toward her. Behind her, the receptionist walked more quietly in her sensible footwear.

"I understand you want to see Mr. Patrizio Gonzaga," the woman said in English. "Can I ask what this is about?"

Lizzie took out one of her business cards and explained her project. "If Mr. Gonzaga is well enough to speak to me, he can answer some questions about the family collection. He has been the principal caretaker of it since after the war."

"Does Mr. Cosimo Gonzaga know that you're here?"

"No," Lizzie answered, "though he is the person who has engaged me to work on this project. I'm sure he would approve of my talking to his uncle," she added, though in fact she had no confidence it was true.

The woman proved to be the hospital administrator and she asked a passing nurse if Patrizio was awake. Hearing that he was, she asked the nurse to escort Lizzie to his room.

The old man was sitting up in his bed watching television and the nurse took the remote control and turned it off without asking his permission. Lizzie resented the action, both the casual insensitivity of it and the fact that introducing herself by once again interrupting his routine seemed a bad way to start the visit.

He seemed happy to see her, however, and asked her, first in Italian, who she was and what she wanted. When he sensed her confusion he immediately asked the same questions in English.

"I'm Lizzie Manning," she said, pulling a chair up to the side of his bed and sitting. "I teach at St. Patrick's College in Boston."

"My grandfather founded that college," Patrizio said. "And I went there."

"I know," Lizzie said. "I'm very interested in your grandfather, I have written a book about him. She pulled another copy of *Patrick Kelliher, Immigrant Industrialist* out of her bag and gave it to him.

"I know this book," Patrizio said. "I've seen it before."

"I sent you a copy when it was published."

"Am I at St. Columba of Bobbio Hospital?" he asked.

"You are. And I see from a plaque at the door that it was dedicated to the memory of your grandfather by your parents."

He nodded. "My mother chose the name. Her father was Irish and St. Columba was an Irish saint who came to Italy in the sixth century and established a mission church at Bobbio." He put his hand up to feel the stubble on his chin. "Why am I here?" he asked. "Did I get hurt?"

"I don't know why you're here."

"Why are you here?"

"Since I wrote that book about your grandfather I've become interested in your family. Do you mind if we talk about them?"

"I think that would be nice," the old man said with a sad sincerity that embarrassed Lizzie.

She turned her face away and made the excuse of taking her computer from her bag. "I have some pictures that your mother gave to the college library in 1959," she said. "I thought you might like to see them."

As each image came up on the screen, Patrizio gave a little sound of recognition and delight. The earliest pictures of his childhood were greeted with laughter as he pointed out the short pants and little cap that he wore. "And look at Adino and Cosimo, trying to look so grown up."

"How much older were they?"

"Adino was seven years older than I, but Cosimo only three."

"He was a senior when you first went to St. Pat's," Lizzie said. "I have a picture from the yearbook in 1939." She showed him the picture of "The Bologna Boys" that Jackie had scanned for her.

"That's me," Patrizio said, pointing to his picture. "And that's Cosimo, Archie, and ..." He paused as he tapped his finger on the last face. "Oh I'm sorry, I can't remember his name."

"It's listed here under the picture," Lizzie said gently. "Guglielmo Gustalla."

"Guli!" he said. "That's right, we called him Guli."

The nurse came in to check Patrizio's vital signs and asked Lizzie how the visit was going. After answering, Lizzie moved to the window to give them some privacy. She wanted to ask him about the collection, but was worried that she might say the wrong thing and set him off into some sort of rage. She also didn't know what sort of response he might have if she just continued on with the family photographs. Would it remain a safe and comfortable topic when they got to the war years and all the painful memories associated with it?

When the rolling table on which her computer sat was pushed back in front of Patrizio, she sat down next to him and asked him about Archie.

"Arcangelo," he answered. "Arcangelo Cussetti. Even though he had been in and out of my house his whole life, I only really got to know him at St. Pat's. My mother had tutored him in English and arranged for him to get a scholarship and travel to Boston with me." He turned to look at Lizzie and smiled. "I was a lazy boy," he said. "Never a hard worker." He closed his eyes and put two fingertips above his nose and tapped softly, as if to help him bring up images of the past. "But Archie, he was something special. He worked hard, and he was so smart." He opened his eyes again. "And he had nothing. His family was poor, his mother did our washing, washed our sheets, our underwear."

He paused again and said, almost with regret. "But my mother saw his talent; she knew he was a genius. She didn't mean to make me feel ashamed that I had so much, the money, the position, and did so little with it, but it was impossible not to feel that she compared me to him and he was the more impressive."

"Is it possible that he worked to impress your mother, to win her favor?"

Patrizio hushed her with a wave of his hand. "Don't speak of Archie that way," he said, not angrily, but with an edge of irritation in his voice. "If I made you think that by what I said, then I am sorry. Archie Cussetti was a faithful friend to me, the most honest man I ever knew. He *did* shame me, by taking his small gifts and making the most of them, but he never did it to make me look bad. He simply was the better man."

In the uncomfortable silence that followed, Lizzie brought up the photograph of the balcony scene from "Romeo and Juliet" on her computer screen.

"I believe this is you and Archie, as Romeo and Tybalt," she said. "Or maybe one of you is Mercutio."

"Ah that day." He touched the picture on the screen. "I was Mercutio, so that I could give that wonderful speech about Queen Mab, but I made a hash out of it. I was never the actor my mother hoped for, but Gianna was a Juliet to make you weep, and Archie was her Romeo."

"Did they fall in love during the play?"

"Maybe Gianna did, but Archie was already very far gone." He told the story of Gianna's schooling in Switzerland while he was away at St. Pat's, which Lizzie had just read about the evening before in Maggie's letter.

"Gianna was a crazy girl when she left for that school, but even in the first year she became very sophisticated. We were all home for the summer in 1939, just a few months before the war started, and Archie and I had become very good friends. He and I were smoking in the courtyard, hiding behind one of the columns so my mother wouldn't see us, and Gianna came down the stairs wearing a white dress." He closed his eyes and Lizzie could tell that he was picturing the moment.

"Archie stepped out from the shadow and just stared at her. I had never known him to be speechless, but he was then. He had opinions on everything and always something to say, but he saw Gianna, standing on the staircase in a white dress, and he practically fell to his knees."

"But she didn't fall in love with him right then?"

"Not so quickly," Patrick answered. "It's funny but he first fell in love with the way she looked in that particular dress, on that staircase, on that summer day in 1939. He began to follow her though, to be able to meet her accidentally on the street, or to help her into the house when she was carrying packages. And Gianna couldn't help but notice."

Lizzie scrolled through other pictures of Archie. "Was he handsome?" she asked.

"Not particularly. He had such a nose on him." Patrizio put his hand about a foot in front of his face and laughed. "At St. Pat's they called him 'the Roman,' because he had such a big nose. But Gianna didn't care about looks, and good thing, since Archie wasn't really handsome."

"He looks good natured," Lizzie said, bringing up another picture.

"He was, before the war. After, everything was different."

"When did Gianna fall in love with him?" Lizzie asked, not wanting to deal yet with Gianna's tragic death, and steering the conversation back in time.

"My sister hadn't ever been in love when she met him, though she had been much pursued, especially that year that we came back from Boston, and by men that many considered to be better than Archie—richer or with a better pedigree. But once the two of them started to talk, they never stopped, not until the day she died."

Patrick's voice grew hoarse. "They talked about art and politics and music and food; they read books together and talked about them in great detail. They went to movies and discussed minute points for longer than the time it took for the movie to run, and they loved plays. They traveled around Europe after they married in January 1942—even with the war on, there were places that continued to produce plays to try and maintain some semblance of normalcy, and Gianna and Archie sought out every opportunity to see plays in multiple languages. Then they would argue about translations and nuances of meaning. They didn't fight, but they disputed points, debated for hours, and loved the process of it, the intellectual nature of the discourse, the wonderful complementary nature of their brains."

Lizzie asked him what his parents had thought of Gianna's relationship with Archie. "Were they hoping she would marry one of those other 'more suitable' men?"

"My father might have, but when he died so unexpectedly, and with the war looming, my mother agreed to let them marry. Gianna was only nineteen, but the two were inseparable and mother had a great fondness for Archie. She had taught him English as a boy and supported him at St. Pat's—though he never returned after that summer. First he said he was going to go to Spain to fight the Fascists there, and then he fell in love with Gianna, and couldn't be separated from her."

"Your mother didn't mind his humble roots?"

"My mother was an American and never had any of the

pretensions of the Italian aristocracy. Even though her father had made a big deal out of her marriage to my father, my parents distanced themselves from any connections to the old titles, and she was very angry that my brothers supported the king. No one in Italy was happier to see the end of the Italian nobility in 1946 than my mother."

Lizzie was unsure which way to navigate the conversation and backtracked again. "Did you have a girlfriend that summer that Gianna and Archie fell in love?"

Patrizio looked confused. "A girlfriend?"

"I read in your mother's correspondence about some visitors that summer, a girl named Theresa Kenney from St. Pat's, who came with her mother."

"Oh yes, Theresa. She wanted to marry me, and her mother wanted it even more. Maybe I should have done it, I have often wondered what my life would have been like if I had."

"And Gianna's German friend, Greta Winkler?"

Patrizio's face turned grey at the mention of the name. "She married a Nazi and got what she deserved," he said softly but intensely. At that, he closed his eyes, crossed his arms, and would not respond to anything more that Lizzie said.

Chapter 18

Ulisse Aldrovandi was one of the greatest collectors of the Renaissance. He amassed something like 50,000 objects in his lifetime, and when they outgrew the space available in his family palazzo, he transferred his collection to the University of Bologna in 1590. Aldrovandi was a man of science, and the purpose of the collection was to capture nature, so that it could be organized into categories and understood. For specimens that could not be possessed, because they were too fragile to be preserved by any of the methods known to him, or those which Aldrovandi had observed but not captured, or which had been described to him but never seen, he hired artists to make small drawings and paintings so that they might still be part of his comprehensive catalog of nature, and there were over 8000 of these representations in the collection.

Unlike the next generation of collectors in Italy, including Ferdinando Cospi and the Gonzagas, Aldrovandi did not collect ethnographic items; he was interested in the world of nature, not the world of humans, and he organized the natural world into three categories: minerals, plants, and animals. In the seventeenth century, the expansion of global trade brought exotic products back to Europe, and collectors like Cospi and the Gonzagas expanded their collecting fields to include them. The new nomenclature of a collection that included both categories was "cabinet of curiosities" and the division of the world was into "natural" curiosities—the sort of thing Aldrovandi had collected and documented—and "artificial" curiosities, the products of human cultures. Many of these collectors were physicians and pharmacists, hoping to find medicinal products among the shriveled plants, earthy minerals, petrified foods, foreign potions, and mummified body parts assembled on their shelves.

There were also great art collectors at the time. Cosimo di Medici established a private museum in the family palazzo in Florence in 1440 and collected paintings and sculpture by artists who were his contemporaries. That branch of the Gonzaga family who were the Dukes of Mantua had made a similar collection, which was dispersed across Europe around 1630. Unlike scholars with their "cabinets," from which they hoped to distill useful and scientific information, aristocrats collected to impress, and in their "Wunder Kammer" or "Wonder Chambers" were fine art, antiquities, and things made of precious metals and gemstones.

As she sat at the library table late in the evening after visiting Patrizio, Lizzie considered the various ways in which Renaissance collections had been organized, and pondered her exhibit. The museum gallery on campus was about the size of the room in which she sat, and she wanted to capture the feel of it somehow if she could. She loved the 1677 drawing of the collection, and still thought it would provide a terrific visual centerpiece for her exhibit, but she now acknowledged that it did not depict any setting in which the collection had actually ever been displayed. That wasn't an insurmountable problem; the collection was both a physical entity and an intellectual one, and the drawing captured the latter well and the former in its component parts if not in its actual physical construction. Most importantly, it documented things that had been in the collection at that specific time, establishing very early dates for key artifacts.

Though Aldrovandi had written a whole book on minerals, the rocks on the shelves in this room simply did not have the visual appeal of other parts of the collection as far as Lizzie was concerned, and visual appeal was going to be important for her exhibit. She wanted people to come into the gallery and be wowed by what they saw. Aldrovandi's book, however—a beautiful copy of which Maggie Gonzaga had given to the college almost a century before—could be exhibited with a few choice examples, and Lizzie decided to identify three or four of the stony hunks in the room that either had interesting descriptions in the catalog, or were particularly wonderful to look at.

She would also need to choose some of the prepared plant materials, though again, the visual appeal of centuries-old dried plants was minimal. It was difficult to distinguish one from another at this point, but many of them were preserved in beautiful old glass jars, with paper labels attached that identified the contents in a flowing Italian script. Again, she would see if any of them had a provenance that made them particularly interesting, and would otherwise choose the ones that looked best. There were numerous seed pods, small sticks, and pieces of bark, some of which, Lizzie found when consulting the catalog list, were actually examples of spices, including cinnamon, mace, nutmeg and vanilla.

It was easier to choose among the animals and animal parts, because so many of them were big, impressive, and readily recognizable from the old drawing. Among the smaller animal mounts were several that were completely charming, including the *Draco dandinii* that her assistant Jimmy had identified as his favorite. There were several fish skeletons, beautifully mounted, and various skulls and bones of animals large and small, including blowfish, chameleons, tusks of elephants and hippopotamus, and rhinoceros horns. The preserved skin of a gigantic snake went on the list. It hung on the wall here in the library, and could be mounted above the cases in the exhibit in Boston.

It might be difficult to transport marine specimens in jars, but she wanted to include some if possible, especially a large eel, whose head was pressed against the glass, its teeth visible through the liquid solution in which it had been submerged for eons. Eggs, long drained of their contents, though fragile, could be transported with care; they ranged in size from the large ostrich eggs to four tiny speckled eggs, preserved in their nest and tucked into a corner of one of the cases.

In making a choice among the ethnographic items from all over the world, Lizzie wanted to show as much of a geographical range as possible. Her list already included things made by ancient Etruscans and Romans, and artists and artisans from China, Egypt, Mexico and the Marquesas. Some of the spears and clubs could be arranged into decorative patterns by the exhibit designer, but others were so rare they needed to be set apart and highlighted.

Now that Lizzie had the luxury of the ledger book of the collection open before her, she spent time perusing the list of objects in it. It was begun in 1659 by Adino Gonzaga, who updated it very regularly for over twenty years, carefully adding entries as new things came into his collection. Adino's son Lorenzo kept up the work, and after him there were other heirs who, in spurts of enthusiasm, added to either the collection or the document or both, but there were many gaps, some longer than a century, when no work was done. Maggie's husband and his father, and she and her son Patrick had added additional information in side notes over the years as well, and Lizzie marked those places where she wanted to ask Carmine to translate for her. Most of these things had to do with where objects in the collection had been obtained, including names of travelers and vendors.

Lizzie took the list again that had been sent by Maggie Gonzaga to St. Pat's College, on which she had presumably worked with Patrizio, and compared it to the ledger. The two were mostly the same; the notes in Maggie's hand in English were often translations of marginalia made by earlier catalogers, though there were additional notes on the list like "cannot locate" to indicate items that had been lost over time.

Lizzie worked long into the night, slept for a few hours and rose early, with thoughts of how the exhibit would be organized still running through her brain. Things could not be randomly placed on shelves, or simply arranged in order of size or color. The way a museum visitor processed information about an object or artwork was very strongly influenced by what was next to it on the wall or in a case.

These were ideas that needed coffee and food to attend to so early in the morning and Lizzie went to a café opposite St. Petronio's, where she had noticed some delicious-looking pastries in the window. As Carmine would not join her today, she decided to buy both rolls and sweet pastry, as well as sliced meat and cheese to take her through the whole day. She got two large cups of coffee and proceeded back across the Piazza Maggiore to the house.

The courtyard was brighter this morning than it had been at any time since her arrival, and setting her food on the steps and taking one of the cups of coffee with her, Lizzie ambled around the area that was in the recess behind the arches. There was much more archaeological material than she had noted the day she'd stood there with Patrizio. A number of engraved stone plaques were cemented directly to the walls, many of which appeared to be memorial or gravestones.

One enigmatic plaque showed a naked young boy, his finger to his lips in a gesture of silence. His other hand had broken off, but there was still a remnant of a branch that he had held in it. There were large stones that had been cut into disks, a few feet in diameter and several inches thick. These were deeply carved with images of chariots being pulled by winged horses, and by toga-clad men shaking hands with angels. Around the circumference of each were patterns of leafy vines, or waves lapping against each other.

There was a pile of amphora in one corner of the courtyard, many of them in pieces. These ancient jars had no flat bottom, but were designed to stick into soft sand when a ship came up to offload its cargo on a beach. There were three of these visible in the 1677 picture of the Gonzaga collection, and Lizzie made a mental note to have Carmine choose that same number from this pile to be sent to Boston. She came around the square to the Etruscan sarcophagi and once more felt the power of how beloved these people must have been to those who survived them, to have been memorialized so sweetly in these stones.

There were occasional niches in the wall of the courtyard where Roman statues had been placed. Lizzie wondered if she should even ask if they could include one of those. So far she hadn't seen any marble carvings that didn't seem to be firmly attached to either their niche or the staircase, but she put that on her growing list of questions to ask Carmine.

After another long day of work, Lizzie felt confident that she had a good list of what would go into the exhibit, with enough flexibility to delete anything that Carmine might find unsuitable to travel. When next they met they would be able to plunge into the work.

Chapter 19

As her first week in Bologna came to an end, Lizzie was able to survey the work that she had done with great satisfaction. She and Carmine had taken a quick look at every piece on her list, and though he had occasionally suggested a replacement, there was nothing important to her that couldn't be shipped to Boston for her exhibit.

For two days, Carmine had brought in a team of two helpers to carry in and set up saw horses and worktables. They had also brought in two tall folding ladders and removed the alligator from its long-held position on the ceiling. The iron rod on which the animal was mounted had been fixed to the ceiling on four sturdy hooks and Carmine had replicated those on a frame in the ballroom, so that the alligator would continue to hang until he could build an appropriate container to support it during shipping.

"It isn't as heavy as it looks," he said to Lizzie as he and his workers positioned it in its new temporary home. "The skin is completely dry and there's not much inside it. I think at some point it must have had straw or sawdust inside it to keep its shape, but that was taken out years ago."

A special table was constructed to hold the sarcophagus while Carmine worked on it, so that he wouldn't be forced to work on his hands and knees. It took the five of them in the room, Lizzie, Carmine, the two assistants from the museum, and the security guard Cosimo had hired, to lift the box from the floor onto the board, some three feet off the ground. Carmine had devised a flexible sling that he slid under the sarcophagus to minimize any need to touch it in the process of moving it. He had also provided a specially coated work surface so that there would be no chemical interaction between the painted exterior of the box and a raw piece of wood, which contained damaging acidity.

As they positioned it on the table, Lizzie felt something inside the box slide and come to rest against the side. "It isn't empty like we thought," she said to Carmine.

"I know," he said. "I felt it too."

"Is it a mummy?" one of his assistants asked.

"No way to tell until we open it, and we can't open it until we remove the glue that's holding it shut."

Both the assistant and the security guard seemed disappointed that they wouldn't immediately open the box to see what was in it, and Lizzie was sympathetic. She knew Carmine had to go through a careful and well-documented process of conservation before they could see the contents, but that didn't make her less curious. What she had felt move in the box was solid and it was big. It was definitely not fragments of bone and wrapping.

It took another day of hard work before everything on Lizzie's list had been transferred from the library to the ballroom and laid out on worktables. Carmine's assistants then brought in the drawers of the cabinet from the Chinese Salon, and then the piece of furniture itself. They also brought the Chinese vases that Lizzie had indicated as her preference.

"The Etruscan burial boxes will stay in the courtyard," Carmine told Lizzie as they surveyed their work. "There is no need to bring such heavy things up and down the stairs. I'll crate them down there."

"And the gigantic marble foot?" Lizzie asked.

"That too," Carmine answered.

When everything had been moved, Lizzie thanked the museum workers and the security guard, and took them down to the door of the courtyard. They would come back to help when the collection was packed for shipping, but she wouldn't see them again while she was here. The rest of her time in Bologna would be spent making a condition report for every piece, with measurements, photographs, and Carmine's conservation assessment.

When Lizzie came back upstairs, Carmine had poured

them each a glass of wine. He stood on the balcony of the ballroom with his back to the courtyard and held a glass out to Lizzie. She tapped it against his upraised glass.

"To a wonderful exhibit," he said.

"I will certainly drink to that," she said. She looked around the room at all the marvelous things assembled there. "I am extraordinarily lucky to have been given this job. This is a dream collection for me, and to be given the time and support to work on it for the better part of a year is sort of miraculous." She turned to him and raised her glass again. "And to you, my colleague and friend. I appreciate someone who knows his business and has a good time doing it."

He gave her a slight bow and took a long sip of the wine. "We still have a lot of work to do, though," he said. "Beginning with the sarcophagus. I did an analysis of the glue and it is the worst kind of thing anyone could have put on it. It's from the 60s and highly acidic. I'll have to get it out of there before it eats away at the wood."

"Do that before I go, if you don't mind," Lizzie said. "I want to see what's inside."

Carmine agreed that if she could start with the measurements of each object, he would begin with the mummy case on Monday morning.

Over the weekend, Lizzie decided to visit Patrizio again. This time she wanted to look at the pictures of the house and of the collection that Maggie Gonzaga had sent in 1959, to see what he would say about them. She had a copy of the inventory list in her bag, but did not intend to show it to him unless he seemed particularly chatty and affable.

He did not remember her from any previous meeting either as herself or as Theresa Kenney. Once again she introduced herself as a faculty member from St. Pat's College, once again he said that his grandfather had founded the place and he had gone to school there. The copy she had brought on her last visit of *Patrick Kelliher, Immigrant Industrialist* was on his bedside table and she reached for it and handed it to him.

"I wrote this book about your grandfather," she said. "I am fascinated by him, and by your mother."

He seemed pleased with her company and babbled on a bit

about his parents and grandparents, but not so coherently as during their last conversation. Lizzie powered up her laptop and once again placed it on the rolling tray in front of him, then opened the file of pictures that Maggie Gonzaga had sent of the house in 1959.

"Can I show you some pictures of your house?"

He looked with interest at the picture of the courtyard, with several of the archaeological fragments visible. "This stone I found with my father, in the hills on the way to Marzabotto. We went there frequently on expeditions with him, as he had with his father." Lizzie struggled to see the piece to which he was referring, and he turned the screen toward her and pointed to several pieces from that same source.

She hit the button to bring up the next image, a picture of the Entrance Hall, and Patrizio began to speak immediately, about the great fresco of the family tree first, and then of the portraits, identifying several individuals. Lizzie did not think she could pull out her notebook and start taking notes without making him suspicious, but it occurred to her that she could use the voice recorder on her cell phone to capture whatever Patrick had to say, so she carefully took the device from her bag and turned it on.

From the Entrance Hall to the Yellow Salon, Patrizio kept up his constant stream of information, talking about the paintings, the tromp l'oeil and plaster decorations, and the furnishings and decorative objects. The table in that room, much smaller than the table in the dining room, but ample for eight or ten people, had come from Mantua, the only item thus far that Lizzie had heard of in Bologna from that great collection of the Gonzaga's more famous relations.

When she brought up a picture of the Chinese Salon, he pointed first to the harpsichord. "There is a signature in it, of Giuseppe Verdi, the great composer," he said. "He once visited the house and played the instrument and someone asked him to sign it as a reminder of his visit." He gave a low rumbling laugh. "My mother told me a funny story about it, that when she first came to live here, she saw that signature and immediately translated it into English. She asked my father 'Who's Joe Green?' It was one of their favorite jokes."

He spoke of the wallpaper and of the vases, which he had pointed out to her on her first day in the house, before his outburst. She looked at him carefully to see if he might have any memory of that episode, but it was clear that he didn't.

The dining room picture, unfortunately, was missing the most important feature in the room, the painted ceiling, and Lizzie moved quickly past it. With a deep breath, she pushed the button that brought the library onto the screen. She braced herself for an outburst, but it never came. Instead Patrick pointed out several pieces and gave her anecdotal information that would be useful in her exhibit labels and catalog.

She felt very fortunate to have gotten so much information, but it was obvious that he was tiring, and she closed her computer and began to put it in her bag. Patrizio's eyes were closed and she thought he had fallen asleep, so she packed her things as quietly as possible. Before she rose from the chair he opened his eyes and said, "Did you ask about Greta?"

"Yes," she whispered hesitantly.

"I loved her, you know. I really loved her."

Lizzie paused indecisively. "But she was German," she whispered.

Patrizio nodded.

"A Nazi?"

"She married Hoffman, that Nazi bastard."

Again his eyes were closed and Lizzie waited several minutes, finally convinced he was no longer conscious of her presence. She rose very softly and almost missed the last thing he said: "She informed on Gianna and got her killed."

Chapter 20

The death of Gianna Gonzaga Cussetti had been described by Tony Tessitore as an execution, and that word stayed with Lizzie, nagging at her with its horrific implications. What had her last moments been like? And how had the knowledge of the manner of her death haunted her husband and mother and brother?

It was difficult to reconcile the image of Gianna as a broken corpse being thrown out of a truck with the picture of her as a vivacious Juliet, standing in the arms of her mother and smiling at her lover and her brother on the courtyard staircase. Lizzie looked again at all the photographs of Gianna in the collection on her laptop.

Wanting to see again the picture of Gianna on the Resistance monument, Lizzie put on her coat and walked across the Piazza Galvani and alongside St. Petronio's to the Piazza Maggiore, and across the square to the collection of photographs mounted on the wall. She was struck by how young and innocent Gianna looked in this picture and realized that she was only 21 when she was murdered in October 1944.

There was a café at the corner of the Piazza Maggiore, and Lizzie chose a seat where she could look past the Neptune Fountain at the wall with the photographs. Though she couldn't actually see Gianna's face on the wall from this distance, she knew exactly where her picture was and she continually looked up to visually mark the spot as she drank a cup of coffee. She had brought her book bag with her e-reader and she took it out to look again at Maggie's letters. She wanted to know more about how the progress of the war had impacted the Gonzagas, and of the sequence of events that led to Gianna's horrific death.

Though Patrizio had told her that his father died in 1941, and though she had read that date in several other locations, the fact of it, and of the impact his loss had on Maggie and her children, had not really occurred to Lizzie until she read an account of his illness in one of Maggie's letters to her brother.

November 21, 1941

Dearest Tommy,

I'm sure you read about the progress of the war in all the papers there. The unholy alliance between Mussolini and Hitler has dragged us into such a chaos of fighting in Greece and North Africa. If the U.S. enters the war, which it must at some point, then I will be put in the extraordinarily difficult position of having my native country at war with my adopted country and I cannot tell you how painful that prospect is. At this point I can only be thankful that none of my sons are involved in active fighting and I pray to God every day to keep them out of it.

Margherita gave birth to a little girl yesterday and having our first grandchild has given Renzo and me some hope for the future. This is good, because Renzo's health has not been well. He has a deep cough that does not seem to go away and fear of the war finding us here has dispirited him, as it has all of us.

The next letter was dated a week later and it was not in Maggie's hand or on her usual plain stationary. This paper was edged in black and embossed with a crown at the top. Lizzie looked quickly to the signature before reading it. It was from Adino Gonzaga, Maggie's son, and he wrote to inform his uncle of the death of his father. "My mother is disconsolate," it said, "and we are somewhat concerned about her. My father died of pneumonia, and the doctors do not think there is any possibility of my mother having it, but she lies in bed much of the day, which you know is not at all like her usual self. We do not expect any of you to come from Boston for the funeral, especially with the conflicts currently disrupting travel in the Mediterranean, but details were sent to you by telegram, which I expect you have received by this time. My mother has specifically requested that you keep Patrick there, and she asks that you have a special mass said for my father at the College, so that Patrick and her American relations can attend."

Tony Tessitore had said that one of his earliest memories was of the funeral of Lorenzo Gonzaga, and that he had seen the coffin with a crown on it. Lizzie suspected that must have been Adino's handiwork. From everything Lizzie had read and heard, Maggie did not subscribe at all to the trappings of nobility, but she had mentioned in an earlier letter to her brother that both Adino and his younger brother Cosimo supported the monarchy.

Lizzie's suspicion was confirmed in the next letter, which Maggie wrote on December 16, 1941.

Dear Tommy,

What a terrible series of disasters has befallen us, both inside and outside of this house. I am only now beginning to get my bearings and consider what my life will be like without Renzo, my partner, confidante, lover and friend of almost thirty years. My comfort in the last few weeks has been Gianna, who has frequently slipped into bed with me when I stayed there for too many hours, and the baby Anna. One of the last things Renzo said was that the baby made him feel there was a future to look forward to, past whatever difficulties we might currently find ourselves in. I try to keep that thought with me as we head into war.

Of course I heard about Pearl Harbor with terrible dismay, and the declaration of war against the

United States by Hitler and Mussolini pulled me finally from my bed. I'm not sure how much longer I will be able to write to you without censorship or suspicion, but with the loss of my husband, I need you my dear brother, and look to you more than ever for counsel and consolation. I am disappointed in my older sons. Adino has tried to take charge in a most officious and irritating way. Renzo's funeral was full of the royal fripperies, which he would have despised, and I blame myself for not taking a bigger hand in it.

I think Adino would turn me out of this house as his inherited property if his father had not specifically willed it to me for the remainder of my life, and for any of my children who might be living with me at that time. At 26 he is already arrogant and grasping and Cosimo follows his lead. It is terrible to be saying these things about my own sons, but I cannot afford to be blind to their faults at this serious time. They have allied themselves with the Fascists, and in that I oppose them. I'm glad Pat is still in Boston and wonder if he can be kept there for some time after graduation. I am concerned not only about his safety, but of the influence that his older brothers might have on him if he were home.

Do not worry too much about me. Many families are divided in time of war, both by politics and by exigent circumstances.

There were only a few letters from 1942, which Lizzie presumed was caused by the disruption of the postal service or by the censorship that Maggie had feared. She managed to inform her brother of Gianna's marriage and of another baby girl for Margherita. She spoke of Archie, her new son-in-law, in the warmest terms. She didn't quite come out and say that he was a member of the growing resistance against Fascism and the Nazis, but in retrospect, Lizzie felt she could read that between the lines.

On February 19, 1943, Maggie wrote again. "I feel very

fortunate, my dear brother, to be able to write you a real letter and put it into safe hands for delivery. One of our local priests is traveling to Switzerland and will post this to you there."

The loss of Italian troops in Russia has led to conscription here and I fear for the safety of Pat and Archie. I wish Pat had stayed in Boston, but if he must be influenced by one of the men in this family I'm glad it's his brother-in-law and not one of his brothers. Neither Pat nor Archie will respond to a draft; they are very active in the Resistance, as is Gianna, and to my great concern she plays it like a game. She often goes to meetings dressed as a man and calling herself "Balthazar, a young lawyer from Bologna," in reference to the disguise used by Portia in "The Merchant of Venice." I have absolutely forbidden her to go on patrols. Archie tells me they frequently have no orders, no recognizable superiors, and among the resistance there are factions that do not work well together. Some declare their allegiance to the King, some are ardent Communists. Whenever Gianna and the boys come back to the house I go to the chapel and thank God.

In anticipation that Bologna might be bombed when the Allies finally get here, the churches are removing stained glass windows and other treasures and moving them into their cellars. We have moved the most valuable parts of the collections in the house down to the basement and built a brick wall in front of them. We have also reinforced the walls with boards and put buckets of sand, bottles of water, bedding and food down there, in case we need to move there to protect ourselves. I should hide the Michelangelo angel that was in the chapel in the house, but I find I cannot bear to be without it and have moved it into my bedroom.

Today as I walked across the Piazza Maggiore, just a few blocks from my house, I saw workmen dismantling the gigantic statue of Neptune from

the fountain on the square. They tell me it will be
stored in the communal laundry.

"Michelangelo angel," Lizzie said softly, then repeated the
two words several more times. There had been two angels on
the altar in the house chapel in 1677; there were none there
today. She knew that one of them was the dell'Arca angel at
St. Pat's that would appear in her exhibit. Was this the other
one?

She looked again at Neptune, standing on the top of his
fountain just a few yards from where she sat. She tried to
imagine what it must have meant to Maggie to see one of the
great icons of the city being dismantled, and to face the prospect of impending bombs. "But she could not bear to hide the
Michelangelo angel," Lizzie said softly to herself. "So where
is it?"

Chapter 21

Carmine found Lizzie at the café and told her he had been doing some research on the cement that sealed the coffin and had come up with a plan for removing it. He sat down and she shifted from coffee to wine.

"I was just reading about the dismantling of this fountain during the war." She indicated the Neptune fountain as she spoke. She wanted to burst out that the Gonzagas had a sculpture by Michelangelo, but decided to wait until she knew more.

Carmine said that he had seen pictures of the process. "Where are you reading about it?"

"In Maggie Gonzaga's letters to her family in Boston."

"Does she give information about the collection?"

"When I first started reading them I thought she might, but then I just found I liked her, and now I'm getting caught up in the progress of the war in Bologna."

"Can you put it aside for a while and let me talk to you about some of the arrangements I'm making?"

Lizzie agreed and the two walked back to the Palazzo Gonzaga.

Carmine had created a bar-code cataloging system that would allow them to affix an inventory sticker to each piece. "And these are designed to come off without leaving any mark on the artifact," he said, looking at the sarcophagus with its tenacious glue. "I'll start on this tomorrow if you will mark each of the other pieces and start the data entry."

"Absolutely," Lizzie said enthusiastically. "I'll even buy the coffee!"

"And do I need to know anything more about Cosimo's

nephew? I think I heard him say that he's going to be here when the collection is shipped?"

Lizzie answered that Justin hadn't been much help so far. "I can understand why Cosimo thinks this is a good job for him, I mean he does go to the college, and this collection was made by his ancestors. But beyond finding a way to declare himself a prince, I haven't found that Justin, aka Beppe, has much interest in the project. Don't let him touch anything, and don't let him enter anything into the computer, as we are likely to lose valuable work."

"So what *can* he do?"

"I think that he could operate a clipboard and check off boxes as they get loaded into a truck."

Carmine gave her a puzzled look, but said he would manage, and Lizzie was glad to transfer the responsibility.

The next morning they began early, with Lizzie describing, measuring, photographing and marking the more than two hundred pieces on her list, and comparing each piece to the ledger and subsequent inventory lists. Every piece of information that had been noted on the various sources now came together on the same page. Carmine worked on the sarcophagus, sitting on a rolling chair so that he had the seam between the bottom and the top of the box at eye level, and looking at the work he did through a magnifying lens.

It took three days for him to remove the glue on the box and he called out to Lizzie at the far end of the ballroom when he finished. She was carefully placing barcodes on glass jars full of plant and animal material.

"I'm done," he said.

"Now what?"

"Let's open it." He gave her a pair of latex gloves and showed her where he had placed several small wedges as the glue came out. Moving from one side to the other and from the top to the bottom, he replaced each wedge with a larger one, inching the box open and allowing him to make sure that all the glue had been removed and that there was no damage to the wood or the paint in the process. Eventually they felt the lid shift and as the first air was exchanged between the box and the ballroom they had a strong whiff of pine pitch.

"Is that from the wood?" Lizzie asked.

"No," Carmine answered. "It's from the mummy."

As he spoke they lifted the top off the box and moved it to the separate table that he had prepared for it. Lizzie then went back and looked into the sarcophagus at a perfectly intact mummy.

"I'm astonished," she said. "I was so prepared for there to be either no mummy or only bits and pieces. Is it possible that this has been in this case since the seventeenth century?" She thought about that for a moment and then added, "or the Eighteenth Dynasty?"

"I have no idea. You'll need an Egyptologist for that."

"Fortunately, I have one," Lizzie said, taking out her camera. "I will send him pictures right away."

"Of course you also have a problem."

Lizzie gave him a quizzical look.

"Do you want to ship the mummy to Boston in the sarcophagus? It might require some specialized conservation."

"Hmm. My colleague John Haworth told me that for any human remains I would need a whole different import license, and I don't think I really want to go through the paperwork necessary to ship a corpse back and forth across the Atlantic." She thought about what a mummy would add to her exhibit. "It would be cool to have the mummy, but I think not."

Carmine ran his gloved hands along the dark linen wrappings of the coffin's occupant. "It seems pretty stiff. Let me set up another table and we can move it out of the box."

The corpse was petite, not more than five feet long, and it wasn't particularly heavy. After they had moved it to a new table, Lizzie walked along the length of it and examined the wrapping, which was very tightly wound around the body and soaked in a resin that still retained its pine-pitch smell.

"I'm amazed at how strong the scent is of the pitch after what, three thousand years? If I remember correctly, the Eighteenth Dynasty was around 1300-1500 B.C."

Carmine agreed that it was surprising. "Look at some of these black spots," he said, pointing to a large patch on the feet of the mummy. "It looks like it's been burned."

"At what point in its history do you think that happened?"

"Again, you need your Egyptologist. What I can tell you is that this box was glued in the twentieth century, not the seventeenth and certainly not the thirteenth B.C."

They took a break for lunch and went into the dining room where Lizzie had left some food for them. Though she never saw Graziella, the housekeeper took away Lizzie's dirty dishes and garbage, and restocked the small stockpile of clean plates and cutlery on the table. On an impulse, Lizzie had bought a bouquet at a flower stall a few days earlier, and left a note that said "Grazie Graziella!" The next day a coffee maker joined the serving pieces.

"I'm rather surprised that you don't want to more aggressively pursue the option of having the mummy," Carmine said as they ate. "It seems right up your alley."

"Ordinarily it would be, but I think it would take attention away from other things. The sarcophagus appears in the old drawing, but the mummy itself isn't visible, and in truth, I have already written a description of the medicinal uses of mummy for the catalog and now I'm having to rethink it." She had been composing a message to John Haworth in her brain ever since they opened the coffin.

"So it isn't the display of human remains that bothers you?"

"In fact, though I admit to a macabre streak, I do have some hesitation about it. I have always been disconcerted by the display of Egyptian mummies. It seems that people who devoted so much attention to insuring that they would face eternity in a certain way ending up in an exhibit case in London or Boston..." She searched for words. "It's not religious," she concluded. "It simply seems disrespectful somehow. And I'm just as uncomfortable with the flayed corpses in the recent 'Body World' exhibits, plasticated and posed for millions of gawkers."

"It's natural though, to be interested in what happens to our bodies after death."

"Here I think we have very different cultural backgrounds," she responded. "Italians seem to celebrate the public display of their corpses. The bones organized into decorative patterns in churches, the piles of skulls, the mummified remains pulled out of graves and stood up on exhibit..." She stopped suddenly, afraid that Carmine might think she was criticizing Italians, but he laughed.

"We are morbid!" he said. "I think your macabre streak cannot match ours. But we use the excuse that we are preserving the relics of saints."

"Not entirely. When I Googled 'Italian' plus 'mummies' I came upon an article about a church in Venzone where corpses put into the limestone vault beneath a church were naturally mummified because of the dehydrating properties of the place. And when they discovered it, the locals pulled the corpses up from the crypt and stood them around the church with their names attached."

"I've been to that church," Carmine said.

"Well then you know that these aren't pretty mummies like the one we have in the ballroom, nicely wrapped with no visible features or body parts. These guys are all contorted into writhing postures and ghastly expressions. Can you imagine if they brought grandpa up like that and exhibited him with his name on a sign around his neck?"

"That is what happens to corpses. Is it better not to know?"

"It might be better not to know them personally. I think I would be curious to see John Doe's grandfather, but not my own."

This conversation reminded Lizzie that she had never shown Carmine the chapel or spoken to him about the reliquaries. "This will now sound very contrary, but I would actually like to include three reliquaries in the exhibit."

"With or without body parts?"

"With, of course, a reliquary is no good without the relic in it."

"And the display of these doesn't bother you?"

"No, and I guess I am being rather inconsistent. I don't know what the original intention of the supposed saint was when his or her bones were placed in a reliquary, but certainly as works of art these pieces were made for display."

"And veneration."

"Would it bother you if I took them and exhibited them? Because I did ask Father O'Toole, the president of my college, if he thought it would be sacrilegious to put them in a secular exhibit, and he basically approved it because the museum is on the campus of a Catholic college."

"I certainly don't object," Carmine said. "I see so many of these things that I am fairly neutral about them. Mostly they come into my workshop as artifacts needing conservation and they sometimes pose special problems because of the mix of organic and inorganic materials."

He asked if the relics would require the same special import license as the mummy and she explained that Father O'Toole had told her that he and his friend the cardinal would take care of it.

"Come see the collection in the chapel," she said. "And you can tell me instantly if any of them need to be rejected for conservation reasons."

He went back to the ballroom to get some gloves and his magnifying lens as Lizzie repackaged the food and made as neat a pile as she could of the used dishes.

She had gone into the chapel several times since Patrizio left the house and looked more closely around the room, so she was able to point out the main features to Carmine. The corpse under the altar was, at this point, mostly just a skeleton lying in armor and he gave it only the most cursory look before turning his attention to the wall of relics.

"You have a fine assortment to choose from here," he said. "What are your criteria for selection?"

"Either they are visually compelling because of their beauty or their strangeness," Lizzie said, "or they have an interesting story."

"What do you mean by 'strangeness?'"

"I'm going by an American definition here. Most of the visitors to my exhibit will never have seen anything like this, so this one, for instance," she said, touching the base of an arm reliquary with the long bone of an arm readily visible, "will seem quite strange."

"And you find strangeness to be desirable in something on exhibit?"

"Anything that draws someone across a room to look more closely is desirable, and I believe this would."

He handed her a pair of gloves. "Don't touch the metal with your hands, please," he said with mock sternness.

"Don't you find that arm bone, encased in silver and studded with jewels, strange?" she said hesitantly.

"Of course. Just because I am more accustomed to seeing these things than you doesn't mean that I don't recognize the strangeness of the practice." He reached up and carefully removed the arm reliquary from the shelf and placed it on the altar.

There was no denying that the thing was beautifully crafted. It was an arm, upraised with an open palm, all made of silver. Folds and creases of fabric had been molded into the metal of the sleeve. Around the base of the arm, where it stood on the altar, and at the cuff of the sleeve, were gold bands, inset with semi-precious stones in squares, circles and ovals; a similar bracelet was around the slender forearm. In the palm of the hand was a gold-set pale-blue jewel. The long silver fingers stretched heavenward.

Had that been the extent of the piece there would have been no element of the strangeness that so intrigued and confounded Lizzie. But it was not simply a lovely sculpture of an arm. The thing was hollow, and strikingly visible through an open panel was an old bone—and it wasn't even a clean white bone. It looked as though it still had the dirt of a grave clinging to it. The contrast between the earthiness of the bone and sumptuousness of the silver and jewels was what gave it its strangeness.

Lizzie held her tongue.

"Don't worry about offending me," Carmine said, giving her a slight bump with his elbow. "I told you I am inured to these things after years of working with them, and I acknowledge that most of the relics are fakes."

Lizzie gave him a smile of relief. She put on the gloves and slowly turned the silver arm around. "They may be fakes as relics of saints, but it is still the arm bone of an actual person. Is there any identification of whose arm this is?"

"When there is a crystal covering the relic, then a paper or fabric slip is usually put inside to identify the saint, but in this case the silversmith has actually given us the name on one of the bands that holds the bone in place: St. Cecilia, it says."

"The patron saint of music," Lizzie said.

"So this is the arm with which she played the harp," Carmine joked.

"Let's put this on the list," she said. "I haven't seen it yet, but I understand the Gonzaga chapel at St. Paolo Maggiore has a fresco of musicians, and I can make a nice connection in the catalog."

They turned back to the display. "What else?" Carmine asked.

"A tooth would be nice." There were three large reliquaries that each held a tooth on a silver pick in the center of a carved piece of crystal.

Carmine asked her if she had a favorite and pulled the nearest one off its shelf and put it on the altar. Each of the three examples was about two feet high, gold, and made in three parts: a base that looked much like the base of a chalice, the central cage which held the crystal, and a finial of some kind. On the simplest of these, the finial was a gold cross sitting on a gilded church tower; the most complex had an enameled crucifixion scene on a gold disk with a dark blue background, surmounted by a cross.

"Once again I have to ask who the donors were before I can make a decision."

Carmine needed his magnifying lens to decipher the tiny writing embedded inside the crystal. "This one is John the Baptist," he said of the first. He retrieved the other two and put them on the altar for examination. "This one is Mary Magdalene, and the other is St. Bartholomew."

"That's interesting," Lizzie said. "The Metropolitan Museum in New York has a tooth of Mary Magdalene, and the Chicago Art Institute has one of John the Baptist. I don't remember the details well enough to know if the artists were the same, but I do remember that there are several heads of John the Baptist in collections all over Europe."

"The steeple effect here is very nicely done," Carmine said of the first one they had looked at. "I would choose it over the others, and it is St. Bartholomew, who isn't already represented in a museum in the U.S."

"Done!" Lizzie said.

"I think that I will choose this as my third reliquary," she added, pointing to a column of crystal capped on either end with a gold crown. It was difficult to see what was inside the crystal, but Lizzie had seen a similar piece years before in Bruges and believed she knew what it was.

"The Holy Blood, I think," she said.

Carmine took it off the shelf and placed it carefully on the altar. The central column of rock crystal was about six inches long and two inches in diameter. It had been drilled through to allow for the placement of a tiny scrap of fabric, really just a few threads. These were said to have been part of the cloth used by Joseph of Arimathea to wash the body of Christ before he was laid in the tomb, and to have captured some of his blood.

"The one in Bruges was given to the Count of Flanders in Jerusalem during the Crusades and has a really terrific provenance for the last thousand years," she said, and then added that she was more suspicious of where it had been for the thousand years between the death of Christ and its acquisition by Count Baldwin.

"I don't suppose you have found a list of the relics here?" Carmine asked.

"Not in the ledger, or in any of the related lists, but there are other manuscripts in that part of the library that I haven't yet surveyed."

"I'd suggest you look for a bible, if there is an old one associated with this chapel." They both looked at the bible lying nearby on the altar, but it was clearly new.

"I'll put it on my list of things to do this evening," she said. "There is a sketch of this chapel made by the same artist who drew the cabinet, which I will show you when we go back downstairs. The Guido Reni painting of the Madonna and Child used to be here, and the dell'Arca angel that is also in our campus chapel."

"I'm very interested in the drawing," Carmine said, and when they returned to the library Lizzie opened her computer and showed him the image that Cosimo had sent her several weeks earlier. She pointed out the two angels.

"One of them is the dell'Arca that you have in Boston?" Carmine asked.

Lizzie nodded, then said hesitantly, "Maggie Gonzaga described a Michelangelo angel from the chapel that she moved to her bedroom during the war. Could that have been it?"

Carmine looked closely at the picture again. "It's impossible to tell from this sketch," he said. "But I can show you a Michelangelo angel holding a candlestick at the church of St. Dominic."

"Is it possible that it is the one from this house?"

Carmine shook his head. "No. The one at the church has been there for centuries and is well documented."

"I wonder where it is?" Lizzie said. She remembered that Father O'Toole had mentioned that the Gonzagas might have lost valuable works of art to Nazi looting during the war, but she hadn't been able to verify it. "Is it possible that such a thing could have been looted during the war?" she asked.

"One hears talk," her companion said. "But no details that I know of. If the Gonzagas had artworks looted by the Nazis they never made a claim to find them or have them repatriated."

"Too bad. A sculpture by Michelangelo would be the crown jewel in my exhibit!"

Chapter 22

Late in the night, Lizzie found the ancient bible on the same locked shelf where Patrizio kept the ledger. It was gigantic and heavy, with a gold-embossed leather cover and a big clasp to hold it closed.

With some difficulty, she wrestled it off the shelf and onto the table. Turning over the cover, she saw a genealogy of the Gonzaga family, with entries for births, marriages and deaths for more than three hundred years. She closed the book and opened it again from the back. In a tiny script covering two pages was a list of the relics, many of which had been gifts to their relations from the cardinals and bishops in the family. Even though the list was in Latin, Lizzie recognized the names of Maria Maddalena, Giovanni il Battista, and "Santo Sangue," the Holy Blood. She would need Carmine to translate the details for her, but they seemed to have been acquired from Jerusalem, Constantinople and Rome.

With that, Lizzie felt her final choices for what would be in the exhibit were complete; now she could turn her attention to writing the catalogue. Martin would arrive in two days and she was ahead enough of the planned schedule to be able to spend a few days walking around the town with him, a prospect to which she looked forward with delight. She would also take some time away from the house tomorrow to visit Patrizio again. Though she had found almost everything that would be included in the exhibit in one or another of the documents available to her, she hoped that there might be family lore associated with some of them and that the old man might, if feeling talkative, be prompted to share those anecdotes.

She did not want to be caught unaware in any interview with him by information that she might be able to get by reading about him in his mother's letters, and she was anxious to get back to the story of Gianna and Archie anyway, so she once again took the letters to bed and read Maggie's account of the war.

August 10, 1943

Dear Tommy,

I have found someone who is going to England and I write this in haste in the hope of putting it into her hands tomorrow. We follow the news on the BBC radio, turned down very low and all of us sitting in the basement of the house. Bologna has become a very dangerous place. Strikes by workers in March protesting their living conditions and criticizing the Fascist government brought unwelcome attention our way and there are large numbers of German forces entrenched in the area. As I'm sure you must know we were heavily bombed in mid-July, by English planes at night and by American planes during the day. The bombs on July 16 and 24 damaged or destroyed many buildings in the center of the city as well as the railroad station. There were many people killed and some great historic works of architecture and the artworks in them are gone forever. I'm sorry to say that it did not make any of us feel better to hear Churchill and Roosevelt urging us on the radio to overthrow the Fascists and take our place among the righteous nations.

It was strange that on the same day that we were bombed, the king finally did something good and threw Mussolini out of power. Marshall Pietro Badoglio is now nominally in control of the government, but the Germans don't answer to him and so it doesn't have much effect on us here. Adino has gone to Rome to follow the king and good luck to him, but you know too much of my feelings on this matter for me to say them all again. Cosimo has left Bologna and I wouldn't be surprised if he showed up on your doorstep, or sets himself up in New York for the rest of the war.

My dear trio of partisans simultaneously terrify me with the danger of their actions and make me enormously proud. I try to aid the cause in small ways with food and supplies, but we have little to spare and there are now more than one hundred people living in my house and I am careful not to bring the Nazis storming in on all of them. I cannot, with a house still standing, turn away people whose houses are gone.

Eleonora and Margherita have property outside the city and are growing food to try to keep us supplied, but their farms are often raided by German troops, or by poor hungry people moving through the area. We have each been given a ration card with stickers to get access to staples like flour and rice, but there is less and less available.

I can read your mind right now, my dear brother, and know that you would wish me in Boston, but as long as Gianna, Pat and Archie are here I cannot go. And I think their work is crucial to securing us a future when the war is over.

October 8, 1943

Dear Tommy,

I cannot tell you how frustrating it is that I must wait until I know there will be a secure way to send you a letter before I even begin to write. As of September ninth we have been officially occupied by the German Army. Roads into the city are closed and there are great fears of arrests and the executions of partisans. There have been several raids in the city to flush them out and I am fearful of being caught with any information that identifies the dangerous activities of those I love. And yet, I want you to know how much the partisans are now doing in this region. What began as a resistance to Fascism has now become a resistance against the Nazi occupation. The people involved are an interesting mix, including large numbers of escaped Allied prisoners, who live in the hills around the city and are aided by local people.

I was visited last week by an S.S. officer named Hoffman, who identified himself as the husband of Greta Winkler, Gianna's old school friend. He is almost a caricature of a Nazi and looks like one of those big blond handsome men that populate the German propaganda posters. He was friendly enough and brought us some much-appreciated food, but I couldn't help thinking that he was really looking to gather information. He asked to speak to Gianna, said he had messages for her from Greta, and became quite insistent. I fear that Gianna is becoming too well known for her role in the movement and Archie has certainly been identified as one of the leaders.

There are mixed feelings here about the armistice with the Allies signed by Badoglio and the king last month. We are in such a squeeze between the Allied advances and the entrenched Germans and there is a general depression on the part of everyone I know. We all want peace, but how shall we get it?

There was a newspaper in the collection that Roscoe had scanned along with the letters. On September 12, 1943, it announced the German rescue of Mussolini from prison and the creation of a new Fascist state in northern Italy. In the south, the Allies, with the king and Badoglio, were forming another provisional government.

In this morass of conflicting claims of authority and violent chaos, Maggie learned that her son Adino was shot and killed in Rome on October 13, 1943. "My grief is matched only by my guilt for being angry at him at the end," she wrote to her brother. "Our politics were so different. I had heard that he approached the king practically as a kinsman, bragging of his noble blood, and then went to the Americans claiming them as his countrymen because he was born in Boston. By trying to gain an advantage from every side he ended up making enemies everywhere and it isn't even known which faction murdered him—I guess it doesn't matter now that he is gone. I received a telegram from one of his friends telling me I cannot have his body because there is no transportation available, and he will be buried in Rome. Oh Tommy, how sad is the progression of our lives right now. This morning I sat and looked at pictures of Adino as a little boy and remembered how sweet natured he was when he was my bambino, and the tears flowed."

Chapter 23

"Your friend is here," the nurse at the hospital told Patrizio, fumbling through the English and smiling broadly at Lizzie.

He greeted her in a very friendly tone. He seemed to understand that Lizzie had visited him before, but he didn't remember her. They restaged their now familiar routine: she taught at St. Patrick's College; his grandfather founded it; he went to school there; and then she once again located the copy of *Patrick Kelliher, Immigrant Industrialist* on his nightstand and handed it to him.

"You wrote this?" he said enthusiastically. "I love this book."

Lizzie decided to try a new tactic. "This is the hundredth anniversary of the founding of the college and we would like to have an exhibit in honor of your family," she started. "Could we borrow some things from the collection in your house?"

"Of course," he said. It was a wonderful idea, how could he help, just tell him what to do. His response could not have been more agreeable.

"Can I ask you about some of the things in the Wonder Chamber?"

He repeated the word with glee and agreed. Lizzie started her questions with the alligator and once again he told her it had been captured in Florida and transported on a Spanish ship.

"How did your family get these Spanish things?" she asked.

"Through Venice. When my ancestors came to Bologna from Mantua, they developed a network of trade that brought things from Venice into the interior. Bologna had a series of canals then and connections throughout the region. My family owned ships in the Mediterranean and they regularly sailed to Spanish ports."

"Is that how the Mexican box got into the collection?" she asked, "and the Marquesan club?"

Patrizio told her that he had heard that many of the things with a Spanish provenance had come through the same source, a Spanish trader with his own cabinet of curiosities, who traded many specimens with the Gonzagas.

"Do you know when that was?"

"I think about 1650."

"And do you have a name?"

Patrizio shook his head and apologized. "I can't remember things anymore, but I think there might be some correspondence with him in a book in my library at home and when I get there I can find it for you."

Lizzie thanked him. "What about the narwhal tusk, the unicorn horn?"

"That came from the collection of Ferdinando Cospi— there is a document that mentions the trade that got it, and likewise, one of the blowfish was given to my ancestor by Ulisse Aldrovandi."

"Excellent! If you don't mind, I will put them on my exhibit list."

Lizzie had not yet gone thoroughly through the bookcase that had the ledger and the bible in it, but she would do so as soon as she returned to the house. She went through several more things on the list and got useable information on about half of them.

"What about the mummy?" she asked finally.

"Do you mean the sarcophagus?" he answered.

"Yes, the sarcophagus," she said, wondering if he knew there was a mummy in it.

"It came through Venice, too," he said. "I don't remember the date, but it was one of the first things acquired for the Wonder Chamber."

"Was there a mummy in it?"

"I don't know if there was a mummy in it when it first

came," he said. He seemed to be working to remember something as he spoke, and then shook his head and was silent.

Lizzie waited for him to speak again.

"My mother took me and Archie to Egypt after the war," he said, breaking the silence unexpectedly and excitedly. "We saw hundreds of mummies there. When we came back I took a class on Egyptian archaeology with Agostini, who had been a student of my father. I considered becoming an Egyptologist."

Lizzie wondered if maybe he had acquired the mummy then, and put it in the sarcophagus. But why would he glue it shut? Perhaps it was to keep the young Cosimo from playing with it—Cosimo had told Lizzie that Patrizio beat him once when he found him touching the case. Or maybe Patrizio had stolen the mummy from the University's collection; in the aftermath of the war, it would be difficult to know where missing artifacts had gone.

"I've heard that your family had a marble carving by Michelangelo," she asked finally.

"An angel holding a candlestick," he said. "It was stolen during the war. My mother should have hidden it in the cellar, but it was a favorite of my father and she couldn't bear not to be able to see it, especially at such a hard time."

"Did you try to recover it?"

"My mother knew who stole it and said she would take care of it herself. I promised never to speak of it."

He was as good as his promise because at the end of the sentence he clamped his mouth shut and would say no more, not even a "ciao" when Lizzie finally left the room.

Chapter 24

"I am a much better tour guide than any of the locals I have met," Lizzie announced to Martin as they drove into the city. She had rented a car to pick him up at the airport and to make it possible for them to drive out into the countryside if the opportunity arose, and the Sunday traffic was easy to negotiate. "Both of the Bolognans who have driven me around, Pina Corelli and Cosimo Gonzaga, are very lazy about pointing things out and my Roman friend, Carmine, is knowledgeable and enthusiastic about the city, but we have only walked around our own neighborhood."

"I know he can't show you around the city," Martin said, "But what about the old man, Patrick, has he improved on knowing him?"

"He is an absolutely essential source for me on understanding the collection, but unfortunately he has lost most of his marbles and is very unpredictable. He has never recognized me, not once, unless he thinks I'm some girl who went to school with him seventy years ago." She told him that she had given him the same copy of *Patrick Kelliher, Immigrant Industrialist* at least five times.

"I don't suppose you could just pretend to be that girl he knew," Martin said, half joking.

"I'm ashamed to admit it, but I tried that," Lizzie confessed. "At one point he started to apologize for having fallen in love with somebody else and I realized I was in over my head."

As they came into the city she gave him an orientation around the Medieval Walls, pointed out the porticos, especially the long covered walkway that went up to the top of a hill where there was an eleventh-century church. "It is the Madonna di San Luca," Lizzie said, "and they have a Byzantine painting there which is supposed to be a portrait of the Virgin Mary, painted from life by St. Luke. There is an eighteenth-century basilica there now and it is an important place of pilgrimage."

"Have you seen it?" Martin asked.

"No, that is a pleasure that I saved to share with you."

"I know the story about Luke painting Mary, because it is the subject of a couple of great Renaissance paintings."

"Carmine, the conservator I'm working with, tells me there are at least forty paintings in Europe that are said to be *the* painting painted by Luke, but that any known dates make all the attributions impossible. And Luke was born after Jesus, so he certainly couldn't have painted him as a baby."

Martin bent his head down to look up to the top of the hill through the windshield. "It looks like a beautiful church and you know I am always ready to visit a beautiful church."

Pina had given Lizzie the code to the garage and she turned into the Piazza Galvani and entered it on the keypad to lift the gate and open the garage door. "I haven't spent any time down here," Lizzie said when they got out of the car in the garage, "but if you don't mind I'd like to take a quick look around. In her letters, Maggie said that they used this as a bomb shelter during the war, and hid their collection down here behind a brick wall."

There were only a few bare-bulb light fixtures hanging in the space, but Lizzie and Martin each had a fairly powerful flashlight application on their cell phones and they used them to bring light into the dark cellar as they moved around the space.

"These boards must have been used to shore up the walls when they were afraid of bombs taking them down," Martin said, running a beam of light up a two-by-four and across another board that ran along the ceiling.

"And here are the last vestiges of the false wall they built," Lizzie said. "Maggie wrote that they hid their collections behind it, by which I assume she meant paintings, silver and other valuables, and maybe some of the cabinet of curiosities, though I doubt they were very worried about the Germans running off with their alligator. Unfortunately, the best piece of all, a small Michelangelo sculpture, did not get hidden and was stolen during the war."

"Wow! How come this is the first I'm hearing of a missing Michelangelo?"

"The details are only now beginning to fall into place, and I'm not sure I'll ever have more information about it because Patrick won't talk about it. I'll ask Cosimo when the time is right."

Martin asked how extensively the city had been bombed. "That's a pretty good way to destroy both works of art and their documentation."

"According to Maggie's letters, the center of the city was hit several times, and she had more than a hundred people living in the house whose own homes had been destroyed."

Lizzie led him to the elevator. "It will be easiest to just take your bags up to the third floor, where we sleep, but the first view into the courtyard really is a grand one from the front entrance."

"From what you've already told me, to see it first from the balcony of the dining room might be even more impressive, and I'm keen to see the Carracci fresco on the ceiling."

"Excellent idea! We'll view the courtyard from the dining room, and then I'll show you what I have been working on."

The courtyard perspective gave Lizzie a chance to describe the Shakespeare plays that Maggie had produced, and to point out the staircase on the opposite wall, where the balcony scene from "Romeo and Juliet" had been staged. She had to compete for his attention with the ceiling of the room, and it was only by promising that he could come back and lie on the table and view it to his heart's content at a later time that she got him to move on to the ballroom.

Martin's artist's eye was always useful to Lizzie, especially on projects like this one, where she wanted the exhibit to have a strong visual impact. The great accumulation in the ballroom impressed him just as Lizzie hoped it would, and after looking at the whole of the collection he began to suggest juxtapositions of certain artifacts that she found inspired. When evening had come along and the natural light was fading, they walked through the rooms he had not yet seen. Lizzie went first and turned on the chandeliers in the Chinese Salon, Yellow Salon, and Entrance Hall so that he could have the full effect.

In the Yellow Salon he turned around and around the room, a puzzled look on his face. He walked up to and backed away from several paintings. "Where's the Ruysdael?" he asked finally. "And the Backhuysen? I saw them in that photograph you showed me, but they're not here."

"I don't know," she said, pointing out the plasterwork and painting that surrounded each frame. "I hadn't looked for them, but you'd have to replace any painting here with something exactly the same size." She was disappointed in herself that she hadn't noticed this first and explained that she hadn't paid attention to this room because she didn't plan to use anything here for her exhibit.

Martin looked closely at one of the frames. "They did a good job matching the size here," he said, indicating the line around an oval frame of substantial size, "but it isn't exact."

"Are you suggesting that something isn't kosher here?"

"Not at all. I don't know why paintings would be swapped, but it seems like there are more legitimate reasons for doing so than suspicious ones. They might have needed money, who knows? I was just looking forward to seeing those two paintings and am a bit disappointed."

The next morning, with the light of day, Martin and Lizzie went back to the Yellow Salon with Carmine and compared the pictures on the walls with those that appeared in the 1959 photograph.

"You're certainly right that several of these frames are not the ones that were here when the fresco around them was first painted," Carmine said. "And some of the background painting has been altered."

Martin looked from the picture on Lizzie's laptop to the paintings on the wall several times. "If you ask me, the most valuable paintings are gone, replaced by secondary works by secondary artists. There is more Italian stuff, and less of the Dutch and Flemish work than was here before."

Carmine agreed. "I've never seen anything in the recent literature about the Gonzagas selling off any portion of their collection, but they might have replaced things discretely after the war, when everyone needed money."

"I don't know when these photographs were taken," Lizzie said, "but I think it was long after the war. Maggie Gonzaga sent them to the college in 1959."

As this was not a puzzle that could be solved by discussion, and as Martin was eager to see the conservation work that Carmine was doing, the three walked back to the ballroom. "What's happening with the mummy?" he asked Carmine. He had already heard everything Lizzie knew about it.

"I think I will make a packing case for the mummy itself and just push it back against the wall. It isn't going to Boston and it seems to be in pretty stable condition, so I am not going to worry about it. As to the sarcophagus," he continued. "It has the usual problems of painted wood of such antiquity, but is overall in remarkably good condition. It will still require the greatest amount of my time of anything in the exhibit, though."

"Ah, the challenges of the conservator!" Martin responded with a smile.

"Do you know that I read about one of your murals in the very first conservation class I ever took? And the story has stayed with me ever since because it raised such interesting questions."

Martin chuckled. "Oh no! That damned mural on the wall of the community college in L.A. You cannot imagine how that thing has haunted me since it got written up in that conservation journal."

Carmine confirmed that was where he had learned about it.

"I hope you understand that it was my very first commission," Martin said, "and that I knew very little about the chemistry of paint at the time. All the big sections of color were done with latex interior house paint, and it simply couldn't stand up to being outside for twenty-five years. Good Lord! I never thought the thing would last that long anyway!"

"Ah the challenges of being a famous artist!" Lizzie said

mockingly. "If the value of your work hadn't gone up so much they probably wouldn't have worked so hard to save it."

"So I'm sure you know from the article that when I learned the college had gotten a grant of more than twenty thousand dollars to conserve the thing, I thought it was just absurd. They only paid me five hundred bucks to paint it in the first place!"

Lizzie described to Carmine how she and Martin had gone to L.A. and shown up at the school.

"And I offered to repaint the wall," Martin continued, "and there was a discussion that went on for days about whether they should continue to work on preserving my original work of art, or let me paint a new mural."

"But if I remember the details correctly, you would have destroyed the original in the process," Carmine said.

"Most of it, anyway. And there were some strong advocates for protecting the original as a historical part of the community."

"Including me," said Lizzie.

"Ultimately I convinced the local people to let me at least remove the latex paint, which honestly wasn't worth saving; to repaint those sections of the wall that were clearly the favorites, and to do it without changing the way they looked; and to add some new material with the assistance of local kids, which is what I mostly like to do now anyway."

"So they got a new and different mural," Carmine said.

"With clear links to the original," Lizzie added.

Martin put his hand on the mummy case. "I would never think to alter this in any way," he said earnestly, "because I respect the integrity of the original artist. But in the L.A. case, *I'm* the artist, and I look upon that wall as something that reflects a changing community."

"It's a terrific case study anyway," Carmine said. He handed Martin a pair of latex gloves. "And please use these if you really don't want to make any changes in the mummy case."

They all laughed.

"I like a man who knows his business," Martin said, snapping the gloves into place.

"As do I."

It was a companionable and productive morning, with Martin making suggestions on ways to think about some of the objects that were helpful for Lizzie, and providing an extra set of hands for Carmine as he moved the things that had been processed from one end of the ballroom to the other. When they began to talk of breaking for lunch, Carmine asked if they would like to walk over to the Basilica di San Domenico.

"The tomb of St. Dominic there has the Michelangelo I told you about, Lizzie, and it was largely designed by Niccolo dell'Arca." he said.

"Did Lizzie tell you that there is a dell'Arca statue at St. Patrick's College that will go into the exhibit?" Martin asked.

"Of course," Lizzie said. "And I'd love to see his work in its original setting."

"He is called 'Arca' because he designed the canopy or 'arch' over the top of the tomb," Carmine explained. "His real name was Niccolo de Bari. The ceiling of that same chapel is by Guido Reni, and I think you said you have a painting by him as well."

"Tell me about the Michelangelo." Martin said.

Carmine smiled. "There are three Michelangelo statues on the tomb, including one of St. Petronio."

"Ah," Lizzie said, "the cover of your book!"

The Basilica was only three blocks from the Gonzaga house and they strolled there in just a few minutes. The tomb of St. Dominic, founder of the Dominican order, was along the right side of the nave, set off by a large black and gilded gate, and by a flight of stairs. Made of marble and framed by a rotunda ceiling and semicircular wall of paintings, the tomb itself had several tiers, with sculptures and bas reliefs of the life of the saint. Two exquisite angels were on the front corners and Carmine pointed out that the one on the left was by dell'Arca, and the one on the right by his student, Michelangelo.

Lizzie stepped up to the dell'Arca angel and was immediately struck by its resemblance to the one in the chapel at St. Patrick's College. She held out her arms to measure it.

"This is astonishing!" she said. "I think that this angel and the one at St. Pat's are a pair!"

Martin and Carmine had been talking about the statue of St. Petronio, but turned to look at her. It was obvious from their expressions that neither thought she could be correct.

"How could that be possible?" Martin asked.

"I don't know," Lizzie said, "but they are. This is a mirror image of the one at St. Pat's."

She explained how she had put her arms around that angel to see if it could be lifted and it was just the same size as this one. "Plus the faces are just alike, the placement of the candlestick on the knee, the long hair, the feathered wings. They are a pair, I'm sure of it."

Carmine was thoughtful for a moment before he spoke. "In researching the St. Petronio statue I found references to two pairs of angels holding candlesticks that were made for this tomb, one by dell'Arca and one by Michelangelo, but the presumed wisdom has always been that dell'Arca didn't finish the work here and Michelangelo was hired to complete it."

"What does that mean, though?" Lizzie asked. She moved to the other side of the altar to look at the Michelangelo angel. "He certainly didn't try to copy the dell'Arca figure; this angel doesn't look anything like the other. He's a man, not a boy, much more masculine looking, and the candlesticks, while similar, don't match."

"Completing a pair doesn't necessarily mean making them identical," Martin said. "Michelangelo was no copyist. Whoever hired him wouldn't expect him to make a replica of the dell'Arca."

"Did dell'Arca die before this was finished?" Lizzie asked. "Is that why Michelangelo had to be brought in?"

Carmine shook his head. "That is the story one usually hears, but in fact one can't be certain about the dates. Michelangelo came here around 1494, and that is the year that dell'Arca died."

"But if dell'Arca was commissioned to make a pair of angels holding candlesticks, how could one of them have gone missing?" Martin asked.

"There are actually a number of plausible explanations for that," Carmine answered. "Someone could have seen it in his studio and offered a good sum of cash for it before he brought it to the church, or they could have offered the church enough money to break up the set." He explained that there had been earlier sculptures on the tomb that were sold when dell'Arca took up the restoration. "There are angels at the Louvre in Paris and at the Victoria and Albert Museum in London that used to be in this church, and I think a couple of carvings from St. Dominic's are even at your Museum of Fine Arts in Boston."

"If the church had two pairs of angels, they could have sold one from each set," Lizzie said. "And the other Michelangelo could have gone with the dell'Arca to the Gonzagas and be the statue stolen from their house during the war."

"Why isn't there more information about this?" Carmine asked. "How could there be a missing Michelangelo that isn't talked about?"

"Patrizio said that his mother knew who stole it and didn't want anyone to know it."

Martin suggested that maybe it was someone in her family.

"That's an interesting thought," Lizzie said. "But who?"

It was difficult to turn their attention to any other topic, but Lizzie paid Carmine the compliment of noting the statue of St. Petronio on the next tier up on the tomb. "Will that be the star of your catalog?" she asked.

"Of course. He was designed and begun by dell'Arca and finished by Michelangelo, and that is clearly documented."

On the ceiling of the chapel was a fresco called "St. Dominic's Glory" painted around 1615 by Guido Reni. "He was a real Bolognese artist," Carmine explained. "He was born and died here."

"I think that Lorenzo Gonzaga had these things in mind when he made his gifts to St. Pat's. He wanted the pieces he gave to represent his home city."

They stopped for lunch at a small restaurant along the Via Garibaldi and as they walked home, Lizzie asked if they might also stop into the Church of St. Paolo Maggiore, which was close by. It had been the family church of the Gonzagas.

"It is a much newer church than St. Dominic's," Carmine answered, "and worth seeing for that reason. The art is quite different."

Whereas St. Dominic had lived on the site of his church and died there in the early thirteenth century, the church of St. Paolo Maggiore wasn't built until four hundred years later, around the time that the Gonzagas moved to Bologna. The three entered and walked to the altar where there was a dramatic larger-than-life-size carving of the beheading of St. Paul. The executioner was a muscular man, dressed only in a cloth that went over one shoulder and around his waist. In his right hand was a sword, his arm raised across his bare chest. One foot was braced behind the other, as if to give more power to the swing of the sword. St. Paul sat before him, his head tilted down, looking off in the opposite direction from the man who would murder him. His long beard came down to his bare chest, and his crossed hands were bound with a cord and resting on his knee.

"This is extraordinary," Lizzie whispered to her companions. "I don't see the usual crucifix."

"This is certainly a powerful alternative," Martin answered. "Still a biblical execution, but somehow seems more violent."

This church had a greater range of things with modern connections than St. Dominic's. One chapel had been turned into a stone grotto to resemble the place where Bernadette had her vision of the Blessed Virgin in 1858.

The Gonzaga chapel was not what Lizzie expected, but she was only now beginning to realize that though the churches in Bologna were filled with bones of saints, they were not the tombs of ordinary family members. In England, where she had spent a fair amount of time in churches both large and small, local people were crowded into the floors when they died, or buried in tombs that were built along the walls; the excess population spilled out into an adjacent graveyard. Here that was not the case.

"I expected to see the tombs of the old Gonzagas here, and maybe even Lorenzo, Maggie and Gianna."

"It's not the tradition here. They are in a cemetery outside of town."

"Do you want to go there?" Martin asked her.

"No, I don't particularly need to see it."

They admired the various paintings in the chapel, but concluded that the most interesting things associated with the family were, or had been, in the house and they returned there to continue the work.

Lizzie had much to keep her busy, but still could not keep the angels from buzzing around her head.

Chapter 25

A few days after Maggie wrote to her brother informing him of the murder of her son, Adino, a local newspaper reported that Jewish students and teachers would no longer be welcome in Bologna schools and on November 6, 1943, the first Jews were transported to Auschwitz. Unsure of what was happening to Jewish friends, Maggie reported to her brother that the Resistance fighters were providing false documents and helping people to escape capture.

"There is now a very large population of people hiding in the hills around Bologna," she wrote in late November.

> Thousands of Allied prisoners of war have escaped, and partisans are leading them to Switzerland along paths that many of them used before the war to smuggle goods out of the country. Many Bolognese have moved out of the city, I'm not sure to where. Everything is difficult to obtain now and we are worried as winter approaches about how we will keep heat in the house. In the summer, we had about eighty people camped out in our courtyard, but now they are all gradually moving up into the ballroom and then out to other rooms in the house. Food is scarce, as is fuel for cooking and lamps. We no longer have electricity.
>
> In addition to the families staying here more-or-less permanently, we have a constant stream of people at the door hoping we can provide them with a much-needed meal or something to wrap around themselves to keep them warm. We have, each of

us in my family, reduced ourselves to two outfits of clothing and given the rest away. Clothes, shoes, all the basics are seriously wanting, and every now and then there is a banging on the front door and the Germans swarm in and take anything they can find of value, making themselves quite at home, stripping naked in the laundry to wash their clothes and eating everything in the kitchen.

I do not mean to burden you, my dear brother, by telling you what life is like here now, but to inform you, and through you other Americans, about what is happening in Italy as we wait for the Allies to come to our aid. The fact that we continue to be bombed by British and American planes makes this very hard to take, as I'm sure you can understand.

On Christmas Eve she wrote again.

I have now been warned of a new law that calls for the arrest of all American and English women in Italy, and for their transportation to concentration camps. What am I? I ask myself. Certainly many people here know that I am an American by birth, but I have lived so long in Italy that you would not know by my accent. Of course I cannot leave here. Perhaps the strangest thing in all this chaos is the change in myself. Having rejected everything having to do with the position of Renzo's family for so long, I now feel some responsibility on behalf of the Gonzagas to provide for the people in this community. I actually feel that if a Nazi officer showed up here to arrest me I could draw myself up and with a fearsome accent claim the nobility of the Gonzagas. It would not fool Colonel Hoffman, of course, who knows my history through his wife, Greta.

She has, by the way, written to Gianna. I have passed the letters along and hope that Gianna, if she has responded, has done so cautiously. That her actions are too bold for her safety is my constant fear. In this I am joined by Archie, who has worked very hard to keep any attention away from my house.

January 31, 1944

Dear Tommy,

Two days ago the Archiginnasio Library, directly across the Galvani Plaza from my house, was hit by a bomb. The explosion when it hit was ferocious; it knocked me right out of my bed. We very timidly opened the door yesterday to see what was left and found the whole front of that great old building gone. My emotions were very strong and very mixed. On the one hand, I saw how lucky I was that the bomb hadn't been let loose a fraction of a second later than it was, in which case it would be my house that was destroyed and I would be dead. The great church of St. Petronio is so near that it also could easily have been the victim. On the other hand, the destruction of the Library, the original home of the University of Bologna, has distressed me more than I can say.

March 17, 1944

Dear Tommy,

It's St. Paddy's Day in Boston and I am thinking about the parade and celebration on the campus. Our dear old papa will be well remembered today, and I know you and all of our family will be gathered there together. It is so strange to think of normalcy there when all semblance of it is gone here. (I know I should not speak of normalcy to either you or Frank, who have sons fighting.) I wish I could get some real word from you. I imagine and hope that you are writing me and those letters are somewhere in transit across the Atlantic and across Europe, though when I think of all the bags of mail that are sent awry because of the war I wonder if I will ever see anything from you that tells me how you are right now. My own letters wait for known opportunities to send, when someone I know is traveling into neutral Switzerland, or is likely to meet up with an American soldier who is still with a unit that might be able to send messages.

Water is in short supply here now. We no longer have it coming into the house and are getting it from either the Neptune fountain or the old canals, and then boiling it before we drink it or cook with it. Shops are mostly closed, stripped of their contents either by Germans, by partisans, or by starving citizens, and no new stock is coming in.

The next page was in a much shakier hand.

Since I wrote the last I have had terrible news. Patrick has been captured as a partisan. This is the great fear I have lived with for the last year. The Germans have shot, hanged or imprisoned dozens of partisans in the last year and they seem to be increasing their raiding parties to round them up. With so much desperation, homelessness and hunger, hopelessness is the worst malady, and it has led people to do things they would never have done in ordinary circumstances. Patrick may have been betrayed by someone he knew well and trusted, but whose fear of the Nazis was greater than any other feeling.

Gianna is here in the house with me and tells me that Archie is working on a prisoner exchange, which is a common way to deal with the Fascists, but not so common, I think, as a way to deal with the Germans. I must end this now as the courier I expected is here and leaving immediately for Switzerland. When I write again I hope it will be with better news.

April 14, 1944

Dear Tom,

I wish I knew if you were receiving my letters. I guess I write as much for myself, as I feel I need to be keeping some sort of record of what is happening here and I am fearful of keeping a journal lest it be found by the Germans.

The tale I began in such a frenzy of fear last month has been resolved favorably, I'm happy to say. Archie and a small group of partisans captured Col. Franz Hoffman and exchanged him for Patrick's freedom. Patrick is now confined to my house, and Archie and Gianna have gone so far underground that I do not expect to see them for the remainder of the war. German sentries are now a permanent fixture in Galvani Plaza and I know they are there to watch my house. I am extraordinarily lucky to have so many good and trusted friends, but to carry information at this time puts people in danger of immediate execution and I do not want to put anyone in that position; consequently I ask no questions.

September 12, 1944

Dear Tommy,

It has been a hard summer with very little opportunity to get news or send it. The Germans took the radio that we used to listen to the BBC, so we do not know where the Allied armies are on their march through Italy, except with very rare messages. There have been a number of strikes in the factories against the poor working conditions, and they have been brutally suppressed. Many people have returned to the city after depleting the produce and stock in the countryside, and in expectation of an Allied advance, and we have been able to get some much-needed supplies in the process. Not only have Eleonora and Margherita sent us baskets of vegetables and fruits, but the relations of many of the people staying in the house have brought gifts of food for all to share. It seems like such a bounty to see it all piled up on the table, but I know that with the crowd we have we could easily go through it all in a day, and so I am trying to develop some good way to ration it.

I haven't seen my dear Gianna or Archie in more than forty days and messages are simply cryptic declarations of their safety. Patrick would sneak out of the house to join them if he could, but Col. Hoffman has said that I will pay the price if Patrick is not here anytime a German officer stops to check on his whereabouts. Maybe Patrick is relieved to be out of it, I'm not sure. He might have been a supporter of Badoglio or even a monarchist, but too intimidated by Archie and Gianna's ardent communism to ever admit that he thought there might be some advantage to supporting the king.

Hoffman has, of course, not come here since the prisoner exchange, and his viciousness toward the partisans in particular, and Italian people in general, just grows over time. I am wondering how Greta, who was such a lovely girl, could have married such a brute.

October 10, 1944

Word has reached us of a horrifying massacre at Marzabotto, about five miles to the south of us. Some say as many as 1000 of the citizens have been massacred by the Germans in retaliation for their

support of the Resistance, including many women
and children and the five priests in the village. I
am very fearful for Gianna and Archie. That area
is well known to them both, to Gianna especially as
the hills around that town are filled with Etruscan
and Roman ruins and Renzo often took the children there when they were young. If anyone could
hide there, it would be they, but having no word is
terrifying.

10/11/44

I add a quick note to this and will send it to you,
that I have heard G & A are well.

The next letter, dated October 13, 1944, was addressed to
Thomas Kelliher from Giorgio Faccini, an Archaeology professor at the University of Bologna. "Dear Mr. Kelliher," it
began. "I am a friend of your sister, and of her late husband,
and write to tell you what she cannot, the devastating news
that her daughter, Gianna, was murdered yesterday. The
crime was particularly brutal, which makes the telling of the
details extraordinarily painful, but I feel that you must know
all, so that you can support your sister with the full knowledge of her suffering, and because the beasts who did this
must be known for the full extent of their cruelty."

I think you know that Gianna and her husband
Arcangelo have been active members of the Resistance almost since their marriage. Their politics
were no secret in Bologna and though Maggie
herself always remained neutral in her speech and
actions, there was knowledge that she supported
the partisans and their work. Gianna often dis-
guised herself in men's clothing, and she went
frequently to Marzabotto with pamphlets for
distribution there. She knew the hills between
there and Bologna well, and it is believed that she
and A. operated mostly from there, though A. is

known to have traveled much farther and he was
away when she was captured. She had printed
partisan materials with her and could easily have
been arrested, quickly tried, and shot or hanged,
but she was taken to some location where she was
beaten and raped.

The violation of women by German soldiers
happens frequently here, but it is a crime about
which few people speak. Even in war, with violence
so fierce all around us, we let shame keep us from
acknowledging the rape of women. Gianna's body
was so broken and bruised that several people tried
to prevent Maggie from seeing her, but she would
not be kept from taking Gianna up in her arms
and carrying her into the courtyard of the house
where she sat weeping over that sad corpse for the
better part of the day. I was called by Patrizio,
whom I'm sure you know is a rather simple creature. He could not comfort his mother, but neither
could her daughters, who were also called to come
to the house, nor anyone, though your sister has
many friends and is much loved for her kindness.
In the midst of her anguish, the Nazis came again,
demanding that Arcangelo be given to them. The
leader of the group was a particularly nasty brute,
Col. Franz Hoffman, who has some history with
Gianna through his wife. He told Maggie that he
had not only witnessed Gianna's rape, but had
participated in it with others. Had the weight of her
daughter's body not kept her from rising instantly
she would have done something that might have
gotten her killed as well, and I don't think it would
have mattered to her at all.

Arcangelo's whereabouts are not known, though
this attack was aimed to bring him out as much as
to punish Gianna for her crimes. I think that the
only thing that keeps Maggie conscious of her surroundings now is her fear that he will be captured
and killed. I do not think she could survive such a

blow and pray that he will not come storming back to kill Hoffman.

I am sorry to be the bearer of such terrible news. I would wish that you could take your sister into your care, but she insists she will not leave Bologna. We hope for liberation from the Allies, but for the present we are very strongly under the thumb of our German occupiers.

There were no more letters from Maggie to her brother, but Roscoe had scanned one last item from the file, an article from the *Boston Globe* from April 1945, describing the Allies' entry into Bologna.

Chapter 26

When she had measured the last object on the list, photographed it, and entered the data in her computer, Lizzie stood and walked to where Carmine and Martin were examining the mummy case inch by inch with magnifying lenses.

"I'm done," she said.

Martin straightened and put his hand on his lower back. "Done for the day? Or done done?"

"I have finished everything that needs to be done in Bologna, and believe that I can do the rest of my research and writing at home. You, of course, still have a mountain of work to do before everything ships," she said to Carmine.

"Ah, but I'll have prince Beppe here to help!"

Lizzie laughed and reminded him not to let Justin touch anything.

"We have one more full day here before we leave," Martin said to Lizzie. "I'd like to meet Patrizio. Can we do that and still have time to see some paintings?"

Lizzie assured him that they could and the next morning they went to the museums and churches where Martin had identified paintings he wanted to see. In the early afternoon they went to the hospital to see Patrizio.

"I don't know how he'll respond to meeting you," Lizzie said to her husband. "I was almost getting to the point where I thought he recognized me some of the time, but his memory is very unpredictable."

"My curiosity is piqued."

When they walked into his room Patrizio was sitting up in his chair. He looked up and smiled at Lizzie. "I'm so glad you came back. I was hoping you'd visit me again."

Lizzie took his hand and squeezed it. "I'm happy to see you again," she said. When she introduced Martin the old man looked first surprised and then relieved.

He shook Martin's hand vigorously. "I didn't know that you had married," he said to Lizzie. "But I am glad you didn't spend your life alone."

Martin gave his wife a look of confusion and she shook her head almost imperceptibly to keep him from saying anything to Patrizio. She had already told him about the frequent confusion between herself and Theresa Kenney.

"I hope you found love too," Martin said, pulling a chair out and sitting in front of Patrizio. Lizzie sat on the side of the bed.

The old man ran the back of his hand along his jaw and then waved it into the air, as if he took some thought that he would have said and dispersed it instead. He adjusted himself in his seat so that his elbows rested on the arms; he clasped his hands and looked hard at Martin. "I thought I had," he said, his voice hoarse and barely above a whisper. "A German girl, a friend of my sister."

Martin met his eyes but did not say anything.

"I should have married you, Theresa," Patrizio said. He began to laugh but it turned into coughing and Lizzie put a hand on his shoulder until it stopped. He reached up and patted her hand. "You were a good girl, and I think you liked me."

"I did," she said. "I do."

He thanked her. "That other woman," he continued softly, "Greta Winkler. She didn't really like me. It was a game for her and after a summer of flirting she went back to Germany and married an officer named Franz Hoffman. He came here, you know, to Bologna during the war."

Lizzie and Martin each murmured something about knowing of Hoffman and Patrizio seemed surprised. "How do you know?" he said, a tinge of urgency or fear in his voice.

"Your mother wrote about him in a letter," Lizzie answered. "That he was in Bologna."

This seemed to satisfy Patrizio and he nodded. "Of course. It would have been my mother. But how much did she tell you?"

"Only that he was in Bologna and that he had married Gianna's friend."

He seemed very frail, his hands like claws as he twisted them around and around each other. "May I tell you what happened?" he asked. "I have never told anyone."

Lizzie nodded.

"Archie killed Hoffman," he said abruptly, stopping the motion of his hands and squeezing them tightly together. "Even though the bastard never went anywhere without guards, Archie waited and waited for him, each day lying on a rooftop with a rifle pointed at the Strada Maggiore, knowing he must eventually pass that way. Archie wanted to capture Hoffman and torture him, as he had tortured Gianna—and he didn't care if he was himself killed in the attempt—but he wanted to be sure that Hoffman died at his hands and thought that this was the only way he could be sure."

Franz Hoffman had, eventually, driven down that street and Archie received news of it even before the car left the German headquarters. "He was so calm and steady," Patrizio said. "I was with him that day and I was so nervous and jumpy. He tried to get me to go away, but I wouldn't, and I was lying beside him as he pulled the trigger that sent the bullet into Hoffman's heart. It was a beautiful shot," he said hoarsely. "Right through the window of his car and into his heart. If I hadn't already believed in the righteousness of retribution, I would have been converted at that moment. We scrambled away and there were partisans all along our path who covered our tracks and protected us. No one was sorry to see Hoffman die."

"Greta?" Martin said, almost to himself. "I wonder if she was sorry."

At that, the old man put one hand in front of his eyes and began to cry. "Ah Greta," he sobbed. "Archie believed that she had informed on Gianna to her husband, even though my mother tried to convince him that it wasn't so. Mama thought that Greta was also a victim of Hoffman, but Archie wouldn't have it. When she came here..." His shoulders convulsed as he wept, and the sound, little more than a whimper, was so pitiful that Lizzie and Martin looked at each other anxiously. Finally Lizzie asked him when Greta had returned to Bologna.

"In 1955," he said. He began to speak rapidly in Italian, gesturing with his hands to indicate directions traveled and at one point made a motion of firing a pistol. Lizzie reached into her bag and turned on the recording function on her cell phone. He spoke in a constant stream for over twenty minutes, while his audience sat frozen at either side, fearing that any motion would break the flow, with consequences that they could not predict. There was finally a point at which he seemed to finish his narrative and then he looked from one of them to the other and nodded. He folded his hands in his lap and closed his eyes.

Lizzie and Martin continued to sit motionless for another several minutes, looking at each other, trying to silently communicate their questions about whether they should sneak away or try to speak again to Patrizio. Finally a nurse came in and told them it was time for her patient to return to his bed. He opened his eyes and saw Lizzie.

"Hello," he said. "I'm so happy you came again to see me. You are from St. Patrick's College aren't you?"

She said that she was.

"My grandfather founded St. Pat's," he said. "And I was a student there."

"I know that," she said. She could not help looking to see if the copy she had brought of *Patrick Kelliher, Immigrant Industrialist* was still in the room, then thought better of giving it to him again. She leaned down and kissed the old man on the forehead. "And now you are the patriarch of the family," she said.

"Si," he said. "Sono il capofamiglia—but Cosimo doesn't think so."

The nurse stepped between them just as Lizzie was about to ask Patrick to elaborate and the moment was lost.

"What do you think that was about?" Martin asked as they walked to the car.

"I have no idea whatsoever."

"And I guess we'll never know."

Lizzie admitted that she had recorded the whole of Patrizio's soliloquy. "When I get it translated, I think we will hear a very interesting story."

Chapter 27

The last image that Lizzie had of the library at the Gonzaga Palazzo was a startling contrast to the first sight of it. Gone was the alligator, leaving a bare ceiling. The surface of the table was bare—the globes were now in the ballroom being packed for shipping to Boston. Many of the cases were empty. She had replaced the ledgers on the shelf, locked the grate that covered it and slipped the key back into its customary spot at the edge of the shelf.

Patrizio had been sitting here the first time she entered the room, and she couldn't help thinking with regret of how the old man would feel to see the alteration in his library, his life. He had once called her a thief, and he would certainly do so again if he saw her here now. But she had strong doubts that he would come home. He certainly couldn't go back to living here with Graziella after everything that had transpired. If he came back to the house he would need more support.

From the library, Lizzie went into the ballroom and here her regrets turned to excitement. The collection would be a sensation in Boston, she had no doubt of that. She said good-bye to Carmine, with the hope that he would be able to come see the exhibit soon after its installation and they had a last word about the management of Justin when he arrived in a few months.

It was strange to enter the familiar library of St. Patrick's College the next day. Lizzie was still drowsy from the overnight flight, but she could not wait to bring Jackie and her assistants up to date on the work she had done in Bologna. Now that the object list was finalized, the work turned to researching each object and writing the catalog.

Justin wasn't clear exactly why he was still expected to go

to Bologna, and Lizzie wasn't either, but off he went at the end
of April to meet Carmine and be lectured by his uncle. Lizzie did not, of course, trust him to have anything to do with
the packing and shipping of the collection. Carmine would
supervise the packing and a fine arts shipping firm had been
hired to help. They had already devised a system for marking
each object and the crate in which it would be shipped. Lizzie
gave Justin a copy of the master list, with instructions to mark
off each object when it left the house.

A few weeks later she went to Logan Airport to meet the
Al Italia flight with Father O'Toole, her interns, the exhibit
designer, and the College's attorney, who had completed the
customs paperwork. The Italian consul to Boston met them
there and greeted Father O'Toole with an embrace of arms
and kisses on both cheeks.

It had been necessary to have declarations for each piece,
along with licenses from the Italian government to remove
works of art with significant cultural value, even for a loan
exhibition, as well as paperwork saying that the items would
be returned, that none would be confiscated while in the U.S.

The campus museum had undergone extensive renova-
tions to receive the valuable Gonzaga collections. The galler-
ies had been upgraded with new temperature and humidity
controls, and a state-of-the-art security system had been installed. When the collection arrived, each crate was removed
from the truck to the loading dock and the bar codes applied by Carmine and the shipping company were scanned.
Crate after crate was moved into the exhibit staging area and
opened; the more fragile objects would rest in their crates for
a few days to adjust to the conditions in the museum. The
photographer, who would take the pictures that would appear
in the catalog, pestered Lizzie with questions about which
objects would need to appear in color and which in black and
white, and began to set up a place to do his work at one end
of the staging area.

It was a few days before everything had been placed on tables in the staging area and Lizzie finally found herself alone
with the collection after a long day of work. She had not yet
had a chance to be able to contemplate the artifacts in their

new surroundings and it was still strange to see the alligator, the giant marble foot, the narwhal tusk and the Marquesan club here.

"Everything okay here, Prof. Manning?"

She jumped when the security guard spoke. "Yes thanks," she said. "I'm going to stay and work for an hour or so more."

When the guard left she went from object to object. In the flurry of activity surrounding the unpacking of the crates it was impossible to ponder the exquisite character of individual works, but now she moved very slowly along the table on which the things had been laid out. The three reliquaries stood together at one long end of the first table. There was the magnificent Reni portrait of the Madonna and the dell'Arca angel, which had been moved here from the chapel. Beside them the *Draco dandinii* smiled upon his perch, and the eel looked out from its watery jar. She had chosen five Chinese vases in different sizes, but all with blue and white designs, and they were placed rather randomly in and among the two large globes, various skeletons, and bronze figures and containers large and small.

Lizzie moved all the marble figures and fragments away from the fragile glass items, though as she gently placed the ancient Etruscan blue-glass bracelet on the table she had to acknowledge that it was sturdier than it looked. The objective of the day had been to make everything visible and be sure that everything on the object list had arrived in good condition. Tomorrow they would start to put like things together for a last conservation inspection, and then organize them by their arrangement in the exhibit.

At the end of one table the sarcophagus was still strapped to a wheeled cart. Within the next few days she would need to invite Prof. Haworth to examine it with her and to make a final translation of the hieroglyphs so that she could write the label. He had already made some comments from her photos, but he was anxious to see the real thing. Colleagues from local museums had also asked to have a close look at some of the items before they went into exhibit cases and she would have Roscoe set up a schedule for that as well. Tomorrow,

Father O'Toole, the Italian consul, members of the Kelliher family and major donors would make an official visit to acknowledge the arrival of the collection. Usually this was a tiresome but necessary part of the process, but Lizzie looked forward to sharing what she had learned with Father O'Toole.

There was still one crate in the back of the loading dock, but it wasn't on her list and Lizzie couldn't find a bar code or shipping label on it. She didn't think it could have come in with her shipment, but she also didn't remember seeing it there when she had inspected the space to make sure it was set up to receive the collections. The tools that the workers had used to unpack the boxes were still lying on the floor and she took a crowbar and carefully pried off the lid. Inside, a large object was carefully fitted into a Styrofoam mold. Moving the covering Lizzie found herself looking at the mummy.

"Shit!" she said angrily. "Shit, shit, shit!" If she had not been alone she would have insisted that someone instantly get Justin Carrere so that she could shake him. "Calm yourself," she said quietly. "You cannot attack a student, especially one whose family is paying for this exhibit, but Shit! What an idiot!" She called Jackie to complain. "That idiot Carrera! I gave him a *very* short list of assignments related to this project, and the first thing on the list was don't send anything that isn't on the final list."

"Can I come see the mummy?" Jackie answered predictably.

"I guess so," Lizzie said. "There isn't anyone here but me."

"And your mummy!" Jackie added.

"Yes, just me and my mummy. Come visit."

Lizzie continued to sort through the collection, moving some things from one table to another so that she could see how they looked together. When Jackie called to tell her that she was at the outside door, Lizzie went to open it and found that John Haworth was with her.

"I called John," Jackie said. "He'd like to meet your mummy too."

Lizzie gestured for them to come in and led the way. They stopped first at the sarcophagus, which John was very excited to see.

"It's in superb condition, just like you said. I've already written some things about it for your catalog from the pictures you sent me."

"Where's the mummy?" Jackie said insistently.

Lizzie pointed to the crate lying open on the floor across the room. "You warned me, John, that I would need a special permit to bring it here and I don't have anything like it. I did *no* paperwork for it; it wasn't supposed to be shipped and it doesn't even have a proper shipping label."

He rubbed his hands together gleefully. "Then we'll have an even better story to tell!" He stopped short when he looked into the box. "What is it?" he asked unexpectedly.

"It's a mummy of course," Jackie answered.

"From where?"

"Isn't it an Egyptian mummy of the eighteenth dynasty?" Lizzie asked. "Isn't it the mummy that was in that case?"

John dropped to his knees and touched the head of the mummy. "I'm not sure what it is, but it isn't the mummy that came in that case." He turned and looked up at Lizzie. "I told you that the original mummy was probably brought to Europe to be ground into medical potions. This is ..." He stopped for a moment and ran his hands along the length of the corpse. "I'm not sure what this is. Can we take it out of the box?"

Lizzie cleared a table that had only a few artifacts on it and the three of them moved the mummy onto it.

"Come on, John," Jackie said insistently. "It's obviously a mummy!"

John rolled his head as if trying to nod in assent but ending up shaking it in a gesture of disagreement. "There's something wrong here. It is a human corpse that has been desiccated somehow and wrapped in linen soaked in a resin. But the materials don't seem right, and the wrapping mostly follows the right pattern but there is just something weird about it."

"What should we do?" Lizzie asked.

"Let's get it x-rayed," John answered. "Let's just take it over to the campus clinic and run it through the fluoroscope." He touched the mummy's head again, pressing along the ridge of the nose. "I'm sorry we don't have a CT scan or an MRI, we could get better detail."

Lizzie paused. "I don't have permission to do anything like that. This thing isn't even supposed to be here."

"Oh come on, Lizzie," Jackie urged. "You have a mystery here and can find out more about it."

"I don't know," she said. "How will we even transport it? Do we need to call an ambulance? Or a hearse?"

John laughed. "Of course not. I'm an archaeologist; I have a truck. I'll just go get it and bring it up to the loading dock door." He was already halfway across the room as he finished. "I'll call Ross Wiley to meet us; he's a radiologist and is on call at the clinic."

"Oy!" Lizzie turned to Jackie with a look of helplessness. "What have you gotten me into?"

Jackie smiled broadly in return. "Something interesting, I hope."

"Is Ross Wiley any relation to Roscoe, my intern?"

"His father, I think."

"Well, at least we can try to keep this in the family while I figure out what I need to do to make it all legal and proper."

When John came back he carried a backboard, the sort of thing used to carry an injured person out of the wilderness. "I always keep it in my van in case someone gets hurt in the field." With the help of Lizzie and Jackie, he lifted the mummy onto it, and with him on one side and Lizzie and Jackie on the other they carried it to his waiting vehicle.

"Good thing he wasn't very big or heavy," Jackie said.

"He was bigger and heavier when he was alive," John explained. "But he was pretty short, as were most Egyptians. Ramses the Great was six feet tall, but most of the other pharaohs were in the five-foot range." He continued to talk about matters of this sort as they made the short drive across campus to Health Services.

It was a slow evening and there was no doctor on duty, but the nurse recognized the three when they came in with their strange request. John Haworth was a not-infrequent visitor with various items that needed a closer look for identification.

"Ross Wiley is meeting us," he explained to the nurse. Then he turned to Lizzie and Jackie and whispered, "Probably best to leave the body in the van until Ross is ready for it."

The three sat side-by-side in the molded plastic chairs of the waiting room. Jackie was ecstatic, John was interested, and Lizzie was worried—worried that there might be repercussions to this that would at the very least take her away from the work that had to be done to get the exhibit completed, and at the very worst damage her reputation and the College's.

When Ross Wiley arrived, his son Roscoe and Jimmy Moe were with him. Jimmy was even more excited than Jackie at the prospect of seeing the mummy.

"I thought the mummy wasn't coming," he said, adding that he was glad Lizzie had changed her mind and brought it.

"I didn't," she said, pulling her interns aside. "The mummy got shipped by mistake. I'm not sure yet how to handle this, but I need you two to promise me that you won't say anything about this to anyone else."

As they nodded, Roscoe's father came up and put a hand on his son's shoulder. He asked for an introduction, which was quickly given.

"I hope you don't mind that I brought the boys along. They were working on your project at our house when John called me."

Lizzie gave a forced smile and lied. "No problem," she said, "but I've asked them not to talk about it outside this circle."

Dr. Wiley winked at her and smiled. "Of course. So where is this mummy?"

As they spoke, John Haworth led Roscoe and Jimmy out to his van and soon after they came through the automatic doors of the clinic with the mummy on the backboard. Dr. Wiley led them to the x-ray suite where they laid it on a bed that had a machine mounted above it that could be moved over any part of the body.

"We'll have to do this in several stages to get the whole corpse," he said. "Where do you want to start, head or feet?"

He directed the question at Lizzie, but John Haworth answered it.

"Feet," he said. "It has been charred there and I'm curious to see if there is any damage inside the wrapping." He turned to Lizzie and said, "It's probably a fake and the wrappings were burned on purpose to make it look old."

"If we are just having a look for our own interest, we'll use the fluoroscope and not bother with a permanent image," Ross Wiley explained as he aimed the machine at the mummy's feet. "Then we won't have to worry about who will pay for it. You will all have to step outside for a minute."

When they returned, there was an image on the screen showing the bones of two feet and the calf bones attached to them. "Nothing out of the ordinary here," the doctor said. "A healthy person of maybe thirty or so, no damage from the charring you saw on the wrapping."

The process was repeated at the knees, thighs, and pelvis.

"I was already suspecting this was a female from the alignment of the femur to the knees, but now I can confirm it," he said as he pointed at the pelvic arch on the screen.

"Had it been a man, the penis would have been wrapped separately and be very obvious," John Haworth added.

"You give us so much to think about, John," Jackie said as they once again left the room and the x-ray machine was moved up to the abdominal and then chest areas, which had been emptied of the major organs.

"The heart was left," John pointed out. "It was thought to be the source of both love and intellect. The other organs were usually mummified separately and placed in a series of four canopic jars."

"What about the brain?" Jimmy asked.

"That was usually removed piece by piece through the nose."

Various looks of surprise, disgust and awe were exchanged among the party.

"Well I'm ready to do the head now," Dr. Wiley announced, sending them once again from the room. "When you come back we'll see if that was done to this corpse."

There was animated chatter among the five people waiting in the anteroom regarding mummies, the removal of brains, upcoming tasks that needed to be done for the exhibit, and how John Haworth's essay would fit into Lizzie's catalog. When the door opened they all stood up to see the x-rayed head of the mummy, but Dr. Wiley said he only wanted to see John. "And perhaps you better come too, Lizzie," he added after a few seconds.

Jackie and Jimmy were clearly disappointed that they were being left out of learning something that must be interesting if it had to be secret, and both said so, but Lizzie ignored them as she went back into the room where the mummy lay stretched out under the x-ray machine.

"What do you know about this mummy?" the doctor asked as he closed the door.

"Only that it comes from the collection of a family in Bologna," Lizzie said. "I don't know when or how they acquired it."

"It's no ancient Egyptian."

"I knew that," John Haworth said. "So what or who is it?"

Ross Wiley used a pencil to point at the image on the screen, but before had a chance to speak John gave a gasp of surprise, and even Lizzie had seen enough of her own dental x-rays to recognize that this mummy had fillings.

"I didn't realize they had dentistry in Egypt," she said hesitantly.

"They didn't, not like this," John said with authority.

"There's more," Ross said. "Look at this." He pointed to a small white mass at the back of the skull. "There was some attempt to pull the brains out, and there has been a resin of some type poured back in, but the murderer failed to get the bullet."

John nodded as if he had recognized it, but Lizzie was totally shocked by the news. "Bullet?" she said, and then "murderer?" She felt her legs weaken and reached out to hold onto the table. "What are you saying?"

"I'm saying that this is the corpse of a young woman who was murdered. She was shot below her right ear with a small caliber gun."

"When?" Lizzie asked, her voice shaking from the news.

"I don't know," Ross answered. "I can send the film of the head to a forensic dentist I know who might be able to date the material and the method of the fillings, but you realize that I have to call the police."

"Of course," Lizzie said. She moved to the only chair in the room and sat down. Her first thoughts were of the meeting tomorrow with Father O'Toole, Jim Kelliher and the cardinal. They were all coming to see the collection. "What should we do with it, or rather her?" she asked.

"I suspect that even though the victim clearly wasn't killed here and the crime probably isn't in the jurisdiction of the Boston Police Department, the coroner's office will still want to take the corpse and do an autopsy," Ross Wiley answered.

"So they'll have to unwrap the mummy," John Haworth said. "I think I'll offer my services for that."

"'Unwrap' is probably a nicety they won't bother with. They'll probably just cut the cloth off."

"If that's so, then I'm going to take a few samples of the cloth and the resin back to my lab and see what they're made of."

Neither Lizzie nor the doctor objected, and John found a pair of scissors in one of the drawers, as well as forceps and a small plastic cup for the samples.

"What should we tell the boys?" Ross asked.

"As little as possible," Lizzie answered. "I know this will sound uncharitable in light of discovering the nature of this poor woman's violent death, but it couldn't come at a worse time as far as my exhibit is concerned. It is bound to hit the news in a fairly sensational way."

"Who do you think she is?" John asked.

"I have no idea," Lizzie answered, then asked him questions of her own. "How long ago do you think she was mummified? Can you tell by the bandages?"

He shook his head. "Probably decades ago, but how many I just can't say. Ross's dentist friend is probably our best bet in establishing a timeline."

While they spoke, Ross called the police and when he hung up he said they would be there within a half hour. "Someone needs to take the boys home," he said. "Would your friend Jackie do that?"

"Only if she can come back. Jackie will not like being sent away when she learns about this."

Lizzie went into the waiting area and pulled Jackie aside to explain the situation, then told Roscoe and Wiley only that there was something strange about the mummy and they would need to do more work on it.

"I'm coming back!" Jackie whispered to Lizzie as she left.

Lizzie called Martin to tell him she would be late coming home. It was almost six o'clock and as she turned off her cell phone she heard the police arriving.

The campus policeman on duty arrived at the same time as the Boston Police cruiser with two uniformed patrolmen. They said that a couple of homicide detectives were also on their way, as they understood a murder had taken place.

"Where is the victim?" one of the officers asked.

Ross led them to the bed where the mummy lay.

"Is this a joke?"

"Of course not," Ross answered angrily. "It's not a recent murder, but it is a murder."

"From a thousand years ago?"

"No. It's not an ancient Egyptian."

John could not help interjecting that the mummies of ancient Egyptians were a lot more than a thousand years old. "From about 2600 B.C. to about 360 A.D.," he said.

Ross rolled his eyes and interrupted to explain that the victim was a modern woman. As he pointed to the image of the bullet on the fluoroscope the detectives arrived.

"So this was recent?" one asked, approaching the mummy and putting on a pair of latex gloves.

"She was shot in the head," John said bluntly.

"When?"

"We don't know."

"Today?"

"No."

"This week?"

"No."

"Do you know where the murder took place?"

"I believe it was in or near Bologna, Italy," Lizzie said. "That's where the mummy came from."

One of the detectives turned to her and handed her his card. "Who are you?" he asked.

Lizzie explained her connection to the corpse. "St. Pat's College is borrowing a number of things from an Italian family for an exhibition that opens in September. This mummy was in an Egyptian sarcophagus and wasn't actually supposed to be shipped here." She was afraid he was going to ask her about export permits and human remains and was preparing her answers, but he quickly moved on.

"So the victim wasn't shot here in Boston."

"Definitely not."

"Okay," he said slowly, turning to Ross. "You're the doctor here?"

Ross said that he was.

"Any idea on a time of death?"

"None whatsoever."

"Not even to a decade or a century?"

"She has fillings in her teeth, so I assume she was killed in the twentieth century, but without more evidence I wouldn't care to speculate as to a decade."

The coroner arrived and the same information was exchanged again as the mummy was transferred to their gurney and taken away.

"Alrighty then," the head detective said, closing the book in which he had been taking notes. "Let's see what the coroner has to say."

Chapter 28

Jackie insisted on coming home with Lizzie that evening to talk about the strange turn of events with the mummy.

"Who do you think it is?" she asked over and over again.

"How could I possibly know the answer to that?" Lizzie answered just as often.

Martin asked her if she should contact someone in the Gonzaga family to warn them in case the police contacted them.

"Oh my god! I should call Father O'Toole and warn him! He's coming to see the collection tomorrow." She dialed the personal number of the college president and when he answered she began to explain.

"What do you mean it was shipped accidentally?" was his first question. His voice was so controlled that Lizzie couldn't tell if he was angry.

"The conservator and I removed the mummy from the sarcophagus because I didn't think it was essential for the exhibit, and consequently I didn't go through the process of getting the required paperwork to bring it here. He made a box to store it in and it was in a separate part of the room and never even had a shipping label put on it. But somehow it got sent anyway." She longed to add, "It must be that idiot Justin Carrere, who I knew was going to be a problem the first day I met him!" Instead she waited silently for him to respond.

"And explain again why the police are involved?"

"Professor Haworth and I had been corresponding about the sarcophagus and I told him about the mummy. He came to see it, it seemed odd to him, and we decided to take it to the infirmary to x-ray it. That's when we found that it wasn't an ancient Egyptian, but a more modern person who had been shot in the head."

"Do you have any idea who it is?"

"I'm sorry, father, but I don't."

"Can you please figure that out very quickly so that we can control this situation?" He hung up the phone before Lizzie had a chance to respond.

She looked at Martin and Jackie. "He wants me to identify the corpse."

"Hold on a second," Martin said. "You will recall that you have been in situations not unlike this before and were almost killed. If there's a murder victim, then there is a murderer, and he might not be so happy that his well-concealed corpse has suddenly been discovered."

"If he's still alive," Jackie added. "You need to figure out when the victim died."

"Ross Wiley said that a forensic dentist might be able to say something about when and where her fillings were put in. I think I'll call him."

"And I think we should get John Haworth over here to help us," Jackie added. "He's the mummy specialist," she said as an aside to Martin.

"This could be a mafia thing," Martin said. "You have no idea what you are getting into."

Lizzie put her hand up as a plea for silence. "Let me just think for a minute. Why would the mafia store a corpse in the Gonzaga house?"

"Hiding in plain sight?" Jackie offered.

Lizzie put her hand up again and shook her head. "No. If the books and movies are right, they want bodies to disappear."

She had to put her hand up a third time as both her companions began to object. "I know, we can't depend on novels and movies for factual information, but let me just continue to work through this." She walked back and forth across the room and thought through her visit to the Gonzaga house from the day she arrived in Bologna. What had she heard about the mummy case?

"It must be Patrick," she said. "Patrizio Gonzaga. He beat

his nephew once for trying to open the sarcophagus, and he even told me that he went to Egypt, and studied the subject at the University." She clapped her hands together and looked from Martin to Jackie and back. "I think he might actually have told me that he knew enough about mummies to make one!"

"That crazy old man?" Martin tried to rein in her enthusiasm. "Are you saying he's a murderer?"

"Not necessarily," Lizzie answered, saying the word so slowly that she hissed through the start of each syllable. Then she thought aloud, speaking as much to herself as to the others. "What if he just wanted to make a mummy as an experiment, wanted to see what it was like, and got hold of a corpse to try it."

"How would he get the corpse of a murder victim?" Martin asked.

Lizzie stopped her pacing and turned to him again. "During the war!" she said. "He could easily have gotten a corpse during the war."

"And where would he have made the mummy? You told me that there were a hundred people living in the house then, so it certainly wasn't there."

"That is a problem," Lizzie said, starting to pace again. "And even the caves around the city were filled with people then, partisans, escaped prisoners, people fleeing bombs..."

"Would the coroner ever have given him an unclaimed body for such a grisly experiment?" Jackie asked.

Lizzie thought about this for a moment. "He certainly had good contacts at the University, and they have a big anatomical collection, but beyond that, I don't know." She rotated on her heel and looked at Jackie. "That would mean that this wasn't during the war, but either before or after."

"Which seems more likely?"

"Af-ter," she said, again dividing her words into their separate components as she thought and talked at the same time. "After the war. He went to Egypt with his mother after the war, and that's when he got interested in mummies."

There was a knock at the door and Martin went to answer it, returning a few minutes later with one of the two detectives who had come to claim the corpse at the campus clinic. He

was accompanied by a woman he introduced as Ann Crandall, another homicide detective. Ann asked a few questions
of everyone in the room and then requested a private audience with Lizzie.

As she shook Lizzie's hand, Ann explained that she frequently was part of investigations where the victim was a
young woman, especially if there were extraordinary circumstances. "Mummification definitely counts as an extraordinary circumstance," she said. "From what I've heard so far,
this is probably not going to be a high priority for my department, as it seems likely that the crime was committed outside
our jurisdiction. But until we are certain of that, I want to get
the investigation started."

"Of course," Lizzie said, nodding.

"Do you have any idea who she is?"

The detective looked steadily at Lizzie, holding her gaze
until Lizzie looked away, thinking that this must be a very
effective way to either catch guilty people in lies, or make
innocent people feel guilty.

She looked down at her hands, then up to meet Ann's
steady gaze. "I don't know who she is."

"Do you have a hunch?"

"No. Not even the slightest notion of who she might be."

Ann made a quick note on the pad she carried. "Do you
know who killed her?"

Again Lizzie said no. Even if she thought that Patrizio
might have mummified the corpse, she couldn't imagine him
shooting a woman in the head. Her thought must have made
some small change in the movement of her eyes or hands, or
some alteration in her expression, because Ann seemed to
sense that she might actually know something that could be
important but was hesitant to share it.

"What is it?" she asked softly, then waited silently for Lizzie to answer.

"I don't want to say anything that will make you suspicious
of a person who is probably innocent of all wrongdoing," Lizzie said.

"Tell me what you are thinking and I'll tell you if it is relevant," Ann said.

"I have an *idea* of who might have mummified her, but I don't necessarily think that should make him a suspect in her death."

"Why would he mummify her if he didn't kill her?"

"As an experiment."

"And how would he get her body for such an experiment?"

"From the coroner, or from the University of Bologna's anatomy lab—which might have been given her corpse if she were unidentified and unclaimed."

"When would this have been?" Ann asked.

Lizzie answered that she suspected it had happened in the 1950s or 60s.

"I believe you said that you found this mummy in a private house?" Ann continued.

Lizzie nodded and Ann asked her for the details. As she gave the detective information to contact Cosimo Gonzaga, Lizzie realized that she had better call him immediately so that he would know what was happening when the Italian police began banging on his door.

When Ann left, Lizzie did just that. She knew she would catch Cosimo in the middle of the night, but had such a feeling of urgency about the situation that she dialed directly to his personal number without hesitating.

"Salve," came the answer, in a voice that indicated he had been waked from sleeping.

"Cosimo," Lizzie said urgently. "A situation has developed here that you need to know about."

"Who is this?" he demanded.

"It's Lizzie Manning," she answered. "I'm calling from Boston."

He began to sound both more awake and more civil. "Lizzie," he said, "how can I help you? Has something happened in the shipping of the collection?"

"Yes, but be assured that nothing is damaged. Unexpectedly, the mummy was sent here."

"The mummy?" He was clearly confused. "You weren't expecting it?"

"No. For several reasons I decided to leave it behind. It required a special license and there were other complications that I didn't want to deal with. Carmine made a case to store it in while the sarcophagus was traveling, and by accident it was shipped here."

"Beppe..." he started.

Later she would love to surrender Justin to his uncle for punishment, but knew this was not the time.

"The mummy is not an ancient Egyptian," she said quickly, before he could ask about his nephew. She explained everything that had happened as concisely as she could, cringing as she admitted that she had allowed the mummy to be x-rayed without his permission. "I'm afraid that you will be contacted about this by the police," she said, concluding her speech. There was a long silence and then he spoke angrily in Italian and hung up the phone. The only word she had recognized was the name of his uncle, Patrizio.

# Chapter 29

The coroner confirmed what they already expected. The victim was a woman in her thirties, shot in the head with a small caliber bullet.

"The bullet was homemade," Ann Crandall explained to Lizzie. "Our lab says a mixture of metals formed in a mold."

"Could it have been left over from World War II?" Lizzie asked.

"I don't know, but I have people checking on it."

"What about the fillings? Were you able to give her a date from them?"

The detective opened her notebook. "Apparently this woman had her first fillings in Germany in the 1930s." She glanced up at Lizzie. "The forensic dentist gave me an earful about 'amalgam wars,' when a German scientist began to sound the alarm about mercury poisoning from fillings and the composition of the materials in the amalgam changed. There is also some acrylic bonding material in her mouth that is recognizable as work pioneered in Switzerland in the late 40s or early 50s."

"I don't suppose they can identify her from dental records," Lizzie said.

Ann shook her head. "We have sent a copy of what we have to Interpol, but the agent I spoke to there says that pre-war records from Germany are very sketchy, and unless we can give them some idea of who the woman is they don't really have a good place to start." She once again gave Lizzie the detective's gaze. "Do you want to tell me anything more about the man you think might have mummified the victim?"

It sounded so strange to be calling the mummy "the victim." Lizzie had previously thought of it as an artifact. She had actually picked it up and moved it around both in Bologna and Boston. It had been so easy to disconnect herself from the notion of the mummy as a corpse, a "victim." And what about Patrizio? He was such a pathetic old man, and from things she had read about him in Maggie's correspondence he had always been a follower rather than a leader. Would he have had the imagination to mummify a corpse on his own?

"I'm hesitant to speak about any of this," Lizzie said. "I don't think that my opinion is relevant, and I don't want to cast suspicion on someone merely because he is eccentric." She hesitated. "I'm sorry I mentioned this to you, because I really don't know anything about what happened to this women... the victim."

Ann spared her the look, but spoke intensely. "I think that your instincts on this might be very helpful. They might help me get closer to the facts." She looked up again to catch Lizzie's eye. "And just because you give me a name doesn't mean that man gets arrested and charged with a crime. He might be a link, though, to whoever killed this poor woman." Another pause. "Even if she died a long ago time ago and far away she deserves our time and consideration."

"You're good at this," Lizzie said admiringly. "You make me want to tell you, even against my own judgment."

"Well, until Mr. Cosimo Gonzaga arrives from Italy this evening, you're all I have."

The room seemed to darken and Lizzie groaned. "Oh no. Cosimo is on his way here?"

The morning had been awful, trying to explain to Father O'Toole, Jim Kelliher, the cardinal and the Italian Consulate that the corpse of a murder victim had inadvertently been shipped to Boston to be part of her exhibit. They had been confused, angry, self-important and judgmental. Cosimo would be much, much worse. He had always had a slick patina of stylish niceness in Lizzie's company in Bologna, but she had a feeling that under that could be a dark, dark interior.

"Oh no," she said again.

Ann Crandall waited. "Are you going to tell me something?" she asked finally.

"No," Lizzie said emphatically. "I am going to see what Cosimo Gonzaga has to say about it first." She did not think she was under any obligation to answer the detective's questions. She wasn't a suspect in the case, but she could see that Ann was surprised by her sudden change of heart. She rose abruptly and went to the door.

"I'm sorry I need to meet with students in a few minutes," she said.

Ann gave her the detective's look, shook hands and left the room.

It was very hard to concentrate for the rest of the day on everything that still needed to be done on the exhibit. The designer and fabricators were busy building the cases and mounts and she wanted to be there whenever anyone was handling the collection. Jimmy and Roscoe had been faithful to their word and she heard no mention of the mummy as she worked with them and the museum staff.

John Haworth came in at the end of the day and was not so circumspect. "I did a quick glance under the microscope at the linen and resin samples I took from the mummy, and compared them to the data bases on those materials," he said, talking as he came into the room. "You won't be surprised to learn that they are Italian manufactures. The resin is the same stuff they use on violin bows, a pine sap, and chemically not at all similar to the bitumen found in the Egyptian desert. It's hard to put a date to it, but the linen is consistent with what got produced on twentieth-century industrial looms."

Lizzie took him aside and whispered to him what she had learned from Detective Ann Crandall. "Keep this quiet, John," she said earnestly. "All I need is for this to show up on someone's Facebook page and it will be all over the Internet."

"And you don't think that would create more interest in your exhibit when it opens?"

"I don't want that kind of interest, and the mummy is not going to be on exhibit anyway." She put her hand to her face and massaged her temple with her fingertips. "Gad," she said. "Father O'Toole is going to freak out when Cosimo Gonzaga gets here, which should be any minute now."

She went back to her work: alligator, check, it had traveled safely, been beautifully restored by Carmine Moreale and would be one of the first things visitors would see when they came into the exhibit. Dell'Arca angel, check. Lizzie resisted putting her hand on the smooth marble of the carving as she checked it against her list. She had been rigorous in her instructions with her interns and everyone else involved in the process that nothing was to be touched with bare hands. Latex gloves were required for everything. She looked at the narwhal tusk and its fabulous stand, at the jars of bugs and reptiles, the books and prints, the Marquesan club, the Madonna painting by Guido Reni. The collection was wonderful, the exhibit would be the highlight of her career, a fitting way to celebrate the college's centennial. A scandal over the mummified corpse of a murder victim being included in the collection would now probably overwhelm every other story about it. The only question was when the story would become public.

The answer came soon enough. Jackie called to tell her that the *Boston Globe* website had the story in advance of their print edition, and Jimmy rather sheepishly approached her to tell her that he had gotten a number of messages from friends who knew he was working on the exhibit and had seen the story on numerous Internet sites. When she looked at her own email at the end of the workday there were more than twenty messages, including several from local television stations and both the *Boston Globe* and the *New York Times*. There was also a message from the director of public relations for the College, saying he would like to speak to her about how to respond to the story. Reluctantly, she picked up her phone and called him; he said he would come right over, with Cosimo Gonzaga and Father O'Toole, who were in his office.

"Shit, shit, shit," she said. She wished for the old days of a heavy phone with a receiver that could be slammed onto the hook, but she sensed that she was being watched by Jimmy and Roscoe, who were now the only other people left in the room.

"I promise you I didn't say anything," Jimmy said, his voice a mixture of fear and hope. Roscoe quietly echoed the comment.

She looked at the two young men who had come to stand

before her and assured them that she didn't hold either of them responsible. "Once a police report got filed someone was bound to see it," she said. "I trust both of you. Don't worry." She tried to sound calm, even assured. "You guys have worked so hard and I appreciate it." She told them they should go, as she didn't want them here when Cosimo Gonzaga arrived.

The door swung out as they left, and back in with Cosimo Gonzaga, Father O'Toole, and the college's PR director.

The three men greeted her politely. Cosimo was even friendly.

"Elizabeta," he said, kissing her hand. He had never called her that when she met him in Bologna.

"Cosimo," she said, nodding her head. "I'm glad to see you again, I'm just sorry about this weird business with the mummy."

"Have you figured out who it is?" Father O'Toole asked her.

She shook her head. "I'm sorry Father. I don't even know where to start on this."

Cosimo took her arm and walked a few steps with her. "Let us talk about this and see what we can come up with."

Lizzie allowed him to lead her further away from the other men, on the pretext that they were looking at various parts of the collection spread out on the tables.

When he spoke again it was very softly and directly into her ear. "It was Patrizio you know."

Lizzie gave a very slight nod. "I know," she whispered back. "But I can't believe he murdered her."

"Then what?"

"He mummified her."

"Why?"

"I'm not sure." She pulled away from him, and turned around.

Father O'Toole and his companion were pretending to give them privacy, but it was obvious that the priest was very tuned in to what was happening on the far side of the room.

Cosimo smiled broadly. "Do you gentlemen mind if I take Professor Manning to dinner?" he asked.

The PR man began to say that they still needed to agree on how information about the mummy would be shared with the press, but Father O'Toole gave him a look that silenced him.

"Of course," said the priest. "And when you are finished, Lizzie, I'd like you to call me and give me an update on what is happening with the exhibit."

She nodded. While the three men made plans to meet again the following day, Lizzie called Martin to tell him that she wouldn't be home for dinner. "Cosimo Gonzaga is in town," she said cheerfully for her audience in the room, "and we're going to catch up."

"That sounds ominous," Martin said.

"Oh it is," she said, again in a lighthearted tone.

"Do you need me to come meet you?"

"No thank you dear, I don't think that's necessary."

"Okay then. Text me if you need me."

Lizzie looked up to find herself being scrutinized by each of the men in the room. She flashed her brightest innocent smile and asked Cosimo if he wanted Italian or something else. "I have a friend who has a very nice restaurant in the North End."

He nodded his assent and said goodbye to Father O'Toole, agreeing that they would meet again the following morning.

Cosimo had a limousine waiting outside, and insisted that Lizzie get into the backseat, despite her protestations that it would be easier to take her own car. She could not keep images from various gangster movies from flying through her brain. At least she wasn't told to sit in the front seat.

Neither Cosimo nor his driver asked Lizzie for a destination. In fact, the driver didn't get into the car after closing the door behind Cosimo, but rather stepped aside so the two could talk privately.

"As I said," Cosimo started abruptly, "this was Patrick's doing."

"What was?" Lizzie asked. "Do you really think he killed a woman?"

"You said that you think he might have mummified her. Why?"

Lizzie suddenly felt very foolish. "I am sorry I said anything. It's just that he told me he was interested in mummies, had been to Egypt, and even knew how to make one."

"But why would he?"

"As an experiment maybe?"

Cosimo suggested he might have done it to hide a murder.

"Why are you telling me this?" Lizzie asked him, worried about being brought into a dangerous secret with Cosimo.

"I don't know," Cosimo answered grimly. "But right now you know as much about him, and about my family, as anyone. I want to resolve this without the police, if possible, and the research you have already done, and can do, might lead to the fastest and cleanest solution." He smiled at her. "Historians are detectives, after all."

Lizzie was chilled rather than comforted by the smile. She thought of dolphins, which everyone thought were so friendly because they had that constant smile, but she had seen them once in a feeding frenzy snapping at flying fish that were doing their best to escape.

"I don't see how this can be kept private. There is a very determined detective here who is committed to solving this murder."

"What is his name?" Cosimo asked, as if he could make a quick phone call and remove the problem from the case.

"*Her* name is Ann Crandall," Lizzie answered.

"I think that the Boston Police will not want to continue an investigation if the Bolognese Polizia take it over," he said, "and I am confident they will do that very soon."

And then he would be able to control the investigation, Lizzie thought.

"What do you want me to do?" she asked.

"Solve the crime," he said.

"You make that sound very easy."

"Not at all. If it were easy, anyone could do it. I think that it requires special skills and you have them." He told her that she should take it as a compliment.

She was about to speak again, but he stopped her.

"I don't blame you for any of this," he said. "I know that you and Carmine Moreale both behaved in the most profes-

sional way. I know that it was the negligence of my idiot nephew Beppe that caused this."

Lizzie thanked him for the acknowledgement. "We're not
really going to dinner, are we?" she asked.

"No," he answered. "And I never eat Italian food when I
am abroad."

Lizzie opened the door before Cosimo was able to alert the
driver, and stepped outside the car. "I'll do what I can," she
said.

He gave her the smile again and she jumped like a flying
fish.

Chapter 30

Martin was surprised when Lizzie arrived home. "I thought you were dining with the Godfather," he said.

"You don't know how close you are on that," she said. "At one point this evening I thought I would end up sleeping with the flying fishes."

"That bad?

"Both Cosimo Gonzaga and Father O'Toole think that I can solve a murder that probably happened fifty years ago, in a country where I don't even speak the language. And they think that I can do it before my exhibit opens, a time when I am more busy than I have ever been."

"Can you?"

Lizzie laughed a "ha ha ha ha" laugh.

"Tell me everything you know about this crime so far," Martin said.

"All right," Lizzie said. "I feel like I should have a white board behind me, and photographs of suspects—but the victim's face is obscured by pitch-infused linen bandages, and the only photos I have are of an alligator, a couple of lizards, and some valuable artifacts."

"Do you think this murder has anything to do with the collection?"

"No."

"Then what?"

"The war, maybe." She wished that for just a moment she could peek into Detective Crandall's notebook. She tried to recall what Ann had said about the victim. She had had dental work done in Germany in the 1930s, and again in Switzerland in the late 1940s or early 1950s.

"She was killed after the war," Lizzie said, thinking aloud. "The only person I can think of who fits the bill is Greta Winkler, or Hoffman, who was a friend of Gianna's at school, and who Patrick fell in love with one summer. She married the Nazi officer who raped and murdered Gianna."

"Do you have any evidence that Patrick wanted to kill this Greta?"

"No, but Archie might have. Patrick said that Archie thought Greta had informed on Gianna to her husband."

"That sounds like a motive to me," Martin said.

"Yes, but where is the opportunity?" Lizzie responded. "If this happened after the war, then Greta must have been back in Germany. Why would he drag her back to Bologna to mummify her? And besides," she added with diminishing enthusiasm, "There must be lots of other women with German dentalwork who were murdered in Bologna after the war. For all I know Colonel Hoffman might have had a Bavarian housekeeper, Wanda Schiertz, who fits that description."

"Did he have such a housekeeper?"

"How the hell would I know? Or it might have been an Italian woman who was a collaborator with the Nazis and was killed in retaliation after the war."

"Do you have a name for her too?"

"Let's call her Gianamaria Pipsicatto. My point is, I can't say that it was this Greta woman simply because she is the only one I know of who fits the description. I can't say it to Detective Crandall, or to Father O'Toole, or to Cosimo Gonzaga, because if it is that woman, then either Archie or Patrick must have killed her, and I cannot even suggest that without having any evidence at all."

"I don't suppose at this point that Patrick could even give a confession."

Lizzie sat down and swore. "Oh my God!" she said. "Oh my god, oh my god, oh my god!" She looked up at Martin. "Maybe he did! Maybe that last day in the hospital when he gave us the dissertation in Italian. What did he say?"

Martin shook his head. "I don't know, it went by so fast and I was just trying to recognize some of the words that I know from Spanish."

"But I recorded it," Lizzie said excitedly. She fished her phone out of her purse and pressed the button to play back the recording of Patrick's soliloquy. His voice came spilling out of the tiny speaker in Italian.

"Non avrei mai pensato, come invece ha fatto Archie, che Greta avesse a che fare con la morte di mia sorella. La mamma aveva detto e ridetto ad Archie che Hoffman era un bruto, che aveva picchiato Greta, e che non aveva nessuna privacy nella sua stessa casa, le aveva persino rubato le lettere di Gianna."

Lizzie turned it off and shook her fists in the air. "Can you get *anything* from that?" she asked her husband.

"I recognize the names Archie, Greta, and Gianna. And some other stuff from Spanish that makes me think you need to get a real translator right away."

Lizzie picked up the phone again and called Rose. "I know it's late," she apologized, "but do you think I could see your father tonight? It is really important."

When Martin heard his wife say that she would be right over, he said "You better call Jackie. If there is something important on that recording she will want to be there when it gets translated."

Lizzie made the call and the two of them sped to Tony's house. Rose was already there and Jackie arrived a few minutes later.

"What's up?" she asked.

"I made a recording of Patrizio Gonzaga when I was in Bologna, and I need to have Tony translate it from Italian to English for me."

"What is it about?" Tony asked.

"I'm not exactly sure," Lizzie said, "but I think it is important."

They sat around Tony's dining room table and Lizzie put her phone in the middle. Tony suggested that they play it through a speaker and pointed to where Lizzie could fetch one from a nearby shelf. When they were finally ready, Lizzie played the first part and Tony translated what Patrizio Gonzaga had said a few weeks earlier in Bologna:

"I never thought, like Archie did, that Greta had anything

to do with my sister's death. My mother told Archie over and over that Hoffman was a brute, that he had beaten Greta, that she had had no privacy in her own house, that Hoffman had stolen Gianna's letters from her."

"Who are these people?" Rose asked.

"Gianna Gonzaga was the daughter of the woman you like to refer to as the Principessa Della Gonzaga," her father answered. "Archie—Arcangelo Cussetti was her husband. I don't know who Greta or Hoffman is or was."

Lizzie picked up the story. "Greta Winkler was a German woman who became friends with Gianna in a boarding school in Switzerland. Patrick fell in love with her when she came once to visit his sister. She married a Nazi officer, Franz Hoffman, who was stationed in Bologna during the war." She found herself unable to go on.

"Hoffman ordered the rape and murder of Gianna," Martin said softly.

"What is on this tape?" Tony asked.

Lizzie told him that she had recorded Patrick speaking at his nursing home. "If you don't mind, can you just translate, rather than have me speculate about what he said?"

Tony agreed that made sense and they went on, with the old man translating.

"My mother was in contact with Greta, I knew that, but she never told Archie, because his anger was so ferocious. But Greta wanted to see my mother. She had moved to Switzerland after the war and wrote to Mama, begging her to let her come to Bologna. When she agreed, Mama had to tell Archie.

"'I'll meet her at the station,' Archie said. Mama was very stern with him. She didn't want him to meet her; she wanted to go herself but my sister-in-law was having a baby that very day—Cosimo's wife, and she was old to be having a baby and it was her first." The voice changed and Patrizio said in a deep rasp, "All this happened on the day my nephew Cosimo was born, I never thought of that before." There was a brief silence before he continued. "'You must not hurt Greta,' my mother said to Archie, and then she demanded that I go with him. She knew I had loved Greta, and I think she thought I would protect her from Archie, and I would have, not only because I *had* loved her, but because my mother so rarely trusted me to do anything of consequence." There was a loud cough on the recording as Patrick cleared his throat and continued.

"I couldn't believe it when I saw her, she had aged so. It was fifteen years since I had last seen her. She had been something special, not just pretty but *una personalita' effervescente,* she shimmered with vitality, with flirtatiousness. But that was gone when I saw her on that train platform. She had become dull, flat, as if the life had gone out of her. I wondered what I had loved in her and then wondered if Hoffman had somehow sucked it out of her, or stomped it out. Or if it was just the war that had made her dead inside, like it had so many of us. And it must have been even worse for Germans because their crimes were so horrific.

"I didn't know what her crimes had been, but when she came to me with her arms outstretched, looking for me to embrace her, I stepped back; I could not do it. I don't know if it was the way she looked, or the intense hatred of her that Archie generated like a fog around him, but I felt sorry for Greta then, because she just seemed to deflate. She could feel that energy of rage that emanated from Archie, and she shrunk even more into herself. She followed us meekly to the car, and then Archie drove us up to a cave in the hills that we had used during our days of hiding.

"We hadn't made a plan to go there, but he said he wanted to show her how Gianna had lived during the war. 'That's what you're here for, isn't it?' His voice was so harsh that Greta cowered, shrinking away from him, and honestly, even I was afraid.

"Greta looked at me with terrified eyes and reached out a hand to me but I did not respond, and now I think of it with shame.

"Archie indicated that she should go into the cave and when she turned to follow his instructions, she stood tall again, resolute.

"Everything after that happened so quickly I could hardly comprehend it. We were not far into the cave when Archie pulled a pistol from his pocket and shot Greta in the head."

There was a sob on the recording and a hush in the room.

"The blood spurted out in a torrent on me and Archie and her body just crumpled. I went to her side and she looked right at me, but she was dead. I could not help thinking then that she was a woman I had loved."

Tony's hand shook as he turned off the recording and they all sat silently when he had translated the last phrase.

Rose was the first to speak. "Did you know this was going to be a confession to a murder?" Rose asked. "Because I think you might have warned us." She put a hand protectively on her father's arm.

Lizzie apologized. "I don't know what I was expecting," she said. "I thought it might tell us something about the mummy, and I knew she had been murdered, but I was stupid not to put it together. I'm sorry. I guess I wasn't expecting what we just heard."

"You thought it was Greta, though," Martin said, "and it was."

"Did you ever know her?" Lizzie asked Tony, thinking how terrible it would be for him to have learned of her death in this way if he had.

The old man shook his head. "No. I don't remember ever meeting or even seeing her. But Archie and Patrizio, I remember them well."

"Again, I'm sorry, Tony," Lizzie said, wishing she had thought more carefully about what might be on the recording before she asked him to translate it.

"It's a terrible thing of course," he said. "But I also knew Gianna and saw their terrible grief when she died." He made a gesture, lifting his palms up to show there was nothing to be done now. "I understand Archie completely," he said. "He thought this woman had given information that led to Gianna's torture and execution."

"I can't imagine that this really resolved anything for him though," Martin added.

"What happened to him after this?" Rose asked.

Tony only vaguely remembered that Archie had died young. "Of tuberculosis, I think. He was in his thirties."

"But no one ever linked either of these guys to the murder?" Jackie said, having been uncharacteristically quiet through the whole of the evening. "I wonder if anyone ever even knew she had disappeared?"

"Maggie Gonzaga was certainly waiting for her," Lizzie said. "Tony, do you mind if we listen to the rest of the tape? I'm hesitant to ask because I didn't prepare any of you very well for what we just heard and I think that there is likely to be some grisly stuff to come. These two men almost certainly mummified the corpse of Greta Hoffman."

"I think we can't stop here," Tony said, and everyone agreed.

Patrick's voice was agitated as he described an argument with Archie about what to do to Greta's body. Archie had a hatchet in the trunk of the car and had planned to dismember her and scatter her body parts, with the expectation that animals would consume her.

"But what if someone found some part of her?" Patrick had argued. "There would have to be an investigation, and mother would be sure to be suspicious."

Archie agreed, but only because he feared being found out by Maggie. Patrick made it clear that Archie feared neither the law nor death, only his mother-in-law. She would disown him if she knew he had murdered Greta, and that was a fate that Archie could not bear even to consider.

"We will have to tell her that she simply wasn't on the train," he said to Patrick. "I will dump her trunk in the canal."

It was Patrick who suggested that they mummify the corpse and hide it in the sarcophagus, and once he got it into his head to do so, he proceeded to make a methodical plan. He sent Archie to fetch four fifty-pound bags of salt, and while his companion was away, Patrick lovingly laid Greta out on the stony floor at the back of the cave. He undressed her in as chaste a manner as he could, covering her breasts and genitals with her clothing while he eviscerated her with the knife he carried.

When Archie returned, they covered her with salt. Over the next few days they returned with tools from the collection and Patrick washed the corpse and instructed Archie how to remove the brain and the eyeballs while he stood at the mouth of the cave, breathing deeply.

Patrick came back again and again to be sure that no people or animals disturbed the sacred site, and after forty days, the period proscribed by Egyptian tradition, they secretly moved the body to the basement of the Gonzaga house and finished the process. Where he had been unable to get the original ingredients, Patrick made clever substitutions and he applied himself thoroughly and systematically to the process, thinking that by preparing Greta's corpse so perfectly for the afterlife he could establish a relationship with her that had not existed in life. Through all this, Maggie wondered about Greta's absence, but Archie maintained the lie of a calm countenance, and Patrick was finally working enthusiastically on a project—though she did not know the details—and so she allowed herself to be persuaded that Greta could not, after all, face the family of the friend her husband had murdered.

Chapter 31

The knowledge that Arcangelo Cussetti had murdered Greta Hoffman and that Patrizio Gonzaga had mummified her could not be kept a secret, though Lizzie was not sure whom she should tell.

Tony ventured that she shouldn't disclose what they now knew. "It was an action of wartime," he said.

Martin argued that it was a crime of passion, of revenge. "The war had been over for a decade," he said. "While we might sympathize with Archie over his loss, this was a cold-blooded murder."

"And I'm not even convinced that Greta was guilty of what he thought," Jackie added. "Maggie seemed pretty certain that Greta was also a victim of the violence of her husband."

They were all moved by Patrick's description of her at the end. "She seemed so vulnerable, even pathetic," Lizzie said, and Rose said almost the same thing at the same time. "But I'm not sure what to do now," Lizzie continued. "Patrick Gonzaga is certainly in no condition to stand trial. He can't be questioned; he's a senile old man. Even to question him would be cruel, and I'm not sure he would remember any of this."

"I'm not so sure about that," Martin interjected. "I think he may remember the details of this business better than anything else that ever happened in his life."

"This is why we have laws and courts," Rose said determinedly. "So that none of us has to decide how to handle the information."

"Do you think I have to turn the recording over to someone?" Lizzie asked.

Rose, Martin and Jackie immediately said, "Yes."

Tony said, "No."

"Gawd, I hate to think of giving it to Cosimo Gonzaga. He would use it to put Patrizio away for good, but would keep the details from going public," Lizzie said. "And maybe that's not such a bad thing."

Jackie asked if Greta Hoffman had a family that might want to know what happened to her.

"No children," Lizzie answered, "and any siblings would probably be in their nineties if they survive at all."

"She might have surviving nieces or nephews," Rose said.

"And do you think that it would give them any kind of satisfaction to know that their aunt was murdered and mummified?" Lizzie picked up the phone from the table and put it in her purse. "Thank you Tony," she said, embracing the old man and kissing him on the cheek. "I know that this evening can't have been easy for you."

He took her face in his hands and gave her a deep determined look, then nodded and let go.

As the company broke up, Jackie asked Lizzie what she was going to do in the morning.

"Tell Father O'Toole," Lizzie said. "And probably Cosimo Gonzaga, and maybe Ann Crandall, though I may give her the details without the names. She can't do anything about it, but she said something about the victim deserving to have her story known, and we can do that, even if only in a small circle."

Jackie asked what sort of impact this might have on the opening of her exhibit and Lizzie answered defensively that any intention to keep the story from coming out now was not because of that. "The sensational nature of Greta's fate will make her a spectacle on the Internet, and I'm not sure that is a very respectful thing to do."

"It could also bring some aspects of what happened during the war to light."

"Maybe, but I am going to leave it to the morning to decide."

No decision was made during the night and when she went to Father O'Toole's office the next morning it was like a penitent going to confession. There really was no reason why she should feel guilty, she told herself, and yet she did. She thought the priest might relieve her of some of the burden she was carrying, and he did, for he was also a pragmatic businessman, and his concern over the reputation of St. Patrick's College seemed equal to any ethical quandary related to bringing a murderer—or a mummifier—to justice.

"You say you have all this on tape?" he asked Lizzie after she explained what she knew about the woman whose mummy was now in the custody of the Boston Coroner. "Can I hear it?"

"It's in Italian," she said, turning on her phone and handing it to him.

"I think if I press this button I would erase it," he said, then smiled at her. "Don't worry, I won't do it, but it would be easy enough to have an accident and lose the evidence. You say this is Cosimo Gonzaga's uncle speaking?"

Lizzie nodded as the priest held the phone up to his ear and listened to the first several minutes of the recording. "Okay," he said. "I'm going to talk to the College's legal counsel about this, but I'm inclined to think we should let Cosimo hear it. His uncle clearly isn't the killer, and from what you've told me the old man is never going to be able to stand trial for hiding the body, anyway, so we might as well let him deal with it in Italy."

"Can I keep my phone?" Lizzie asked.

"Do you mind if I say no, at least for a day or so?"

She had to agree and as she left Father O'Toole said, "Now you can return to your exhibit work full time without any distractions."

Lizzie gave him a very small smile and walked across campus to the workspace where the Gonzaga collection was being prepared. Jimmy and Roscoe were working with the designer on preparing the labels and placing them next to each object.

"'U'u club," she read. "Collected on the 1595 expedition of Alvaro de Mendaña, this is the oldest artifact known to exist from the Marquesas Islands..."

The beautiful dark wood of the object glowed under the artificial lights, its abstract face stared up from the table on which it lay. Lizzie put her hand on it, breaking her own rule of never touching any part of the collection without gloves. The wood felt warm, smooth. How many hands had touched it over the last four hundred years? Certainly Patrizio Gonzaga had held it in the same hands that had eviscerated and mummified Greta Winkler Hoffman.

And before that, what generations of Gonzaga men and women had held it in their hands, touched the wood as she was doing now? Four hundred years ago a Spanish explorer had taken it from the hands of a Marquesan man to stow on his ship for the long voyage home, and before that some carver had rubbed it with his hands to smooth it. Each person through whose hands the club had passed had a story, each had lived a life full of drama, emotion, love, violence. Lizzie wondered if Patrick had ever put it into the hands of Greta Winkler when he was a young man and she was a young woman to impress. Perhaps those hands, now desiccated and wrapped in resin-soaked linen, had held this club when they were warm and soft and Patrick desired to hold them in his own and put them to his lips.

Lizzie walked quietly around the room, lost in her own thoughts. Jimmy and Roscoe held back, despite the list of questions they had been saving to ask her. She looked again at the alligator, the narwhal tusk and all the other artifacts that had now become a part of her story as well.

When Cosimo Gonzaga came into the room, she asked her assistants to leave, which they did quickly and quietly.

"Father O'Toole played me the tape," he said. "I had never heard any part of that story before."

"Had you heard of Greta Winkler?"

"No. I had heard something once from Pat that a friend of Gianna's had informed on her to the Nazis and that's how she was captured, but my grandmother gave him a smack when he said it and told him never to mention anything about it ever again."

He picked up the Marquesan club and Lizzie didn't say anything. His was another pair of hands upon it, another link in the chain.

"And so the mysteries are all solved," he said, giving her a slight bow. "Grazie."

Lizzie took the club from him and laid it back on the table.

"I still have some questions, if you don't mind answering them," she said.

Cosimo raised an eyebrow and nodded.

"What happened to the Dutch paintings that used to hang in the Yellow Salon?" she asked.

"They are in my house," he said without emotion. "Everything in the palazzo on Galvani Plaza legally belongs to me and I have moved some things out of it. By a quirk of my grandfather's will, his wife, and any of her children living with her could stay there for their lifetimes. Nobody ever expected Patrick to stay there for sixty-plus years after her death. My father wanted the house, which he inherited, and I want it too."

It occurred to her that he might have the Michelangelo angel. "Do you have it?" she asked.

He said that he didn't. "I have never seen it," he said. "My grandmother told me it was stolen during the war and never returned."

"Did you ever try to find it through one of the lost art registries?"

He shook his head. "There was something strange in the circumstances of its loss. My grandmother would not allow it to be pursued, and I don't have any good evidence to show that my family owned it."

"It is on the altar in the chapel in that sketch you sent me," Lizzie said.

"But it isn't recognizable there, and it isn't in the catalog of artworks made after." He put his hand on her arm and looked carefully at her. "Did you find evidence of it in the work you've done?"

"Your grandmother wrote that she moved it into her bedroom during the war, that she didn't want to hide it with the rest of the valuables because it meant so much to her."

"Where did she write this?"

"In a letter to her brother that is in the library collection here at the college."

Cosimo leaned against the table on which a number of valuable artifacts were laid. "Can you find it?" he asked.

"The letter?" she said. "Of course, I can show you a copy right now on my computer."

"No, the statue," Cosimo said earnestly. "Can you find the Michelangelo?"

"How?" Lizzie said, her surprise at the request evident in her tone. "Are you willing to put out a request through the stolen art channels?"

"Again, I have no real evidence, no image of the thing."

Lizzie told him that she thought it might be a pair with the Michelangelo angel on St. Dominic's tomb. She moved down the table to the dell'Arca angel and told him her theory. "I think there may have been two pairs of angels, one pair by each artist, and that somehow they got split between the church and the Gonzaga family."

"I'm impressed. You know a lot more than I thought," Cosimo said. "In fact, you know a lot more about some of my family matters than I do. I don't suppose you can tell me why my grandmother did not want to pursue this after the war?"

"Patrick said that she knew who stole it."

Cosimo was silenced by that bit of information and did not speak again for almost a minute. "Did he say who it was?" he asked finally.

Lizzie shook her head. "Is it possible it is still in the possession of someone in your family?" she asked.

"If it was stolen by someone in my family, it was likely to be either one of my uncles or my father. My uncle Adino was feuding with his mother during the war and considered the house and all its contents to be his personal property. I never met him, but he was described to me by my father as a grasping schemer."

"And he was killed during the war," Lizzie added, "so if he took the statue out of the house it would be very difficult to trace it. There is an impressive *catalog raisonne* of Michelangelo's work in public and private collections and there is nothing in it to suggest that anyone knows of another angel with a candlestick like the one on St. Dominic's tomb."

"If my uncle took it to Rome though, for instance, it could just be in some collection where the current owners don't even know what it is. There is an embarrassment of riches there when it comes to Renaissance statuary."

"What about your own father? Is there any chance that he could have taken it and you wouldn't know?"

"My father wasn't in Italy during most of the war. He didn't want to be conscripted by any of the various parties and he didn't have as much reverence for the resistance as my grandmother. He thought that Gianna was foolish to get involved."

"Well I am pretty sure it wasn't Patrick. Why would he hide it when he has lived his whole life in the house? And he is the one who told me it was stolen."

Cosimo put his hand on the head of the dell'Arca angel and mused. "This is really quite beautiful," he said. "It was a generous gift from my grandfather."

"I have thought that the gift of the angel and the painting must have been an acknowledgment of how deeply he loved Maggie Kelliher."

"Perhaps." He nodded. "If you can find the Michelangelo angel, or good documentation of it belonging to my family, there will be a handsome reward in it for you." He once again caught Lizzie's eye and gave her a very serious look.

She repeated her earlier comment that she didn't see how it could be done without using public sources, but said she would keep it in mind.

"What will happen to Patrick now?" she asked. "Will he be going back to the house on the Piazza Galvani?"

Cosimo made it clear that he wouldn't. "He really can't live on his own anymore, as I think you will agree. He's comfortable at the St. Columba Hospital and will stay there."

She couldn't argue and it wasn't really her business anyway.

"And what about the house and the collection?" she asked. "Will you live there?"

"God no," he exclaimed. "That old wreck! My wife would never live in a house with an alligator on the ceiling. She prefers a more modern house and so do I."

"I hope you won't disperse the collection if you sell the house," Lizzie said earnestly.

"Of course not. Once you have made it famous with this exhibit and book I might donate it to the government though." He laughed. "I'm sure that you are suspicious of me—that I would only consider this with some suspicious motives, to avoid taxes or for some political gain, and I admit we Italians play those games all the time."

Lizzie smiled at him and said in all earnestness, "I don't care why you preserve it, as long as you do."

Chapter 32

Museum's Mummy Murder Mystery" was the closest that any news source got to the story of Greta Winkler Hoffman and her horrible demise. She was never identified in any of the many speculative yarns that got spun on the Internet and in the sensationalist press. Lizzie never even told Detective Ann Crandall who the victim was, and she trusted that everyone who had heard the recording of Patrizio Gonzaga's confession would keep it confidential. Cosimo's connections had worked their magic in both Boston and Bologna, and though there was a great deal of curiosity about the story of the young woman whose mummified corpse had ended up in an Egyptian sarcophagus, no answers ever emerged in public sources.

After several weeks Lizzie stopped getting the endless phone calls and emails asking if the mummy would be on exhibit when the Gonzaga show opened, and as the date of the opening approached there was finally more interest in the collection that *would* be exhibited rather than in the mummy, which would not.

John Haworth's essay in the catalog had beautifully captured both the importance of the early sarcophagus, and the interesting story of the use of mummies as medicine in the Renaissance. Lizzie was pleased with her own efforts as well. The collection was marvelous and looked it in both the catalog and the exhibit, which she walked through a few days before the opening. The designer had used the 1677 image very cleverly, along with both the old black and white images of the house taken in the 1950s and color photographs that Carmine had taken before they dismantled the library. The three amphora from the original image, along with two of the marble busts that stood on top of the case in that picture, were immediately recognizable. The two big globes were mounted near a photograph of Patrizio's library, where they occupied their position on the long table.

The modern cases turned out to be very well suited for the ancient objects. In the library at the Gonzaga palazzo they had seemed at home, part of the furniture, and though someone desiring to be astonished could be if she looked closely, it was possible to walk through the room without realizing what treasures were kept in "The Wonder Chamber." That wasn't possible here. In this exhibit everything seemed special.

The dell'Arca angel was the very first thing seen upon entering and Lizzie looked at it for a long time. She remembered when she had put her arms around it and lifted it off the altar in the chapel, and then thought about the partner angel on the altar of St. Dominic's tomb in Bologna. She had decided to be bold in her label and declare that they were a pair, and that the place of this one on St. Dominic's tomb was now occupied by a replacement made by Michelangelo. She said nothing about the missing partner to that angel.

What had happened to the second Michelangelo angel? She had pondered this question repeatedly since Cosimo Gonzaga had asked her to find it three months earlier.

Walking methodically around the exhibit, she looked again at every item on display and read each label one last time before the public would see them. Jimmy Moe and Roscoe Wiley were cleaning the glass of the cases when she entered, but gradually moved into her wake and followed, first at a distance and then moving closer, like two cats looking to be petted. When she reached the *Draco dandinii* she stopped. The designer had positioned it perfectly. The creature looked up at them with its big grin. With its extended wings and reptilian body, it appeared every bit like the pint-sized dragon Jimmy had hoped for.

"Where's the flame?" Lizzie asked, turning to Roscoe.

"What?"

"You said you would add a flame coming out of its mouth when it went on exhibit."

The momentary look of confusion and fear on the student's face diffused when Lizzie laughed.

"I have the flame!" Jimmy said excitedly. As his companions turned to look at him he rolled up the sleeve of his tee shirt and showed them a new tattoo. While the *Draco dandinii* was recognizable, the creature was made more dramatic and more dragon-like by the addition of claws, an arc to the back, and a few tendrils of red and yellow flame being exhaled onto the pale skin of Jimmy's arm.

Lizzie and Roscoe both howled with delight. "I love it!" Lizzie said. "It's wonderful."

"I think you and Roscoe ought to get one, in honor of our exhibit!" Jimmy said. "I told the tattoo guy to save the pattern so that he could make another one, but told him not to give it to anyone but one of you."

Lizzie was moved by the gesture and said she would think about it.

"You guys have done such a great job," she said to them, giving each a tight hug. "I can't tell you how much I appreciate all your hard work."

When she left the museum she walked across the campus green. The statue of Paddy Kelliher had worn a Hawaiian shirt and sunglasses through most of the summer, but now with the start of the new school year he was dressed in a green "St. Pat's" sweatshirt.

Entering the library, Lizzie saw Jackie packing up the various folders of Gonzaga material that had been spread across two tables for the better part of seven months. She pulled up a chair and began to help reconstruct the files.

"How does the exhibit look?" Jackie asked.

"It is absolutely fabulous," Lizzie said, though she knew she did not sound as enthusiastic as she should.

"Is there something wrong?" Jackie asked.

"Just the usual post-project depression. It is always hard to say goodbye to an enterprise that has provided so much excitement, and this has been a great one. What a collection! I'm not kidding, Jackie, even without the Michelangelo, this is absolutely the most astonishing assemblage of great stuff!"

"What about the Michelangelo? Did anything more ever turn up about it?"

Lizzie answered regretfully, "It seems that the only people who ever knew anything about it were the thief and Maggie, and she never mentioned it again after saying that she was keeping it in her bedroom rather than sending it into hiding during the war."

"She never talked about it in any of the later letters?"

Lizzie froze. When she spoke again her voice was a squeak. "What later letters?"

Jackie picked up a stiff envelope from the table. "It's right here. Gonzaga Correspondence, 1954-1959. This came in about the same time as the photographs and the list. It has been sitting here on the table for several months."

She handed the envelope to Lizzie who pulled a few dozen sheets of paper from it.

"This is the first time I am seeing these," Lizzie said, "and the exhibit catalogs just arrived at the warehouse. They'll be here tomorrow. I hope there isn't anything here that I will wish I knew two months ago."

She wondered aloud why Roscoe hadn't included them in the correspondence he scanned for her early in the process.

"In Roscoe's defense, he scanned the first box of letters as soon as I took it off the shelf, and I didn't find this until later," Jackie said. "Either you or I have to take responsibility for this."

"I thought I had looked at every piece of paper on this table," Lizzie said in response.

"I thought you had too."

There was nothing to be done now but read the letters and a quick scan through them revealed that all were written by Maggie to her brother Tom in Boston. The first several were about family matters, the relationships and occupations of adult children and the frolics of new grandchildren. Maggie worried about Archie's health. "He has never recovered from Gianna's death," she wrote, "but there is something else at work here which we fear is tuberculosis."

"You're turning too fast," Jackie said to Lizzie. "I think there was something interesting there about getting the house back in order."

"Here," Lizzie answered, handing her friend half of the pages. "You take these and I'll read the later ones."

"She mentions here that she and Patrick are making an inventory of the collection in the library as a project to keep him busy. From the way she describes him he might have been fairly loony even when he was young."

"What date is that?" Lizzie asked.

"November, 1954."

"I'm sorry we don't know Cosimo Gonzaga's birthday. Patrick said that Archie murdered Greta on the day Cosimo was born."

Jackie rose from the table and went back to the computer on her desk. "He was born on May 29, 1955," she said, returning to the table. "I have the pages around that date."

"We should start at least a few months earlier, to see if Maggie says anything to her brother about expecting Greta to visit."

The two women sat close together and started with the first letter written in 1955, on February 28.

"Move on," Lizzie said, urging Jackie to turn to the next page.

On March 18, 1955, Maggie wrote the letter they sought.

"I have received an unexpected communication today," she wrote, "from Greta Winkler, who was Gianna's friend from school. It sat on the table in front of me for more than twenty minutes before I could open it. You may remember that she married the Nazi who murdered Gianna. My hand is shaking even to think about him and I cannot write his name, yet I have to tell you this important news. She has my Michelangelo angel, it was her husband who stole it."

Lizzie gasped as she read it and Jackie made the same sound a moment later. They could not read fast enough.

"I had suspected he was the thief—he stormed through the house looking for Gianna just before it went missing—but I never accused him because it was so shortly after that episode that his crimes became so much more vile and horrific. When this monstrous rapist and murderer was himself gunned down by Archie, I did not know what could have happened to my angel."

Lizzie ran her finger under the next lines and read them aloud: "I quietly approached the Allied officers who brought works of art back to Italy after our liberation, but there was nothing like the Michelangelo that had been identified in the various salt mines and hunting lodges where the booty was stored that Hitler and Göring looted from us."

"Oh my God!" Lizzie said softly but intensely. "It must have been in Greta's trunk when Archie and Patrick abducted and killed her."

They read quickly through the next few letters, where Maggie described Greta's plans to bring the angel to Bologna, and about her inability to meet her at the train station. "The timing is unfortunately so awkward. Cosimo and Isabella insist that I must be at the birth of their first child, and as Isabella is already thirty years old and extremely frightened by the whole prospect, I do not feel that I can refuse." She wrote what Lizzie had heard from Patrick, both in person and in his recorded confession, and what Maggie had said in earlier letters, that Archie believed Greta had informed on Gianna's activities in the Resistance. "I still don't think this happened," she wrote, "and I have said it many times to both Archie and Patrick."

Through several more letters over many months, Maggie lamented that Greta had not kept her word and brought her the Michelangelo angel, and that all subsequent letters to her had been returned. She speculated that Greta had been unable to face her after all. If she suspected that either her son-in-law or her son had killed the woman, she never admitted it to her brother.

In the last letters in the folder, she wrote of Archie's death from tuberculosis and Patrick's increasing mental instability. This is what led Maggie to document the collection through an inventory and photographs, and to send them to Boston as a record in 1959.

"Wow," Jackie said, sitting back in her chair and looking at Lizzie. "Wow, wow, wow! What happened to the statute?"

"Did Patrick say anything about it in that recording?"

"I don't remember. I only heard it that once and I was so astonished at the confession that he had murdered and *mummified* a woman that I didn't pay a lot of attention to what happened to her luggage!"

"Me either," Lizzie said. "I transferred the recording from my phone to my computer, which is a good thing because either Cosimo or Father O'Toole erased it from my phone. If we listen to it now, can you translate it?"

Jackie had to admit that her Italian wasn't quite as good as she had claimed earlier. "I think we need to ask Tony again," she said, "and make sure we get it right."

"I'll call him and see if he remembers," Lizzie said. "Would you mind making a scan of these letters? I'll send them to Cosimo."

She stepped outside the door of the library to make her call, looking at the statue of Paddy Kelliher and wondering what he would think if he knew of the antics of his heirs.

Tony answered immediately.

"Hi Tony, it's Lizzie Manning."

"Lizzie," he said, "how delightful to hear your voice."

"I'm sorry that I'm not calling on a happy subject," she said. "It's about that recording that you translated for me."

"Oh," he said, his voice losing its happy tone. "Did they arrest him?"

He seemed relieved when Lizzie told him that Patrick Gonzaga had not been arrested for the murder. She asked if he remembered what had happened to Greta's luggage.

"They threw it into the canal. Patrizio said she had a big trunk that was heavy to shift, and that he and Archie threw it into one of the canals."

"I don't remember seeing a canal in Bologna."

"Most of the old canals are covered over now. I remember a lot more of them when I was a boy than you can see now, but they are a relic of medieval times."

Lizzie swallowed hard and asked him if Patrick had mentioned specifically where they dumped it.

"No," he answered.

"When did they cover the canals?"

"Starting in the 50s," he said. "It was after the war."

"And there were a lot of them?"

"I think something like fifty miles of canals at one time."

She thanked him and turned off her phone. Jackie would be waiting to know what she knew, and she would have to tell Cosimo very soon that his priceless Michelangelo "Angel with a Candlestick" was lying at the bottom of an unknown Bologna canal, possibly under some street or building. She sank down to sit on the library steps and looked again at the sweatshirt-clad statue of the college founder. In three days they would celebrate the hundredth anniversary of his gift, her exhibit would open, and her book would be launched. She felt like a chip of wood in a fast-flowing stream.

Chapter 33

"The Wonder Chamber of the Gonzagas" exhibit and catalog were both launched successfully. The story of the unusual circumstances surrounding the mummy in the sarcophagus continued to bring attention, but didn't overwhelm the fascination that the rest of the collection inspired. Lizzie, a glass of champagne in hand, followed along as first Father O'Toole, then Jim Kelliher, then Cosimo Gonzaga toasted Patrick Kelliher, Maggie and Lorenzo Gonzaga, and themselves for being so generous and inspired.

An hour before the official festivities began, Lizzie gathered a small group of friends and family to thank them and give them copies of the book. She presented the first two to Jimmy Moe and Roscoe Wiley, for having been so dedicated to the project. To each of them she also gave a framed copy of the 1677 image, on the mats of which Martin had drawn comical dragons and alligators, inspired by the ones in the collection.

Carmine had come from Bologna for the launch and she gave him the next copy, then proffered copies to Jackie, Rose, and Tony. Rose immediately saw the dedication: "To the memory of Margaret Kelliher Gonzaga, who connected a family on two continents and cherished this collection." Below that Lizzie had written in Rose's copy: "You were right. She led a much more interesting life than her father."

In Jackie's copy she wrote: "To my dearest friend, who knows better than anyone the mysteries that lurk in libraries." Martin had received his copy the day before, when Lizzie opened the first carton of books, but she gave them, along with warm hugs, to John Haworth and her friend Kate Wentworth.

Lizzie had also prepared a special copy in advance for Cosimo. "Only one piece missing," she wrote, "and now you know where it is."

She signed books, pointed out special features of the collection, and talked to members of the community for an hour before Cosimo asked if he could speak to her outside. They walked from the museum to the green and sat on the base of the statue of Paddy Kelliher.

"Your great-grandfather," she said, nodding her head to the statue. "I hope this is a good day for you. I think it certainly would have been for him, and for your grandmother."

He agreed. He still had a glass of champagne in his hand and he finished it and set the glass on the grass beside him.

"So you found the Michelangelo," he said. "I told you I would pay you handsomely to do that."

Lizzie laughed. "I wouldn't say I actually found it since you can't recover it simply by knowing it was tossed into a canal."

He took an envelope from his pocket and handed it to her. "Nonetheless, I'm glad to know what happened to it."

She wondered how much he thought the information was worth, and if there were any strings attached to it.

"You don't need to pay me for anything. I was doing my job and got my compensation from St. Patrick's College." She did not reach for the envelope and eventually he put it back in his pocket.

"Do you plan to say anything about it? I would hate to cause a mass dredging of the Bologna canals by treasure hunters looking for it," he said.

"Would you make a claim for it if it were found?" She had already thought about this. Italian authorities would certainly make a claim if he didn't. The fact that it had been stolen by a Nazi officer during the war would probably make the Gonzaga claim very strong, and now they had the evidence of Maggie's letters to back it up. But going public with the information would necessitate revealing the details of Greta Winkler Hoffman's murder.

"After you sent me the copy of my grandmother's letter I went to Patrizio to ask him if he would tell me specifically where they dumped Greta's trunk, but he is like a clam about it now." Cosimo turned and looked at her. "And the canals have changed so much since then. I don't think it will ever be recovered."

Lizzie stood and adjusted the tuxedo coat and bowtie that Paddy-Boy's statue was wearing for the occasion. It was a nice touch and she appreciated whoever had done it. As she moved the coat she saw that a tattoo had been painted on the arm, a smiling dragon labeled *Draco dandinii*. She worked very hard not to laugh as she turned again to Cosimo.

"Life's just full of mysteries, isn't it?" She felt happy. Even picturing the marble Michelangelo lying in the mud of a Bologna canal could not diminish her satisfaction on this evening.

Cosimo offered his arm and they walked back to the museum. The exhibit looked splendid. She saw Jimmy and Roscoe leading their own tours and joined for a few minutes to hear Jimmy's enthusiastic descriptions and Roscoe's more measured commentary.

Martin was also listening. "Where is your third assistant? Is he here tonight?"

"I'm happy to say that he wisely decided not to put in an appearance," Lizzie said. She had noted Prince Beppe Carrera's absence early in the program.

They wandered through the exhibit and looked again at the alligator, the Marquesan club, the gigantic marble foot, the sweetly moving Etruscan tomb chests, the rocks and bugs and fish skeletons; and finally stopped at the sarcophagus.

"I wonder who originally occupied this coffin?" Martin said.

"A mid-level functionary of the eighteenth dynasty," Lizzie said automatically, then laughed. "Strange, isn't it, that the further back in time we go the less seriously we take the details of death. Whoever he was, he might have been just as much a victim of passion and violence as Greta Hoffman, but we don't have the same response."

Jackie had joined them and overheard the last statement. "And if you have been following her story in the scandal sheets, she isn't treated very humanely either."

"I wonder if it would make a difference if they knew who she was and what happened to her," Lizzie offered.

"I don't think so," Jackie said.

"You certainly do find a lot of corpses in your work. I think there must be some police detectives who find fewer dead bodies than you," Martin said, slipping an arm around Lizzie's waist.

"Well I'm a historian and that's just what we do," Lizzie responded. "We see dead people."

"I like the concept that history is just one damn thing after another," Jackie said. "Or in your case, one old corpse after another."

They arrived back at the dell'Arca angel, where the exhibit started.

"I prefer to think I deal with objects and documents rather than corpses," Lizzie said. "There are people behind every document and every object, of course, and theirs are the stories I want to tell, but despite what you two may think, I'd rather get at them through something other than their actual corporeal remains."

Lizzie remembered how surprised she was the first time she touched the marble on the angel's wing. It looked so warm but had an unexpected coolness under her fingers.

"I regret that we can't let every visitor touch the objects," she continued. "The tactile part is crucial to me and I'm lucky that as the curator I get to experience it."

"I think you did the next best thing," Martin said. He had helped her assemble a collection of marble and other raw materials that people could touch, which was mounted on a wall with the introductory text for the exhibit. "We all know that even marble gets worn down from constant touching, and it's less fragile than wood or paint."

"I am a document person as you both know," Jackie interjected, "but I have frequently heard that every object tells a story."

"Every object certainly *has* a story," Lizzie answered, "but unfortunately they frequently don't tell it. You can sometimes read its history on its surface, or speculate about it based on the context or by a comparison to similar objects, but usually you need the documents as well. Take this beautiful thing," she said, nodding at the angel. "We know it was made by an artist named Niccolo de Bari, who became famous for designing the fabulous arch over the tomb of St. Dominic, and is now called dell'Arca for that reason. We can speculate, by comparing this angel to the one on that tomb, that they are a pair, but we don't know why this angel never went on the tomb, and we don't even know how it got into the Gonzaga collection. Everything we know, except the comparison of the two sculptures, is based on documents."

A student waiter came by and offered them each another glass of champagne.

"And we know that one hundred years ago today Lorenzo Gonzaga gave this wonderful angel to the college in honor of Maggie Kelliher. And that is worth a toast."

They clinked glasses.

"I have learned a lesson in all this," Lizzie continued, "about both documents and objects. I have a tendency to judge early and be suspicious. Remember how we leapt to the conclusion that Maggie Kelliher was the unwilling pawn in an arranged marriage just because we didn't think she looked happy in that horrible picture in the *New York Times?*"

"Yes, but that is how you have to start a project," Jackie answered. "You need to have ideas that prompt questions. You kept an open mind and arrived at a very different conclusion."

"I was suspicious when the Dutch paintings were missing from the house," Martin said. "And that turned out to have a completely legitimate explanation." He saw Cosimo Gonzaga looking at them from across the room and raised his glass.

"Now I am just wondering what things got left out that will come back to haunt me!" Lizzie said. "There are always things that are discovered just after the exhibit opens or the book is published."

"Now is not the time to worry about that though," Jackie said. "It is a wonderful exhibit, Lizzie." She lifted her glass again. "To angels and alligators!"

"I'll drink to that," Lizzie said with a laugh, touching her glass first to Jackie's and then to Martin's. "And to the Wonder Chamber of the Gonzagas."

Behind them, the marble of the angel glowed in soft light against a dark fabric background.

An interview with the author

Q. Readers of your first two books might be surprised to find that Lizzie's job has taken her to Bologna in *The Wonder Chamber*. Why did you decide to move the setting of her research from England to Italy?

A. In the previous book, *Paradise Walk*, Lizzie retraced the pilgrimage of "The Wife of Bath," a character from Geoffrey Chaucer's *Canterbury Tales*. In addition to going to Canterbury, Chaucer tells us that "The Wife" made pilgrimages to Rome, Bologna, Jerusalem, Cologne, and Santiago de Compostela. I've decided to follow her to each of those places. I fell in love with Bologna the first time I went there, and the city is important in the history of museums, which is another of my interests, so I took advantage of the opportunity to steer the research for the book in that direction. The biggest part of any of these books is the research and I try to choose subject matter that will sustain my interest over the several years it takes to write the novel.

Q. Can you describe some of the research?

A. I hadn't originally intended to include so much about World War II in this book, but when I realized I was sending the character of Maggie Kelleher to live in Bologna during a time when the city was transformed by war, it became a necessary part of the plot. That meant that I had two rather different topics to research: Renaissance collections and WWII in Italy. The first I was already pretty familiar with; I teach a course on the history of museums at Harvard and am working on a non-fiction book on the topic. Seeing what is left of the collections of Ulisses Aldrovandi and Ferdinando Cospi at two museums in Bologna was absolutely essential to me. It allowed me to give what I hope are good descriptions of real objects.

For my research on World War II and the resistance in Italy, I relied heavily on Iris Origo's *War in Val D'Orcia: An Italian War Diary, 1943-1944.* The author was an Anglo-American woman married to an Italian aristocrat and her diary is filled with perceptive observations of the war unfolding around her. I also really liked Beppe Fenoglio's fictionalized descriptions of his experiences in the Italian Resistance—the novel *A Private Affair,* and his collection of short stories, *The Twenty-three Days of the City of Alba.* In Bologna, I found the Museum of the History of the Resistance (Museo della Resistenza) very useful, and traveled with *A Travel Guide to World War II Sites in Italy: Museums, Monuments, and Battlegrounds,* by Anne Leslie Saunders.

Q. Objects are a source of information in all three Lizzie Manning books, but you stress them more in *The Wonder Chamber.* Why do objects matter?

A. There is a progression over the three books in the way I think about Lizzie's research that is related to my own research projects. When I started *The Wandering Heart,* I was working on a doctoral dissertation and I saw the novel as an antidote to the limitations of non-fiction history writing, which requires that you stick pretty close to your source materials. I started by creating documents for Lizzie to discover, but quickly found that I wanted her to get information from objects and paintings as well. Both are important sources of historical information, but neither are used as often as they might be by historians.

The second book, *Paradise Walk,* starts from a document (a journal of a pilgrimage to Canterbury) and an object (a reliquary of Thomas Becket), but I wanted to use the landscape of the English countryside, as well as literary texts, as additional sources of information. In addition to Chaucer's *Canterbury Tales,* the texts included Arthurian romances, English poetry, modern narratives of long walks, and song lyrics (from ancient ballads to rock and roll). If I were to summarize how I thought about the three Lizzie books, *The Wandering Heart* is about documents and paintings, *Paradise Walk* is about works of literature, and The *Wonder Chamber* is about objects. Obviously, I am especially attracted to objects and what they can and do represent.

I am intrigued by the question of "why objects matter." I think there are two answers. The first is related to the physical properties of objects. We respond to their design, color, shape, and material composition. The other, usually more important answer, is tied to the people, events, and places with which an object is associated. Sometimes we become attached to objects for personal reasons. For example, we often become particularly attached to objects that are acquired through family connections, received as gifts from people we care deeply about, or associated with important memories. An object may also be given heightened value due to its ties to fame or celebrity. This is not just a modern phenomenon. We often appreciate something more if we know it was made or owned by someone famous or because it represents something bigger than itself. Plymouth Rock is the perfect example of this. It is a boulder sitting on a beach that was almost certainly *not* stepped on by pilgrims as they landed in small boats from the *Mayflower,* and yet it has gained iconic status for Americans. At some point, someone carved the date "1620" into it and built a sort of Greek temple around it. We have, over a few centuries, somehow agreed as a group, a culture, to let this stone represent the early Colonial period of our shared history.

Because I say so much about relics in this book, I should mention them as well. Relics represent how we invest faith in objects, even tiny splinters of wood believed to be from the cross on which Jesus was crucified. There were no pieces of the "true cross" circulating for several centuries after Christ and the true cross relics that began to appear after that time are almost certainly all fakes. This should strip them of their meaning, but many people continue to believe in spite of the evidence. That's a powerful object!

Q. This is the third in your Lizzie Manning trilogy. Did you always see this as a trilogy, or can we expect other books in this series?

A. I always conceived of this as a trilogy, but I love the character and her friends, and the research is always fun, so I am willing to consider continuing it if there is a readership to warrant it.

Q. Are you interested in writing other mystery novels?

A. It was actually never my intention to write classic mysteries, where the investigator is usually solving a murder, and I haven't been entirely comfortable with that designation for my books. Nonetheless, Lizzie is a historian and historians *are* detectives, though the puzzles they solve are not generally crimes. That said, historical events often have consequences that linger for generations, which is how Lizzie gets into so much trouble.

The novel I am currently working on is a more straightforward historical novel, set in medieval Ireland, when the English were claiming territory and the Irish clans were fighting among themselves. I love that period. There was such strong intellectual presence in Ireland at that time, and yet, just beneath the surface, a world of fairies who meddled in human activities.

The Author

MARY MALLOY is the author of the novels *The Wandering Heart* and *Paradise Walk*. She is also the author of four maritime history books, including the award-winning *Devil on the Deep Blue Sea: The Notorious Career of Samuel Hill of Boston*. An authority on musical traditions on shipboard, Mary has performed the songs of American mariners at museums and colleges around the world. She appears on four albums of traditional sea music, including the Aaargh-rated *Pirate Songs!* She has a Ph.D. from Brown University and is Professor of Maritime Studies and Director of the Global Ocean Program at the Sea Education Association in Woods Hole, Mass. In addition, Mary teaches Museum Studies at Harvard University, where she won the Shattuck Award for Excellence in Teaching in 2010.

About the Type

This book was set in Plantin, a family of text typefaces inspired by the work of Christophe Plantin (1520-1589.) In 1913, Frank Hinman Pierpont of the English Monotype Corporation directed the Plantin revival. Based on 16th century specimens from the Plantin-Moretus Museum in Antwerp, specifically a type cut by Robert Granjon and a separate cursive Italic, the Plantin typeface was conceived. Plantin was drawn for use in mechanical typesetting on the international publishing markets.

Designed by John Taylor-Convery
Composed at JTC Imagineering, Santa Maria, CA